Robert Verlander was born in Williamstown where much of the action unfolds in *Of White and Shady*. While raised in Melbourne he moved to Sydney in 1986 to pursue a career in Financial Markets. He is married with two sons and lives on the Sydney's Lower North Shore at Neutral Bay. *Of White and Shady* is his first novel.

A NOVEL

OF
WHITE
AND
SHADY

ROBERT VERLANDER

Copyright © 2015 Robert Verlander

ISBN: 978-1-925209-29-7
Published by Vivid Publishing
P.O. Box 948, Fremantle
Western Australia 6959
www.vividpublishing.com.au

National Library of Australia Cataloguing-in-Publication entry
Creator: Verlander, Robert, author.
Title: Of White and Shady / Robert Verlander.
ISBN: 9781925209297 (paperback)
Subjects: Nineteen sixty-nine, A.D.--Fiction.
             Disasters--Australia--Fiction.
             Inheritance and succession--Fiction.
Dewey Number: A823.4

To Andrea, Dash and Digby,
and my mother and father

ACKNOWLEDGEMENTS

The chapters dealing with Tick Tock's diaries draw upon E.E. Dunlop, *The War Diaries of Weary Dunlop: Java and the Burma – Thailand Railway 1942-1945*, (Melbourne, Nelson, 1986)

I thank all my readers for their time and valuable comments. In particular, I thank one of my very first readers, Jan Goldsmith, for her enthusiasm and encouragement and advice on earlier drafts. To Diana Giese, much appreciation for her insights and guidance and professional judgement in steering the manuscript through its various drafts to its final form. And to the team at Vivid Publishing my heartfelt thanks for the quality of their work and collaboration in getting the book published. I love the cover! Finally, to Andrea and Dash and Digby, I couldn't wish for a better team in my corner than you.

PART ONE

MADE IN WILLIAMSTOWN

ONE
LIFE IMITATES ART

'Man Walks On Moon' was the headline on the newspaper on the floor of my bedroom. Neil Armstrong was in the history books for sure, in there with Christopher Columbus and Captain Cook. The only way I'd get into the papers would be to drown or get run over.

My mother called out from downstairs: 'Michel, are you up there?' Of course I was, on my back on my bed right beneath the life-sized poster of Jimi Hendrix. Without waiting for an answer she yelled: 'Your father's about to start.' Before being disturbed I'd been contemplating my existence—or more precisely, the lack of it. When would I amount to anything?

My grandfather Val had died a few days before Neil Armstrong walked on the moon. Everyone knew him as Tick Tock, because whenever he saw anyone wasting time he would mutter, 'tick tock, tick tock.' His story wasn't on the front pages like the Moon walk. It was in the obituaries, right in the middle of the *Herald Sun*, before the classifieds. There were seven notices in an edition that sold a record number of copies. So by dying when he did he had probably come to the attention of more people than he had in his entire life. Lots of people read the obituaries. Mother said so.

'Don't make me come upstairs,' called Mother. 'He's already started.'

My father, Len, was the executor of Tick Tock's will. For the reading of the will he wore a suit, not the black one he wore to the funeral, but one in a vivid shade of paisley green. He had worse in his wardrobe. The safari suits were worse.

Our living room was packed tight with people. There were four rows of makeshift seating, six to a row, about the same as the number of chocolates in a full Cadbury's Milk Tray, which Len would buy for Mother every Friday night. The air was thick with an off-putting mix of Old Spice and Chanel No 5. Uncles were buttoned-up in suits and aunts in best dresses. To a man, each was Brylcreemed and braced.

Len had said to Mother the night before: 'They're like everyone else. They'll measure Tick Tock's love by how much they get.' Mother had replied, that the only thing her father owned of any value was the Ballet Shoe Factory.

The audience was wise to that too. Everyone held their breath as Len's gruff monotone fell temporarily silent. Had he lost his place? Maybe he'd scanned ahead and seen something unexpected. A name that shouldn't be there?

```
'... and  I  Valencia  Michel  Fiorentino
leave  all  my  estate  in  the  property
at  6  Little  Nelson  Place  Williamstown
otherwise  known  as  the  Ballet  Shoe
Factory  and  represented  on  Certificate
of  Title  3980  Folio  2547  to  the  man  to
whom  I  owe  my  greatest  debt,  and  for
whom  no  words  or  gift  can  adequately
express  my  appreciation—  Shady  Green...'
```

Who? The Ballet Shoe Factory, a prized piece of real estate worth a fortune, had been left to some unknown? Shady Green? Was that even a proper name?

But Len wasn't finished:

```
'In the event that he cannot be found
all the title in the property passes to
my grandson, Michel White.'
```

There was a collective gasp as the words of the will rolled through our living room like the fragmenting of a hand grenade. 'An absolute disgrace!' shouted Aunt Myra, to a chorus of *Hear hears*. Uncle Alf, her husband, rocked back and forwards in his chair like a patient in a psychiatric ward. As the chair rocked he eased his braces in and out over his gut as if trying to digest something not too pleasant. 'Shady Green my foot,' I heard him say.

Tick Tock's chickens were the only bequest that I thought I stood a chance of getting. He and I had spent a lot of time together in the chook pens out the back of the Ballet Shoe Factory. No one knew the chooks as well as us.

On the family's last visit to Tick Tock in hospital he had made me promise him to look after his chickens. I told him, 'Honestly, Tick Tock, I sometimes think you love your chooks more than people.' There, out of sight of everyone else, he had slipped the key to the Ballet Shoe Factory into my hand and whispered: '*Remember*.' Which I'd thought was a strange thing to say to a boy not known for forgetting.

Much of my family thought Tick Tock was not quite right in the head, mental. A man who sat for hours in a chook pen talking to chickens and a boy in pidgin-Japanese might give this impression. I guessed what they were thinking: Shady Green was a figment of Tick Tock's imagination. More proof of the damage the War had done to him all those years ago. But I knew different. When I was younger, no more than eight or nine, Tick Tock told me stories of Shady Green in which he had always seemed so real. These were stories of drains and tunnels and jockeys and racehorses and not for a moment did I think Shady was anything but an actual person.

Mother touched me on the shoulder: 'Take these in,' she said, and passed me a large plate of scones, 'it might keep them busy.'

Anger and disappointment hadn't dented the crowd's appetite. When I extended the plate to Aunt Myra, who would normally pepper me with the latest academic achievements of her children—'Suzanne got an A for her latest essay, I think she'll do Medicine,' would be typical, and as Suzanne still hadn't finished playing with dolls, this might have been jumping the gun—selected a scone, but uttered not a word merely fluttering her eyes as if they were covered in an invisible frost. Only Uncle Graham made any general enquiries about my well-being, 'How's that new school going, eh?' To which I lied and told him it was going great. When it came to schools and academic success there was no greater competition than between the cousins.

After I'd done a complete circuit of the living room there was a loud snap, not unlike when Len did his Achilles tendon, trying too hard to beat me at squash. Behind me, Uncle Alf lay sprawled on the carpet, his chair and its shattered leg beneath him. Startled, I all but dropped the near-empty plate on the dining room table. Under her breath, from the kitchen and not aware that Uncle Alf was destroying *her* furniture, Mother declared: 'You'd think they were house bricks the way you treat them.'

If I hadn't been the centre of attention, I might have

scoffed one of the remaining scones. But it struck me that a mouth stuffed with scone might be an image I could do without—greedy-guts. I resisted the temptation.

Len came up beside me. 'I thought I'd see if you'd broken the table. I could put it out in the garage with Alf's chair.'

'I'll try harder next time,' I assured him.

'Who's Shady Green?'

I shrugged. 'You know old Tick Tock.'

Len swallowed the last morsel of a scone, wiping butter from the corners of his mouth that left his lips shiny and red. 'Not as well as you do,' he said and squinted in that way he had of intentionally conveying suspicion.

My right hand felt for the sharp ridges of the key to the Ballet Shoe Factory in the bottom of my pocket.

'Don't bother to answer. Now's not the time,' he said, casting his eyes around the room where conversations had begun to bubble again. 'Make yourself scarce. We'll talk about this later.'

I needed no further invitation, bolting out the front door and grabbing the Malvern Star bike that lay spreadeagled on the lawn. As I raced down the Esplanade Mrs Wilkinson gave me a smile, and old Mrs Murray a little regal wiggling wave. Bud Brown, peered at me through his bottle-thick dark-framed glasses before he stopped reversing out of his drive to let me snake around the rear of his late model shark-finned sedan. Nobody could do a thing in this town without being spotted. I was off to Gerry Nelson's, my best friend, to give him 'The news' and I'd gone no more than one hundred yards and had three eyewitnesses.

For the record Michel was pronounced just like Michael— Mother had insisted on the Italian spelling. For all of my sixteen years I had lived in Beau Vista a western suburb eight miles from the Central Business District of Melbourne.

Much of Beau Vista was resumed swamp. It lay almost cut off from the world, serviced only by a two-carriage spur-line train and the Sitch Bus Company. A suburb held in the jaws of smoke-belching petrol refineries on one side and, on the other side, what passed for a beach. Beau Vista was where the water of Hobsons Bay met its most westerly suburban settlement; where after a sweltering summer's day the southerly change would arrive first, and I would ring our cousins on the other side of Melbourne and say how cool it was out here already, secretly hoping that this might make them jealous of where I lived.

The beach and the great expanse of choppy blue-grey bay could make you forget how unsightly the factories were, even though the beach could hardly be described as spectacular. It wasn't a beach like Williamstown's with its wide and handsome boardwalk. Seaweed and kelp would pile up after heavy weather in drifts so deep I could hardly see the sand. The sulphurous stench would be awful and last for days, covering the whole town like a blanket. When our cousins came over for a swim, I would hope it didn't stink because they would all make such a fuss and say it was worse than not having a beach at all. Still, when the seaweed didn't wash up, and it was blazing hot in the height of summer and the northerlies seemed to blast all the way from the withering Wimmera Mallee scrublands, and the blowflies were as big as ten-cent pieces, I was glad it was there no matter what anyone else might have thought of it.

Gerry lived in a house without a front fence. The lack of a front fence created the impression that the house was abandoned, and that the front yard was a sort of no-man's land. Built of fibro-cement there was a whole sheet of it missing from beneath the lounge window, making it look as if the house had got a punch in the eye.

The front door was chocked open and the fly-wire door shut. The hallway was empty all the way down to the open back door and the plastic-coloured strips of fly screen, blowing in the draught. There was no sound from inside. The Venetian blinds of the lounge room window were open, the big old phonogram on full display where a TV would otherwise be. The Nelsons didn't have a TV. Gerry's father didn't believe in them.

Gerry and his two brothers lived under a military-style regime where a thrashing was never too far away. Gerry's father's great fear was that Gerry or one of his two brothers would disgrace the family. Mr Nelson hung a leather belt on a nail in the kitchen, right near where they pencilled the straight ruled lines on the walls that measured the boys as they grew. There wasn't a week went by that the strap didn't come off the wall. Gerry's father would get out the strap, a fine-looking one made of camel-brown leather and double-stitched the whole way round. He would deliver three or six 'cuts', never more nor less, no matter how minor or major the infraction, three or six that was it. Gerry would ask, 'Three or six?' And he would be told with the authority of an archbishop what was coming.

Gerry's father would beat the boys butt naked, bent double over the kitchen table, trousers around their ankles, telling them while he dealt out the thrashing, why it would do them good, although the only good it seemed to be doing was to Gerry's dad. The curious thing was the more Gerry's dad leathered those boys, the harder and tougher they got, and the more likely they were to do exactly what he feared the most.

I went around the side of the house to the backyard. Like most blocks of land in Beau Vista the Nelsons had a large backyard. *Unlike* most houses in Beau Vista the toilet—the thunderbox—was in the very middle of it. The thunderbox, although old and wooden, was an oasis, covered in lush green vines and a trellising that wove plump passionfruit throughout the foliage. Inside it was dark and cool with just enough natural light to read by. The can filled a round hole in a long wooden bench. On one side of the bench was a pile of newspapers and magazines. On a nail on the wall were stripped sheets of newspaper. In the pile of newspapers and magazines there was always a copy of *Playboy* right at the bottom as if that hid it. Gerry's father could spend most of a Sunday morning in there. It was his favourite place. That wasn't a guess. He told us.

Gerry's blue gym boots stretched out into the doorway of the thunderbox.

'Gerry?' I ventured.

'Who's that?' Came the voice from within.

'It's me.'

Gerry knew who it was. 'Why don't you come over here where I can talk to you?'

'I'm not coming over there while you're on the throne.'

Lately Gerry had taken to sitting on the can for extended periods. I think he thought that this was what all men did. Paper rustled from inside the thunderbox. It might have been the *Playboy*.

'What are you afraid of?' The sound of lips and gums, sucking what turned out to be the soft insides of a passion-fruit, emerged from the thunderbox.

'You're not eating in there, are you?' I was not faking my disgust.

More noises came from the thunderbox, the harsh rasp of paper being rubbed. 'Jesus, do you mind?'

'No.' The toilet flushed and the purple shell of a passionfruit flew out of the open door.

Gerry emerged with a red and black plaid shirt hanging over his jeans. Puberty had come early for Gerry. He had thick sideburns the colour of rusty corrugated iron and hair only his mother could have cut that was always a bit long at the front, and had to be flicked back to keep it from covering his eyes. Mrs Nelson didn't use a bowl, but there was always a definite lopsidedness to it. His hair gave the impression that he had something to hide.

He lifted a leg and scratched his groin.

'Do you have to?' I asked.

'Some of us do, yeah.' He grinned like a sailor going on shore leave.

'Can't you think of something else?'

'Not often. Can you?'

'Of course I can.'

'That's your problem.'

'I don't have a problem.'

'You have a problem. You *know* you have a problem.'

'I need to talk to you about something.'

'OK, what?' Gerry asked.

I told Gerry that Tick Tock had sort of left the Ballet Shoe Factory to me.

Gerry shrugged. 'Who'd want it?'

'Are you crazy? It's got to be worth a mint.'

'S'pose it might help pay for that new swank school of yours.' His face did its best at a sneer. Gerry had still not adjusted to my new school that lay in far-off Essendon and for which he had not quite forgiven my treachery in wanting to attend.

'What's wrong with you?'

'Fancy school…money…doesn't mean you get a girl.'

'Aren't you listening? The whole bloody great Ballet

Shoe Factory might be mine. Don't you know what that could mean?'

Gerry acted as if he didn't care. 'It's just a big old house...'

I finished the sentence for him, '...that's worth a fortune. I'm thinking panel van, trip to Fiji, you and me.'

The mention of a panel van had worked like a dose of smelling salts on an unconscious footballer. 'A shagging wagon would be good,' he mumbled.

'Jet black, surf racks, a chick with tits like Raquel Welch painted on the outside.'

'V-8, Ford, of course?'

'Of course.' I had Gerry in a stupor. For a moment I thought his eyes might roll over into the back of his head as he imagined himself at the wheel of the panel van. 'I'm not sure your mother would let you get away with Raquel Welch.'

'OK, Hayley Mills then.'

Gerry groaned.

'Come on. Let's get down there.'

Gerry flicked the hair from his eyes. 'Yeah s'pose anything to get me out of this place.'

The Ballet Shoe Factory lay four miles away in Williamstown. In no time we had sprinted the length of the Esplanade and were out on the abandoned Williamstown racecourse. Up ahead were the ruins of the old grandstand and beyond that Kororoit Creek and the petro-chemical and oil refineries, and the neat ordered clusters of massive oil storage tanks that were regarded as the border between Beau Vista and Williamstown. The tanks were so big and contained so much oil that I periodically wondered what might happen if they ignited and would the blast make it to where I lived.

We veered right hugging the coastline and skirting the old rifle range until we reached the Williamstown foreshore. Not only did Williamstown have a fancier esplanade than Beau Vista—nineteenth century merchant mansions stretched from one end to the other—but its main streets were as wide as in the City of Melbourne itself. Streets lined with elms so big and broad that they reached out and entangled in one another, forming leafy archways high overhead. Williamstown was not really like Beau Vista at all.

The fastest way to the Ballet Shoe Factory was up a narrow passage between a cluster of grand Victorian shops on Nelson Place. This passage led to a cobblestoned lane known as Little Nelson Place—and one hundred yards along from there was where you would find it.

The Ballet Shoe Factory rose before us tall and magnificent with its massive, grey slate cross-gabled roof commanding our attention. The house, built almost entirely of wooden shingles, was like an elaborate doll's house made of gingerbread. The intricate white tracery beneath the eaves appeared so delicate and brittle that it might snap off as easily as the decorative frosting of a birthday cake. Beautiful rounded oriel windows and the little balconies they circumscribed, hung in the second-storey air, seemingly supported by nothing but the scent of the gardenias that flowered beneath. Painted in a glossy white, it shone self-importantly in the late afternoon sun on its impressively deep, wide and private allotment. Upon the façade just beneath the eaves was the shape of dark, faded letters that spelt: *Gorham's Ballet Shoe Factory*. It was like a house from a children's fable. A place where, if you believed in fairies and goblins you wouldn't be surprised in the least to find them inside.

The Ballet Shoe Factory was a great nineteenth-century boom-time folly with no recognised architectural merit beyond its quirkiness. Both its practical and cavernous working premises, and the chicken pens out the back undermined any pretensions to grandeur. The safety of a Heritage Listing had been denied before and would just as certainly be denied again to anyone who cared to apply.

The working premises, or salon, as Tick Tock had called it, swept along the entire southern side of the Ballet Shoe Factory virtually the width of the block—too big for any domestic use. In it every sound was an echo. Untouched for years, it was preserved like a memory.

Nothing appeared to have changed since we were last here, more dust and cobwebs that was all. The sewing machines were where they had always been. The ballet shoes were on their shelves and the fitting stools scattered about as ready as ever to receive the fine heel-print of a dancer's foot. It was all neat and tidy just the way Tick Tock liked to keep it.

Around the side of the house was the front entrance for which Tick Tock had given me the key. It was in the shape of a ballet shoe with an inscription: My Time Flies. Beneath the inscription was the tiny engraving of a horse in full stride with a jockey on board. Two thin ribbons were threaded through the eyelet of the key. One was pink and the other was green, and both shone with a silky sheen.

The door opened as smoothly as if the lock had been oiled yesterday. Before us was the carpeted imprint of where a desk had once stood, and above that, the faded outline of a painting that had been removed. A picture rail ran head-high the circumference of the entrance hall. The passage on our left led to the salon its door ajar. We entered the wide-open space of the salon. A fourteen feet ceiling and windows that stretched the length of the salon let the light stream in. 'What's up here?' Gerry asked. An open door in the back wall of the salon led to a staircase bathed in the red light of high, stained-glass windows. Royal blue carpet runners swept down in broad pinned folds, leading our eyes up through the mahogany banisters to the upstairs rooms.

Unlike the salon, the rooms upstairs were in a state of disrepair as if they were being dismantled. The living room had been stripped of its flooring. Carpet sat lumped and rolled into corners and beneath the torn-up timber floor the joists lay bare. It seemed the wooden floor had been used as wood for a fire. Inside the fireplace ash had burned to a soft grey and black powder. I stuck my head up the chimney. The flue was covered with dark moist soot. I rubbed my finger along the surface and drew a greasy line.

'Deros,' said Gerry and reached over the iron grate of the fireplace and grasped the only thing of material shape: a lump of wood that was burned through, but somehow whole. He held it up to me and with a hand on either end compressed the wood to the ash it really was. It vaporized with barely a puff into the remnants of the fire. Gerry rubbed his smoky-gray hands together and cleaned them down the sides of his trousers. 'Warm,' he said.

'Yeah be a dero for sure,' I replied with false conviction.

I didn't need a second reading of the will to tell me that if Shady Green couldn't be found that the Ballet Shoe Factory was mine alone. Yet I knew as I stood before the remains of the fire that Shady Green and I would meet. I can't really tell you why I believed that. It's like explaining why I believed Jesus was the Son of God and not, say, poor little Philip Wilkinson who lived down the road with his deaf and dumb mum and dad. And right then it was as if I could see Shady Green with his legs crossed in front of that fireplace.

'Hey, bit of art as well. And some old papers full of writing.'

Gerry clutched a painting in one arm and two bundles

of loose-leafed paper in the other. Both bundles of paper each individually tied with string, were aged and yellowed, and in the unmistakeable handwriting of Tick Tock.

'Where were they?' I asked.

'The painting was on top of the sideboard. The papers underneath the rolled-up carpet.'

The painting was of a jockey in full racing silks and skullcap seated upon a big bay racehorse. The jockey was in profile, facing straight over the head of the horse. Even though one side of his face was visible, I didn't recognise him. His silks were striking pink with green hoops. I opened my fisted hand and examined the key. The key with its inscription My Time Flies twinkled in the light, the little bands of pink and green ribbon tied through the eyelet, spread wave-like over the palm of my hand. The colours of the key's ribbons and the silks of the jockey were identical, more stunning than a normal pink or green. In a racing *Best Bets* guide they would have been magenta and chartreuse.

Memories are funny things. They pop into your head unannounced and unexpected. Tick Tock is speaking quietly to me, and it's a long time ago. I'm on his knee. My attention is absolute. I strain for the words. Tick Tock is very close to me, closer than normal, his mouth above my ear, my straight hair moving under the force of his breath. I can smell the hops of beer and the perfume of loose-pouched tobacco from a packet of Drum in his top pocket. The turned-down corners of his mouth are moist with saliva—too much talking and they'll drip. As his saliva is about to drip, Tick Tock raises an old green jacket sleeve and wipes the drip dry. Behind him a jockey in silks slinks by with a sly grin on his small face. The jockey goes by virtually unnoticed. My eyes are only for Tick Tock.

I gave the painting back to Gerry. 'Looks like it's worth

a bob. Better put it back where you found it.'

'And these?' Gerry asked, holding up the papers that bore the signs of having been chewed by silverfish—holed and frayed and transparently thin.

Like a thief in the night I walked out of the Ballet Shoe Factory with the papers stuffed down my jeans.

TWO

YOU NEVER GET TO PICK YOUR RELATIVES

'Hey!'

It was my mother and she was shaking me awake. Startled, I sat up and swung my feet from the footstool and with that the reclining back of the faulty Jason recliner-rocker sprang bolt upright.

'Where'd you go?'

After hiding the papers in the cavity of the garage wall, I'd slunk in the back door and confirming first impressions that all the relatives had departed, settled into Len's favourite chair for a quick nap.

'With Gerry,' as if that helped much.

My mother looked at me, her arms crossed. 'They're your relatives.'

Of this I needed no reminding. 'They're not getting anything.'

'You don't make things easy. Do you?'

I began to say something. What it would be had not quite formed in my head. Mother waved at me to stop as if she was so angry anything I came up with would only make it worse. My open mouth clammed shut.

I knew she wanted some acknowledgement from me of her and Len's dilemma: a sixteen-year-old with all that wealth and potentially Aunt Myra and Uncle Alf and Uncle Graham and Aunt Daphne, and all the rest of the relos, if you were to believe the whinging, going round forever in cast-offs from St Vinnies. I knew all this. I was smart enough just not wise enough.

For a couple of seconds as she waited, I was tempted to relent and negotiate a way through. Hope was spread thinly on a face corrugated by lines of worry her nose pointed up like a boat in heavy going. I worried she might cry. Only little bastards make their mother cry.

'You just don't care what we think, do you?' She dabbed the corner of an eye with a finger, although I didn't see a tear.

'Why should they get anything? Tick Tock could have given it to them if he'd really wanted to.'

'This town's not that big. How am I supposed to look your uncles and aunts in the face. It's not as if we really need it. Anyway you've seen how money can destroy a family. You don't have to look further than that blasted pair of Nigel and Priscilla for that.'

Nigel and Priscilla were the Beau Vista equivalent of a biblical parable, the son and daughter of a pair of rich builders, a couple that had destroyed the family business and made off with most of the family fortune by unwinding a complex scheme of corporate trusts for which they were only meant to be nominal beneficiaries.

'You wouldn't want to be associated with the likes of them,' she said.

'Nigel and Priscilla? You think I'm like Nigel and Priscilla?'

In repetition the couple sounded like Bonnie and Clyde.

Mother ran her hand through my hair. 'Of course you're not like either of that pair. But…you can't be too careful. People are very touchy when it comes to money.'

When I could just about feel the prospect of money lifting my life of mediocrity up by the laces of my gym boots, Mother has to spoil it by giving me a sense of guilt.

'Mother, what do you want me to do about it?'

Her eyes brightened. 'Well we've given that a little thought,' she said, 'and your father and I think it would be a good idea if we could tell your aunts and uncles that if you should be lucky enough to get the inheritance that you would share it with them.'

'I'm not sure I like the idea of that,' I said, which was a vast understatement of how I actually felt—I loathed the idea.

'Now listen here, Sonny Jim,'—James, my middle name only ever got a mention as a kind of reference to a bad alter ego that I needed to keep under wraps—'there are people here to consider other than just yourself.' She swung around to leave, only to reverse direction and quickly swing back. 'And I told you. I don't want you seeing that Gerry-boy. Have you got that?'

I stepped into the unknown. 'Anyhow, why should you worry? I could be off your hands soon,' I ventured dangerously referring to my by no means certain windfall.

Mother's eyes narrowed, everything soft, feminine and maternal imploded to a dark husk of austere unquestionable authority. 'Oh, will you now? Mr Independent, eh? We'll see about that.'

She stood frozen. Anger bit hard on her bottom lip. Her eyes fixed upon mine waiting for me to relent. My smug little dial sometimes drove her nuts and the less she could do about it the angrier she got. 'Whatever will you amount to? Honestly, I really don't know.' She sighed as if she physically had to lift her heart up and put it back down in a slightly different place. 'I'd keep a low profile if I was you,' was her parting shot.

Gerry was off-limits again. I would have to negotiate life like some kind of double agent.

Fortunately, Mother never did extract from me where I'd been. She didn't know I'd gone to the Ballet Shoe Factory with Gerry in what she would have described as a land-grab. She didn't know that any sense of my elation had been largely dashed by the sight of all those ripped-up floorboards and the dawning fear that this unknown Shady Green might have been responsible. My mediocre existence was destined to continue. What would I ever amount to? Mother had hit the nail on the head and she knew it. My dead-ordinariness appalled me. I grasped this Ballet Shoe Factory bequest like a man in a bushfire grabbed a working hose. It was my ticket to success. Time ticked by, and I could hear every tock and tick as I imagined my worthlessness becoming evident for all to see, and not just to me, in my private hysterical conversations.

Early the next morning I woke beneath an open window and its sleeve of silky breeze, a weak dull light barely illuminating a sky full of grey clouds. My brother Malcolm lay fast in sleep in a single bed on the other side of the room that we shared. After a troubled night in which a vision of Shady Green had wandered uninvited into my dreams it was a relief to be awake.

I got up and went downstairs. Without the characteristic noise of the television the living room was eerily quiet, so I turned the television on to rectify the eeriness. A fist-pumping religious programme was on. I checked the other channel—a Test Pattern. The religious programme would have to do. But the fellow berating the live audience and its viewers was no Catholic Priest, and Catholicism was the only legitimate religion as far as I was concerned. I took it as self-evident that it was the premier league of Christian religions, non-Christian just didn't bear thinking about. All that misery and poverty—and Gandhi's nappy—belonged to a way of life so foreign that for me to embrace it as a white Australian would in all likelihood be regarded as mentally deficient.

A dark-suited man was on the TV. His emphatic speech on sin and sinners seemed appropriate for his black-and-white TV world. He spoke of how the Lord had already saved us and how He would do it again if He had to and by the dire sound of things this was as near as a cast iron certainty as you could get. I didn't believe a word this man was saying. This was snake oil and this was a salesman, not a spokesman for God, let alone the right god. I knew self-promotion when I saw it and turned the TV channel over to the Test Pattern, and contemplated the complex grid of lines in shades of black and white and grey.

As I focused on the intricacies of the Test Pattern, it dawned on me that I had not the vaguest idea of how a TV worked, and for the amount of time I spent watching it, this seemed negligent. Our General Electric TV had been on the blink that week. A TV technician had been duly called and arrived in a van with a sign on the side that said 'TV Repairs', that was his job; that was all he apparently did. He had removed a few screws and in no time levered the backboard off. The guts of it were a total revelation. I'd never seen inside one before, and having had a close look it was not obvious in any way how it produced pictures.

If you'd dropped me back into the nineteenth century, for all the head start that I'd had, and based on what I actually knew now, I could not have advanced civilisation a single minute faster that it'd done without my help.

I was passing through the dining room en route to the kitchen, when the sound of the living approached, accompanied by the flush of a toilet and a creak on the stairs. A word was uttered in anger as someone tripped in the half-light. Moments later there was the pressurised rushing sound of water from a tap turned on full, pouring into the hollowness of an empty kettle and then the clank of the plumbing being sharply shut off. Jiffies scuffed across the coffee-coloured, hexagonal print of the tiled kitchen floor. I waited for the kettle to boil and hoped it would be turned off before it whistled. A minute or two later I heard the bubble of boiling water and smelt burning toast. And through it all, every now and again, there was the distinct sound of a page being turned. I'd be damned if I'd get up and turn it off. The kettle's whistle began to blow loudly and then piercingly. This other person and I were separated only by the width of a wall and were likely back to back. If I rammed my fist through the wall, I'd knock whomever it was out. Shortly after came the merciful dying whine of the kettle.

My older sister Esther materialised in the doorway her eyes nearly shut, layered in pink a cardigan over a thick long cotton nightie, long black witch-like hair streaming down her back, a book tucked under an arm and in her hands a steaming cup of tea and a plate of toast balanced precariously on top. I stood motionless in a darkened corner of the dining room, not inclined to say a word because any unexpected movement or sound and she might drop the lot.

If you didn't know it was my sister her appearance was daunting like meeting someone from another time. Her whole wardrobe was op-shop couture. Esther hadn't felt the direct warmth of the sun since she read that it might age her skin. She wore sunglasses in the outdoors in all weather conditions and a wide-brimmed hat—puce or black were her favourite colours. At close range her skin appeared bleached. I believed that this was the effect of too much time under indoor lights—a minor modern miracle, but a fact to me all the same.

'Well you've done it now,' Esther announced without giving any obvious sign of seeing me.

Play dumb for a bit.

'I know you're there. I can smell you.'

What? I thought, but didn't say anything.

Esther blindly shambled past seeking the window seat in the nook of the dining room. Even from where I was standing I could see the contents of the cup swirling over its brim and slopping down the sides into a filling saucer.

'I think Uncle Alf would be on a drip recovering after yesterday afternoon. Apparently he's in shock,' she said.

'Uncle Alf?' I asked.

Esther officially recognised me with a hooded look of disdain. She dunked the toast into her tea and brought it sopping full to her mouth in a resumption of reading the hardback book that lay on its spine on her lap, munching the wet toast slowly, absentmindedly, as if I'd vanished. Again she dunked the toast.

'Uncle Alf? Something wrong there?' I asked again.

'Mmm,' she said and didn't look up.

What is wrong with people? And why are so many of them related to me? I cursed the damned automobile. If not for the automobile relatives could exist in a misty distance that I never needed to know about, let alone visit. Every Sunday we'd be flung into the back of a big, old, black Vauxhall and hauled across the city to any one of half a dozen uncles or aunts. We'd implore to be allowed to stay at home with the conviction of a death-row inmate begging for a stay of execution. It was the phenomenon of 'The Drive.'

'We're going for a Drive.' Can you imagine it now? I mean I can't. Children look at you bug-eyed if it is so much as suggested we all get in the car together to look at a couple of houses Open for Inspection—that is their modern limit. They do not understand us all getting in the car together and aimlessly wandering the roads, or worse, wantonly and without specific reason visiting relatives who they'd see as accidents of birth. These were people we could only find time to criticize, but every Sunday that's what we did—church, a roast for lunch and then the trek across town. The cars didn't have seatbelts or if they did they were never used so people could be stacked like luggage on the backseat. I'd be in pride of place in the front carsick-prone, head hanging out the window like a dog, everyone hoping the wind in my face would stop the spewing. But Uncle Alf? I should take notice of Uncle Alf? The Uncle Alf who was pensioned off in his forties. The Uncle Alf who'd just run out of the will to work, spluttered one day to a dead stop, backed it up with one spurious medical complaint after another and been on social security ever since.

Esther's eyes reluctantly lifted to me in slits. 'Could have been Tick Tock's funeral all over again,' she said and took a measured mouthful of tea.

'Couldn't have been that bad?'

'Outdone yourself, sport. *Shady Green*? Who are you kidding?' She laughed all mean and snide and if I could have given her a good kicking and got away with it, I would have.

'Shady Green?'

'I'll bet he's long dead, isn't he?'

'How would I know?'

'Tick Tock told you everything, didn't he, sport? Thick as thieves you were out in those filthy chook pens all the time—his little friend.'

'I think you've been reading too many novels.'

Esther was not the type you wanted to unnecessarily provoke, getting on the wrong side of her was something I could do without. My life didn't need her kind of scrutiny. Take having the occasional piss around the side of the house. Look, I knew the toilet was closer, but there was just something about having a slash in the great outdoors that made it better. Esther was onto me but she didn't have firm proof. What she did have was a suspicious patch of grass that was clearly in the throes of dying. An almost perfect circle of balding grass leached to the colour of straw. A circle so perfect that it had either been made by Druids or someone with a urinating fetish. Last week before I'd even the chance to zip up, I heard Esther coming. I had dived under the house to escape detection, but not before I'd crawled through some of the very grass I'd doused. She knew it was me and the fact that the fence itself was shiny and slick in thick Rolf Harris-like brush strokes from over-exuberance on this occasion, meant she had only just failed to catch me red-handed. It was a matter of time before I—and not the less likely culprits of the dog or Malcolm's shaky little bladder—would accurately get the blame. Then Esther would have what she wanted, which was incontrovertible proof that not only was I some kind of Ork, but that I was also deliberately killing Mother's lawn.

This potential exposure hung over my head like a biblical beheading apparatus. The possibility that I could get on even terms using an equally venal and mortifying disclosure against her had emerged as a plan. For months I stalked Esther for incriminating material, but to no avail. She operated with the care of someone who knew she was under surveillance. I needed evidence of a personal and humiliating kind that I could use as contra—a bargaining chip—to negotiate non-proliferation of my offences. I always came up empty-handed. From time to time, I'd just walk into her bedroom without a knock and I'd stand there gormlessly staring at her reading a book in bed, instead of being hopelessly compromised in the arms of a smuggled-in boyfriend. I was like an old-time gumshoe trying to get a compromising shot. I don't know what I was thinking. She'd just smile and say: 'Get out.' She wouldn't shout or even complain. I didn't matter that much.

'Shady Green?' Esther finished her toast. 'A pseudonym?'

A what?

'You think you're clever?'

Not at that moment I didn't.

'It won't work.'

What wouldn't?

'I know what you're up to.'

Please tell me.

'They'll lynch you first.'

I could tell there were some parts of that idea she didn't mind.

'They?' I asked.

'Aunt Myra paid Mother a visit,' Esther said, a note of mischief in her voice. *'Couldn't believe her ears'.* That's what Aunt Myra had said. The words of the will were no less than knives in her and Alf's backs. The very idea of it that a boy just turned sixteen could get all that money. 'You can't possibly let him keep it. Can you?' she'd asked.

Apparently Mother wouldn't have any of it. Although it wasn't lost on me that Mother, as one of Tick Tock's daughters, might have been more than a little surprised that my claim for the family fortune had been staked ahead of her. She would not be shamed into interfering with the clear—mysterious though they might be—words of her father.

As if Esther was reading my mind she said: 'You can see Mother's not quite as greedy as you, you little gold digger.'

This stung because it was too close to the truth.

'You're just jealous.'

The look on Esther's face betrayed a girl who needed convincing. If Shady Green was real then I was worthless. One equalled the other. She was a cobra readied to strike and I was no snake charmer. And she had a track record for inflicting pain dating back to early childhood.

Esther was five and I was three. To this day I am still not positive of the accidental nature of the incident and her innocence. It's my earliest memory. 'Hold it steady,' she'd said and raised the axe above her shoulder. All around us was cut kindling, stacked high in piles against the paling fence. On the ground wood chips, bark and fine splinters mixed with loose earth. I had placed the small log for cutting upon the chopping block right in the middle where the axe blade had made its deepest cuts. Under no circumstances was I to remove my hand. My small arm reached out fearlessly to steady the log. Esther bit her lip in concentration and effort and swung the axe. I didn't make a sound. It must have been the shock and the knife-edge sharpness of the blade. The joint, for a time, hung on only by the thinness of skin tissue. I cupped my other hand beneath the dangling joint and blood dripped exquisitely over the smooth pinkness of my palm. I looked at Esther for some acknowledgement of what she had done, but her face revealed only puzzlement at what had gone wrong. An ageless puzzlement captured perfectly again today as she tried to find out more.

'Your idea? This Shady Green thing?'

I looked genuinely ignorant. 'Sorry?'

'It's something you'd come up with. Get the hounds off the scent. Make the relos focus on someone other than yourself.'

She finished off the cup of tea and levelled a stare that was meant to break me down, the cup dripping into the saucer by way of accompaniment—drip drip drip—so annoying.

'There is always that other matter,' she hinted ominously. 'It would be a shame to let that out.' A long tongue flicked snake-like sweeping her lips clean and wet.

'I haven't got a clue about any Shady Green,' I said.

She wasn't sure if I spoke the truth. Our relationship was not based upon trust. Secrecy and separateness were the rules we lived by.

'What a lucky boy.'

THREE
GEORGIE GREEN

Shady Green rose early. He made sure not to wake the two snoring men in the room of the boarding house that he shared. His brown duffel bag was packed full. Everything he owned of any value was in the bag. Shady shouldered the bag and threaded his way soundlessly through the room and down the dark hallway.

In the pocket of his shirt was the most recent letter from Tick Tock. In it was written,

```
Dear Shady

Knowing as I do your opinion on the
matter I'll make this brief. You've
known for a long time that the Ballet
Shoe Factory would eventually be yours.
The time for arguing to the contrary is
past and the time that it will be yours
is rapidly approaching. I write this
only to put you on your guard for a bit
of the legal hoopla that will no doubt
come your way.
```

You've been the finest of friends and I
wish you well.

All the best
Val

If, for no reason other than the emphysema, Shady had long insisted that he'd be the first to push up the daisies. What was the point in Tick Tock making him the heir to the Ballet Shoe Factory? When last he'd seen him a few months ago—on Tick Tock's annual holiday in Brisbane—he'd been as good as he'd seen him in years. It was almost inconceivable that he might die before him, but that's what the letter seemed to say and Shady couldn't take the chance that his great friend might die without seeing him again.

Shady had kept promising to come to Melbourne, his plans always thwarted by an attack of the emphysema that seemed to flare at the very idea of journeying to a place, he thought responsible for the condition. But with Tick Tock's thin Sicilian blood driving him north to Brisbane every year as reliably as a wildebeest migrating across the Serengeti Plains to the Masai Mara, Shady had always put the journey off.

This year would be very different because Shady had the most wonderful present for Tick Tock. When Shady received the delicate little package he almost boarded a train for Melbourne straightaway. Then the emphysema had hit him hard, putting him in and out of hospital for weeks. Still not fully recovered he booked the first available train to Melbourne. What a shock Tick Tock would get, to see him standing on the doorstep of the Ballet Shoe Factory. What joy and sadness Tick Tock would feel as Shady gave him the precious object that he wore for safety around his neck.

Brisbane Central train station was close enough to walk.

Shady put on clothes fit more for a Melbourne winter—the weather there notoriously fickle. He arrived at the railway station in a sweat. Once aboard the Southern Aurora he quickly found his seat. As day became night and then day again, the Southern Aurora made its way south. Stirred by vivid images of the Ballet Shoe Factory and life in a different time, Shady fell in and out of sleep.

In 1918, a boy, called George, scavenged each day for survival on the streets of Williamstown. All he had was a few coins in his pocket and the worn winter clothes on his back. His stepfather, loaded with drink, again, had hurled him down the front stoop of their rented single-fronted cottage with the declaration: 'If I see you a-bloody 'gain it'll be the hiding of your life.' His mother had come no further than the doorway her face wild with fear that George would further test his strength against a man she needed, but did not love. Behind his stepfather's back, she waved him to move off for all their sakes.

Hands in his pockets, George had shown his anger in a slow, sullen step and a front gate left wide open. From down the street, he could hear his stepfather berating his mother: 'You fill the boy's head up with stuff and nonsense about the stars and the sky, is it any wonder he's the way he is? A dose of the real world is what he needs.' There was, George knew, some truth in his stepfather's words. His mother was all too given to astrology and its charts. Most days he would set off to school with an astrologist's prognostication in his head. 'George, make the most of your chances this week. Jupiter, the planet of good fortune,' and she'd lifted her eyes to the ceiling in acknowledgement of its undoubted presence, 'is ready to help people looking for advancement through good honest toil. Don't let opportunities slip by.'

George would listen attentively—he was naturally disposed to believe—although daily attendance at school did make him wonder what sort of opportunities could come his way.

Being cast out of home caused George neither fear nor sadness. He knew he was strong and healthy, and he had had enough of school. Perhaps the old drunk was right, at fourteen, it was time enough to earn a living. And, curiously, his mother's fascination for living by the stars had given him a sense of his own worldly destiny and significance: 'You were born under a good sign, George, you can be sure of that. Houdini and Nostradamus and Johann Sebastian Bach and you were all born under the same sign—Libran in the seventh house.' The possibility that Genghis Khan or Judas or the warmonger, the Kaiser Wilhelm, might also have been born under the same sign didn't enter their minds.

After walking a few blocks George turned into a lane, its narrowness an invitation for some respite from the wide, windswept street he had struggled along. A glow from a building George knew as the Ballet Shoe Factory beckoned like a hearth from within the lane. Shady lowered his head against the bitter wind and decided upon a closer look.

The enormous back section of the Ballet Shoe Factory was well-lit with no interior signs of life. George hurdled the back fence and took temporary shelter in one of the many nooks the building afforded. Out of the direct lash of the wind and with the occasional comforting cackling of hens from the chook pens as company George had fallen asleep.

'And who have we got here?' said an old woman's voice. For a few moments George forgot where he was and thought the woman was his mother. But it was a large elderly woman—Mrs Gorham was her name—with stout calves and ankles that spoke down to him.

George blinked in the morning light and when he spoke his teeth chattered from the cold: 'Ge Ge Ge George…'

The elderly woman folded her hands across the apron she wore about her waist. 'And what would I be thinking now,' she chastised herself, 'asking questions of a lad in the outdoors on such a frosty morning.'

Mrs Gorham led George inside.

For a house so large he had been struck by its warmth. There were paintings upon the walls and the rooms were dense with furniture. He had briefly caught sight of the 'salon' and its mirrored wall and the many pairs of ballet shoes arrayed on shelves about that vast room. She led him along a corridor into an enormous kitchen with a table at its centre, around which, in every one of its many chairs was a boy of varying age and size with his head buried in a bowl of what looked to be porridge—steaming hot porridge with heaped spoons of sugar melting on top.

The boys all looked up at George as one. 'This is George,' she announced.

'The George that slayed the dragon, I think not,' said one of the older boys.

The boys looked back down at their bowls and resumed eating.

George took a moment to appraise the dirt upon his trousers and the mud upon his boots, feeling somehow dirtier for being inside.

'Quite a menagerie,' the old lady declared while she ladled porridge from a pot to a bowl. She placed the bowl at the only spare setting at the table. 'Come and eat it before it gets cold.'

A mouthful of hot porridge pleasantly singed his tongue.

'Where do you come from, lad?' the old lady asked.

George swallowed the porridge with some difficulty and

told her he came from just down the road. 'The old man threw me out.'

Mrs Gorham shook her head. 'And I suppose you'd be looking for a place to rest your bones.'

'I can look after meself,' he mumbled into the bowl.

'And a grand job you'd be doing of that,' said Mrs Gorham as she balanced a thick slice of bread on the lip of George's bowl. 'Not going to school, no job either, I'll wager.'

George didn't think these were questions.

'I'll give you a pound and ten shillings a week with room and board. For that you'll do the daily deliveries into the city and any odd jobs that require doing around the factory. The arrangement will be reviewed every month and I won't hear another word upon the matter. Harold, here,' she seemed to indicate the eldest boy, 'will show you where you'll sleep.'

Some weeks passed, during which, from time to time, George would sneak home when his stepfather was out and visit his mother. She was invariably surprised at his good health and general condition. He told her that he'd fallen upon his feet and gotten a job at the Ballet Shoe Factory down the road. 'Really,' she'd asked, 'doing what, exactly?' George replied, 'Deliveries mainly. They wanted someone reliable-like.' Her son's good fortune seemed too good to be true. 'I thought they'd gone out of business long ago,' she said. 'Heaven's no Mother, business is booming. A famous Danish ballerina is visiting next week. There's a mad scramble getting ready for that I can tell you.' His mother was puzzled—a ballerina in Williamstown? For her it was a notion as likely as the prime minister coming over for a Sunday roast. 'Son, you'd be pulling my leg.'

Indeed George was not exaggerating. Adeline Genée, billed by the Australian promoters as the Finest Dancer In

The World and touring Sydney and Melbourne for a series of concerts had reserved a time for a fitting of *pointe* ballet shoes at the Ballet Shoe Factory. What George didn't tell his mother was that the lady who owned the Ballet Shoe Factory was an eccentric old thing that regularly took in boys who were strays and provided jobs for them where she could.

For George, who had wished and prayed for better times, his wishes and prayers had been answered. The boys were rascals but he had never had better companions. The bicycle ride to the city by steam ferry to Port Melbourne was a daily adventure and hardly like work. But most unexpectedly he fell in love: not with a girl but with the Ballet Shoe Factory itself. He would admit this to no one, scared they would think him crazy and for a time George thought he might be touched. Touched was a favourite expression of Mrs Gorham for anyone not quite right in the head—which it so happened was what some people thought of her. 'They think I'm batty still making these things,' she'd say to George, holding up a worn, pink, satin ballet shoe. 'The industrial revolution my foot,' she'd say without irony. 'I'll go the way of the glass-blowers over my dead body.' Every time she said this, it made George shiver.

Sometimes on a cloudless night, despite the cold, George would drag his mattress out into the backyard and lie beneath the heavens. He'd recall the Yesternight stories his mother told him. Stories with no beginning and no end, as boundless as the universe where the stars and planets and moons and meteorite showers were the heroes and villains. She'd begin every story exactly the same, not with a, 'Once upon a time,' but with an 'In Yesternight.' For his part he would trace a line through the faraway pinpricks of stars for what he thought was the Southern Cross or the Scorpion or the Crab, and imagine each as the characters in a story. So drawn the Scorpion and the Crab and other celestial marvels would come to life, fighting for good or evil and sometimes to save the world.

On busy nights the light from the Ballet Shoe Factory was so bright that George found it difficult to pick out the stars. Then he would turn his attention to the salon and the old lady inside. Her work was seemingly never done. Long after the other shoemakers had departed, she would return to the salon and ply away with needle, hammer and stitching awl into the early hours of the morning. Unlike his stepfather, the old lady never made him come inside or asked what he might be doing lying on a mattress in the middle of the backyard. Occasionally she'd look through the window into the darkness outside and pinch her nose and adjust her spectacles. Otherwise she paid him no apparent mind.

George thought that the glow of the Ballet Shoe Factory was partly an aura of the old lady herself and not simply that of the many lights that she insisted remained lit all night. George wondered about the lights, and so one day, he asked Harold why Mrs Gorham would not allow them to be extinguished. 'She thinks this place is like a lighthouse in a storm. If a shipwrecked soul should come upon us, they will know they have found a safe place: a home away from home.' George thought the old lady was some kind of saint. He came to believe that if people knew how kind she was and how many good works she did even the Pope in Rome would want her for a saint.

Mrs Gorham called them her elves: cobblers, seam-stresses, even a jolly old fellow from London who insisted that he belonged to the Guild of Cordwainers, makers of bespoke shoes for the well-heeled. The salon itself didn't smell of dainty and pretty things. It smelt distinctively of leather. And no surprise that with great swathes of it piled against the walls and smaller pieces—soles and insoles— already fashioned by cutting, spread across tabletops and workbenches like footprints. There was, however, another curious smell that cut through the leather. The scent, if you could call it that, of Mrs Gorham's magic glue. The glue used to attach the hard toe-box to the point of the ballet shoe that made the base for dancing *en pointe*. The glue that George occasionally helped fetch in the horse and buggy from the abattoirs in Footscray. How he hated those trips, riding shotgun with Harold, the awful haul of boiled horses' remains bouncing in their pots on the boards of the buggy floor.

Mrs Gorham added special ingredients to the glue, one a perfume, to camouflage the stench and another for extra strength. The latter ingredient an orange viscous concoction with a vile smell. She'd ladle and mix the ingredients in pots just inside the back door of the salon. The shoemakers would beg her to take the pots outside. But Mrs Gorham would wag her finger at them and say that she would not leave her magic potion out where it would be a temptation for competitors to steal. 'When ballet people think of *pointe* shoes they think of the Ballet Shoe Factory and that's the way I want to keep it.' No one cared to argue with the old lady. With all the jumping and spinning and heat the dancers' feet generated the glue needed to be especially strong. 'No girl on her tippy toes will be falling off my shoes if I can help it.'

Every second Wednesday was rehearsal day. One end of the salon would be set up like a stage with a raised polished wooden floor for dancing. The local ballet schools would take turns putting on a production. Mrs Gorham and her 'elves' would arrange their working chairs in a semicircle around the stage. Only the dancers and their teachers were allowed in to watch: a private viewing—no mothers allowed. But Mrs Gorham didn't mind her boys sneaking a look. George was the most fascinated of all. He'd press his face up against the window, absorbing every *pas de deux* and *jetté* from the beginning of a rehearsal to the very end.

On those Wednesdays George would be up early. His destination was the Princess Theatre on the other side of the City of Melbourne in Spring Street. Counting the ride on the steam ferry from Newport and depending on traffic the journey might take an hour. On every trip he could have been bowled over. It was a bit like the Wild West. Horses and carts and trams and automobiles, and sometimes herds of animals crowded the streets as their drovers urged them on to the Queen Victoria Market just down the way.

George would be met at the backstage door by a maid of sorts—her hair covered in a scullery cap. She'd hold the door open and wave him inside and down the dark corridors with which he had become familiar. Ushered along at speed, barely able to take in the little 'stars' on the doors and the names inscribed in gold paint, George would be directed to a large wicker basket beneath one of the wings of the stage. Inside were the most precious of things, ballerinas' *pointe* shoes: virtually new, most discarded after just one performance. Sometimes the basket was full to brimming and George would struggle to fit them all inside the two jute bags he'd sling over his shoulder.

It was like Christmas when Mrs Gorham opened up the bags of shoes for the girls. George would watch the girls diving in the bags for a pair that would fit. There would be squeals of delight and tears and sometimes Mrs Gorham would have to clap to bring an end to the jostling, and restore some order. But George could see that the old lady loved these days. Her face would go bright pink with excitement and her eyes behind the thick glasses cloud with tears of joy.

George hadn't known what to expect of a ballerina. In the salon, he had seen customers—usually girls but sometimes women in ballet costume—pirouetting on the wooden practice dance floor or at the barre before the mirrored wall, giving their ballet shoes a thorough trial. But never a prima ballerina and certainly not the greatest dancer in the world: Adeline Genée.

There was, according to one of the boys a framed photograph of her in the salon. George's knowledge of the salon was scant, limited as it was to the occasions he was allowed in to give Mrs Gorham a delivery of shoes or a message, and then hustled out: 'Out with you now and all your dirt and grit,' Mrs Gorham would say to him, 'and away from my beautiful shoes.' So whether or not there was a photograph of Adeline Genée in the salon, he wouldn't know.

As the date for her visit approached, George's interest grew. In his mind, she was no less than a film star. On the appointed day he finished his deliveries early. Unsure how close Mrs Gorham would allow him or any of the boys to get to the ballerina, George decided to hide in a closet of one of the upstairs rooms, and wait there until he heard what was certain to be a commotion upon her arrival. In the scramble of activity that he had no doubt would greet her, he planned to descend the little-used back stairs and get as close to her as he dared. If Mrs Gorham should spy him, he would be off like a shot. She would forgive him as he knew she had a heart of gold.

The commotion happened just as he thought. A flurry of high-pitched, whispering voices and the rustle of fine dresses floated up the stairwell into the closet where George remained hidden in a sparsely furnished room stacked with shoeboxes. In a room that should have been empty of people, he began to hear the most elusive of noises—the soft drop of clothing on a carpeted floor, the broken sounds of a song half-sung half-spoken. George peered through a crack in the door and to his amazement—a lady who could only be Adeline Genée—stood before the closet, gazing at the mirror inset within its door, almost as if she were looking at George himself. For some time George was transfixed by the face of the most amazing creature he had ever seen. Skin the colour of alabaster, her bare shapely arms befitting a Greek goddess…but no…she wasn't…but she was…she was changing into a tutu that he could see she'd cast over the back of the chair behind her. 'I'll be right down,' he heard her say with a distinct accent.

George flew out of the closet before she could remove another stitch of clothing. He heard a frightful scream as he hurtled down the stairs and through the expectant crowd in the salon. Unless he had misheard, the accusation of 'Peeping Tom' was shouted. His first thought was of refuge, a place to hide. They would never find him in the labyrinth of drains that ran like catacombs beneath the Ballet Shoe Factory and the streets of Williamstown. He would hide in there until the storm blew over. And so he did, just for the night, because he was right about Mrs Gorham, she did have a heart of gold. She told the boys to go find Georgie Green and bring him back. Madame Adeline Genée could get her ballet slippers somewhere else if she was going to make a fuss over one of her boys.

When the train pulled in at Spencer Street Station, Shady was already waiting to alight at the door of the train. A conductor smiled at his eagerness, opened the door wide and asked if he needed a hand. Shady replied he was fine and the conductor stepped back, and wished him a pleasant stay in Melbourne. He stepped cautiously onto the platform, his legs stiff and his shoulders sore from the confinement of the journey. The bag was not too heavy, and, of this, he was thankful, as he saw other passengers, struggling with heavy suitcases along the platform in the direction of the exit.

After consulting a train timetable, Shady slowly descended a long flight of stairs and tracked along a tiled, damp underground passageway, following the sign to Platforms 6&7 for the Williamstown and Beau Vista Lines. Soon he was on a blue Harris train and headed west. Thirty minutes later, he was at Williamstown Beach Station where he gave his ticket to the stationmaster and went down the ramp, and then along the street running parallel with the railway tracks for a few hundred yards until he met Parker Street and turned left. Parker Street would take him all the way to Nelson Place and his ultimate destination: the Ballet Shoe Factory.

FOUR
THE WRECKING BALL

The stars in my galaxy shone brighter than ever. Shady Green had still not come forward. I overheard a woman in the butcher's say: 'That boy must have been kissed by a fairy.' The chances of any Shady Green collecting the inheritance were dimming by the day. Len had taken me aside and explained that if the inheritance were shared equally amongst the aunts and uncles, Mother's individual share would still be considerable. I didn't need telling. Arithmetic was not one of my major problems. But that tongue of mine was tied with greed. I couldn't tell him I wanted it all. Besides, why couldn't the relatives accept Tick Tock's clear intentions?

Len suggested we see the bank after school. He suspected, quite correctly, that my head was financially freewheeling with ideas of new guitars, overseas holidays and a set of wheels to be parked in the garage for the better part of two years until I reached driving age. Something had to be done—I heard him say to Mother—to get me on track.

For the meeting with the bank manager, I was decked out in a blue jacket and a blue and white striped tie. The starch

in the collar chafed my neck and the belt in the trousers
was too big for my waist and hung in a half-loop down my
thigh. I had knotted the tie in a double-Windsor to use up
all the slack. It knotted so thick it could have hung a steer.
The pants were my best—not the same colour as the jacket
but close. The pants were pleated in sharp defined ridges all
the way to the cuffs where they flared a little over my size
seven black Grosbys. I had almost bought a silver-buttoned
jacket from Fletcher Jones. My mother thought I looked
like an admiral and so did I. The Fletcher Jones man had
said, 'My you look smart.' The Fletcher Jones man could
shove it. I refused to be a complete spectacle.

Charlie Breen, the bank manager, also came from Beau
Vista. His face was always long and sad as if the bank had
just been robbed. Before we left home Mother said to Len,
'I hope Charlie's all right.' This had something to do with
Charlie's 'attack of nerves.' Charlie had reached the end of
the line with his wife Charlene and the reason for that was
all the shoplifting. Charlene couldn't keep her hands off what
wasn't hers. They were known as Charlie 1 and Charlie 2,
and the pity of it all was they couldn't have a little Charlie
3 no matter how hard they tried. No amount of thieving
would get that.

If there was one thing that banks did well it was intim-
idate. The power of classic marble pillars, soaring vaulted
ceilings and acres of granite floors to drive home the insig-
nificance of the customer and the importance of the bank.
Charlie Breen's office was large and on the seventh floor
of an old building right in the middle of town, the Paris
end of Collins Street. It had windows on three sides, the
blinds drawn back to tight folds in each of the corners.
The cityscape was a raw, voyeuristic view of rooftops and
janitor huts and air conditioning units. Upon one rooftop a

woman sunbaked in a red bikini on a patch of green carpet laid out like a strip of lawn.

Charlie met us at the door of his office. He motioned for us to take a seat in one of the wide, black low-slung chairs that dotted the office. On a teak coffee table was a cigarette box full to brimming with filter tip cigarettes. Charlie offered one to my father who declined with a dismissive hand.

'Given up?'

'Filthy habit.' My father laughed. 'Reformed smoker. We're the worst.'

'You don't mind?'

'Nah. Go ahead.'

Charlie took a cigarette from the box with a shaky hand. He flipped his silver lighter open with a metallic click. One hand held the other as he carefully raised the ominously large naked flame to the shaking cigarette.

Before Len gave up I'd steal the butts and go around the side of the house for a puff. The cancer thing worried me. When I got caught the first time I was told that the fags would give me cancer. I asked how many it took? My mother said if I was unlucky it might only be one. I didn't totally believe the darts could be that lethal but the thought never left me that it mightn't require many to take me out. The fags were good because they provided personality and a veneer of manliness. Benson and Hedges was the brand for me, not the bitter throat-scorching unfiltered Turfs knocked-back at the rate of 40 a day by Aunt Myra. Even if a kid didn't really smoke he couldn't *not* know how. It was a life-skill.

Charlie blew a plume of smoke at the ceiling. 'Sorry to hear about Marg's father. I'm sure that came as a shock.'

Len nodded. 'We're over the worst of it.'

'Would you like something to drink?' Both Len and I

declined in our own fashion, my 'No,' vaporising in spit and a small choking fit.

Charlie shuffled through some papers. 'No mortgage.'

'Good,' Len said.

'Got a caveat though.'

'Caveat?'

'Ah,' Charlie examined a document, 'in the name of a Shady Green.'

I did not have a clue what caveat meant.

'What's that?' Len asked.

'It's a registration of a legal interest in the property for a debt owing to a Shady Green.'

My father shrugged his shoulders. 'Can we get rid of it?'

'Depends.'

'On what?'

'Who is he?'

'Prime beneficiary under the will. Haven't got a clue who he is or where he is. Michel's next in line. Subject to this Shady Green character showing up.'

Charlie looked at me with an appreciative, nervous smile and lit another cigarette. 'Right,' said Charlie regarding me thoughtfully through a small cloud of smoke. 'What are you going to do with all that money, eh?'

Clearly, Charlie meant something beyond a shagging wagon and a room full of guitars. If I said what I thought I'd be revealing myself as the shallow product of a rampant consumer culture—a revelation that my reputation could probably do without. I mean it might be all right to have a shopping list of stuff as yardsticks of success, but not such a great idea to have it out on display as some kind of social manifesto of greed.

Then, suddenly, a massive molten metal wrecking ball appeared out of nowhere, swung past the window and ploughed into the building next door. The noise was not as loud as you'd expect, muffled no doubt by double-glazed windows. The office shook.

'Damn, they've started up again,' said Charlie and he turned to face the window. The wrecking ball passed by the window for a second time. Attached to a hook the size of a man's arm, it shaped an immense metal question mark against the sky. Once again the room shuddered and Charlie Breen shrugged his shoulders. 'What do you do?'

While my father and Charlie Breen discussed the arcane world of caveats, I watched that big metal question mark go backwards and forwards like a hypnotist's fob watch. Over and over it swung and crashed. Every so often I would hear the aftermath, the distant collapse of building material as it hit the earth.

Entranced, I leant back in my chair against the window, so close I felt the heat of the day upon my cheek. I stretched so that my feet no longer reached the floor. I felt this illusory sensation of being outside on the thinnest of ledges, my back braced against the window through which I had somehow imaginatively stepped.

Far below, a big yellow crane was chocked high on long stands of timber. In its cab the operator was faceless, with only the motion of his arms visible. The wrecking ball drew back in a slow arc, and I watched it against the sky, a dull orange on a striking cobalt blue.

Below on the pavement a crowd had gathered to watch. I could make out mouths shaped like little Os as the wrecking ball reached the end of its long descending arc, moments from another blow. But what I saw was not the partially destroyed office block. There, suspended in the air before me, hovered the Ballet Shoe Factory, shimmering and directly in line with the ball's trajectory.

'No,' I said softly in terror. I raised my hands as if to push the ball away my legs shaking. I felt that I might tumble at any moment off the imaginary ledge. As the wrecking ball crashed into the stained glass windows of the Ballet Shoe Factory, I realised that silence had fallen. Len and Charlie Breen were no longer talking. Below us was a dusty oblivion, the roiling cloud of dust the only clue to what had disappeared. That last mighty smash had demolished what remained of the building. It was as if it had never been there at all.

My father and Charlie Breen contemplated my situation and then resumed their talk. The wrecking ball swayed in the air with nothing left to hit—the spirit of progress with nowhere to go. I had witnessed this languid effortless obliteration and felt a shiver of dread. Could the wrecker read my mind? Was I any better than one of my self-serving greedy relatives? Any better than a developer for whom it was merely business to destroy the beautiful and irreplaceable? I had glimpsed a possible future in which I would be oblivious to the rights of Shady Green (whoever he was) and the obscure wishes of my grandfather.

I dug my hands deep into my pockets. In my right pocket, fast inside, I touched the key to the Ballet Shoe Factory. I revolved the key in my fingers. Its shape and hardness were reassuring and suggested all was not yet lost. Each revolution in the tight space of my pocket felt as though I was reeling in a fish I hadn't yet seen.

My father spoke, 'You feel all right?'

'Fine,' I lied.

The key was out of my pocket and my father saw it.

'What's that?' Len took the key from the palm of my hand. 'The Ballet Shoe Factory?' he asked.

I nodded.

'Never seen this before. Beautiful work. Have a look, Charlie.'

My father passed the key to Charlie Breen who held it to the light like a jeweller would appraise a diamond. The silver edges of the key glinted and there was a momentary sparkle of light from its eyelet.

'Yes, beautiful,' agreed Charlie, and returned the key to my father for closer inspection.

'My Time Flies. Do you know what that means?'

'A horse, I think,' I replied although I did not know how I knew.

'A racehorse?'

I nodded again. My father continued to look thoughtfully at the key for some kind of insight.

'So what's the plan?' asked Charlie stubbing out a cigarette.

'No plan yet. We need to know where we stand on this Shady Green and the caveat.'

Charlie leaned back in his chair. 'Shouldn't be a problem getting the caveat removed provided this Green character doesn't turn up.'

All this talk of mortgages and caveats whistled past my ears like bullets at Lone Pine. I knew what I'd seen at the Ballet Shoe Factory and it was probably just a derelict's fire. Should it be my problem that the old building might get demolished? Should it make any difference that I had seen a future that had alerted me to the likelihood of what could happen? Should it be my responsibility to help find the one person who could take it all away from me? Yet as much as I wanted the inheritance, I knew I couldn't make some naked grab without any regard for what Tick Tock might have wanted.

I missed Tick Tock. We were close. 'Chook pen,' he'd say and I'd follow him. It was like our office. Out we'd go and he'd talk to me about the chickens and sometimes the old days and sometimes how hopeless some of his sons-in law were. He gave the impression that I was neither man nor child but that I could be trusted. He'd have me in the chook pen counting to ten in the pidgin-Japanese he'd picked up in the prisoner of war camps. Hectored in a way that I would have taken offence with from anyone else, I'd repeat the numbers after him until I got them right. Esther and Malcolm would poke fun from a distance. I really didn't mind. I'd do it for Tick Tock.

On the drive back from the bank I looked through my side of the Ford Fairmont's windshield and Len looked through his. It was as if the rules of the road prescribed this as a safe form of driving. Len had had non-standard bucket seats fitted as an option and so we sat deep and low-down. Every now and again Len stole a look to see if I had dozed off.

Finally he spoke, 'How's school?'

Len never asked about school. He was not that sort of father. He was old school: you went until the State said you could leave. Except in my case I was not leaving any time soon.

'It's all right.'

'All that trouble to get you in and it's just *all right*?'

Barely twelve months before, with aspirations of higher academic achievement, I'd pushed for a change of school. No longer the sprawling industrial paddocks of Beau Vista North, I now attended school in Essendon, if a little west of its epicentre, in the quarried hills where developing Keilor sprawled and bore down on its older neighbour. Now it took a drive to the station, three trains and a bus before I arrived at my chosen place of learning: St Sebastian's.

Nobody made me leave St Michael's in Beau Vista. I could have coasted through with friends I'd known since kindergarten. Instead I just had to know what a better school was like; just had to understand *how* smart boys from good schools were, boys who made it into Law and Medicine in droves, not as some spectacular exception that would warrant a write-up in the *Beau Vista Star*.

'No it's good.'

The only good thing about going to St Sebastians was the girls I got to meet on the trains I caught to get there. In seemingly no time my contact with girls had gone from the infrequency of a NASA moonshot to almost taken for granted. Girls had ceased to be a phenomenon. I no longer stared at girls as if I was doing some kind of an inventory like they'd lost an arm or an ear or simply forgotten to put a leg on.

'Told anyone about what's going on with the Ballet Shoe Factory?'

'At school?'

There would have been no holding me back at the old school. My impending windfall and climb in financial worth was not something I'd want to keep to myself. But at St Sebastians the only so-called friend I had was the quint-essential smart-arse, John Carson. To John Carson I was 'de Gaulle', or just plain 'Charles' or more generically 'Froggie'. John Carson, who had befriended me in his own oblique way, had got it into his head that Michel was French and that it would be very funny to call someone so obviously on the short side after someone who had been so obviously tall. It might not have been so funny if John Carson's fellow clowns had had some idea of who de Gaulle had been. Such that when I did tuck shop duty, boys would line up at the counter with their right hand tucked *Napoleonically* inside their blue blazers.

John Carson had it in his head that Beau Vista was some sort of slum and that I was some sort of slum-dweller. Of course, he would not have believed in the absolute truth of this, but he would have believed in enough of it to make it a credible source of mirth. But one of the great benefits of living in virtually another world is that people in that other world, only knew what you told them. The social immolation John Carson was capable of meting out if I jumped the gun on any inheritance didn't bear thinking about. I would hold back on telling John Carson about the Ballet Shoe Factory until it was a certainty.

'Do you think I should?'

And with that I turned my eyes upon Len like headlights on high beam. He turned back to the road his face kind of dazed.

When Len's little hazel eyes had locked upon the steel-blue rays of mine there had been a confusion, almost a sadness in them. Not unlike the time with the motor-mower when I was ten and he had offered to let me cut the lawn. My indifference had bordered on dismay that he might think I would want to do it. No greater honour could have been bestowed by Len at such an age. The alarm bells that rang then might well be ringing again, because, if nothing else, I was a consistent child.

The mail lay unopened upon the stand in the hallway. Len picked the envelopes up in a bundle. I could see the largest envelope was from Penguin Pools and I knew more or less what would be inside. I had requisitioned yet another brochure from an in-ground swimming pool manufacturer. I averaged five to six replies a week as we headed into the summer season. To apply pressure on Len I had arranged a rectangular outline of bricks in the backyard so he could imagine how the pool would appear, installed in some land-scaped context.

Len tore the envelope open as he walked down the passage. 'You can't even swim properly,' he said.

'Is there a better way to learn?' I asked. The benefit of receiving dozens of these things was that I got the chance to rehearse the answer based upon prior rejections.

'What about the big thing out the front?' Len referred to that very large body of water called Port Phillip Bay that was directly out the front of our house.

'Dad,' I said, bemused that he'd missed the obvious, 'you can't look out for sharks and learn to swim at the same time. Besides what about all that kicking, that's just the sort of thing that gets their attention.'

'Who'd clean it?'

Len thought he had me.

'It's automatic. A thing crawls around the bottom of the pool. It comes free with the pool. You don't have to do a thing.'

In the movies at about this point the dad says, 'Honey I'm home,' making his presence generally known in a defer-ential way to those already there. Len instead ritually called out, 'Ho ho ho,' although there was nothing seasonal about the greeting, he said it all year round. When Len said he was home, this was the equivalent of a captain reboarding his ship after shore leave and everything but the naval whistle would go off to recognise his return. A chorus of voices duly responded, 'Ho ho ho,' from the far reaches of the dining room.

The whole family were already seated at the dining room table in their assigned positions. Each chair might as well have had a name carved upon it, as it was inconceivable we would sit in any other place. The quietness of the gathering was indicative of expectant news.

Len said an additional muffled, 'Ho,' to my mother as he traversed the carpet and a, 'Smells good whatever it is,' before he sat down. He ruffled Malcolm's hair with his thick stubby fingers. For Esther he reserved a squint.

Mother portioned out the veal cutlets and vegetables. She piled a plateful in front of Len. There was never an occasion in which Len would be served other than first.

'Did you see Lisa today?' asked Malcolm as he ran a cob of corn along a bared set of teeth.

Did I talk in my sleep? Or did the kid have some special gift for divining my every thought and deed?

'Put the corn down when you're talking,' said Mother. 'Who's Lisa?'

Gerry referred to Lisa disparagingly as my girlfriend although he knew I'd never spoken a complete sentence to her. She had been my quest for six months but last Friday I had ended whatever there was to end. Not for the first time I could not absolutely decide if the girl I had set my sights on was who I really wanted.

'Lisa's no one.'

'Doesn't sound like no one,' Len said already making serious inroads into the cutlet. At moments like this there were certain similarities between Henry VIII and Len. If Len had grabbed one of the veal cutlets, gnawed it to the bone and thrown the bone over his shoulder, I was sure nobody would have been overly surprised.

While I had had a spectacular lack of success in my search for Miss Dead Right—there was hardly a queue lining up for the honour—the situation was always a work in progress. I just couldn't give up. I knew I had hurt Lisa. Courage had failed me. I guessed I waited for someone better. In the meantime I would do without, which was all I had ever known, which I would have thought would have made me do something differently to whatever it was I was doing.

Esther planted her elbows on the table. 'Yes, tell us about Lisa. That should be interesting.'

Almost to himself but loud enough to be heard Malcolm said, 'Or maybe Linda?'

Well, Linda X would be more interesting but on the Richter scale of romantic disaster and emotional fallout that scored an easy 10 this was not my idea of family entertainment. 'She's history.'

'All right this Linda, then,' declared Esther.

'Don't you start.' Mother would spare me the inquisition. 'More importantly, though, what about Charlie Breen?'

Len grabbed a cutlet and tore the flesh from the bone. 'A Shady Green has a caveat over the Ballet Shoe Factory.'

I waited to see if he would throw the bone over his shoulder. He didn't but he did lick his fingers.

'Really Len do you have to?' Mother said.

Len grabbed another cutlet.

Mother gave up on the table manners and probably wondered why she ever bothered. 'Shady Green, again, eh? The plot thickens.'

Esther's eyes darted from her book to me and back to her book. 'Maybe you could enlighten us on that, sport?'

The need for a distraction loomed large. 'Do you remember Sister Fishface and the time I almost lost my eye?' I asked.

Esther telegraphed a look that said I wasn't going to get away with running a smokescreen.

Malcolm asked me to tell the story about Sister Fishface.

Esther closed the book in her lap. 'Can't you see what he's doing? He knows all about this Shady Green.'

'You never met Sister Fishface did you?' I said to Malcolm.

'Oh please can someone stop him,' said Esther.

I would try and tell the story no matter what.

It was as if the pitiless Sister Patricia aka Sister Fishface with those colourless piscine eyes stood before us. I recreated the unnerving habit she had of sucking air through her top teeth in a perennial search for non-existent food particles, and told how one day on my way home from school, minding my own business, a state school kid had thrown a yonnie and hit me just below the eye.

'Give it a break, you Freak,' said Esther.

I held up my hand with the missing half finger as if to say if I was a freak who was to blame for that?

Mother hated it when I did this, but she could hardly yell at the person with the upraised digital mutilation. 'Michel,' she said as sweetly as she could, no doubt recalling the axe incident more vividly than she wished, 'could you put your hand down while at the table.'

'She called me a Freak,' I complained.

'Well he is…'

The mutilated hand remained held high in the warm air of the dining room like a curing ham.

'Leave him alone!' demanded Mother. My having half a digit less than the full complement was the only guaranteed route I knew to maternal sympathy. She couldn't bear to look at it. Talking about it was hard enough.

Esher resorted to beseeching hand signals. 'Can't you see what he's doing? Are you blind to him?'

Len unfortunately had had enough. 'I don't want to know any more about this Fishface thing. And stop calling your brother a Freak.'

'OK OK,' pleaded Esther less than remorsefully, 'but

what about this Shady Green? Why don't we find out a bit more about this elusive character?' She was desperate to reveal what a fraud I was.

I looked up from my plate with the hurt saintly expression I dialled up for special emergencies. To emphasise the insult, I held my fork aloft with half a potato and a few smashed peas impaled upon its tines like 'I surrender', and the mutilated finger clearly showing. Cutlery scraped on plates, the dog barked in the backyard. 'Not my Shady Green,' I declared, the food muffling the words.

The book fell off Esther's lap with a clatter. 'Oh, I'll bet. How very convenient for you. How very convenient. Can't you all see?' she implored. 'It's all a pathetic little scheme.'

'Is it?' asked my father.

I almost choked on a big piece of spud going down my throat. 'Scheme?'

'Who is Shady Green?' said Esther.

My eyes opened wide in wonder. 'I don't know.'

'Leaned on the poor old man to get yourself in line for most of what he's got and then threw this Shady Green into the mix to put us all off the scent. Hey presto little Michel White gets it all.'

'That's enough,' said my father.

And at that very moment it was possible they were thinking what a greedy undeserving little bugger they had on their hands.

FIVE

HOWARD STARR AND HIS
TECHNICOLOUR MASTER PLAN

Howard Starr Theatrical Productions operated out of a small makeshift office off a goods ramp behind the University Theatre. It was cold bare concrete surrounded by delivery pallets. An environment less suited to creative endeavour would be hard to imagine. My dreams of fame and fortune receded as I mounted each steep, stained step.

Howard, if not for two years of deferrals, would, on a conventional academic timeline, have been in the third year of a Fine Arts degree. Instead, he was immersed in what he grandly styled the business of an impresario. Windowless, dark and stuffy, the office I poked my head into, was as welcoming as the goods ramp outside. But the office came rent-free, in return for particular unspecified services. Howard's humble headquarters came courtesy of the vice-chancellor himself.

If it was 25 degrees outside it was 15 degrees inside the storeroom. The concrete floor was painted black and the walls another dark colour—maybe Lincoln green. It was as dark as if I'd walked into a cinema in session. Hung on the walls were theatrical posters of past University Theatre productions. If there had been sufficient light from the turned down, green art deco lamp on the old kitchen table that passed for a desk—and given all other light had been effectively absorbed by the colour scheme—I would have seen in small writing in every corner of every poster, *Howard Starr Theatrical Productions Presents.*

The man at the desk sat hunched over and reading. His face was bathed in the green horror show glow of the lamp. I presumed this was Howard Starr, whom I had last encountered, in full costume, on muck-up day four years before. I knocked softly on the wall near the door. So far my outstretched arm was the only part of my body that had dared to enter.

The ghoulish figure shifted in his seat, as if his concentration had been disturbed, if not quite broken. He seemed to turn and smile—the smile let down by his teeth, discoloured and shadowed. He was dressed like a leading architect stepping out of his vintage Morgan at a golf club members' monthly medal. His trousers were woven in a spiralling corkscrew design of puce, aquamarine and canary yellow. His floral shirt was unbuttoned at the collar and for two further buttons beyond that. On his feet he wore a chunky pair of brown shoes laced a lighter brown.

My knock had produced no discernible reaction beyond a slight shifting in his chair. *What now?* I'd screwed up the courage and rung Howard to let him know something of what I had in mind for the Ballet Shoe Factory. *Sure* he'd said *come on over.* So here I was, feeling as awkward and out of place as Commissioner Gordon suddenly alone in the Batcave. I felt glued to the spot, my tongue jammed dry and tight against the roof of my mouth.

Howard loosened the clasp of a large folder on his desk and removed a page. As he examined it in the half-light of the lamp, he simultaneously swept his arm in a gesture that seemed to be welcoming me in.

I hovered on the threshold.

He turned and looked at me. 'I presume you must be Mr White?'

I took a few uncertain steps forward with my hand stuck out. His soft clammy paw curled around my fingers. This was not a handshake Len would have approved of. Howard gazed down on me from a considerable height. *Untidy little scruff* seemed to ooze from his every condescending pore. He waved me to a seat, then picked at some lint on the sleeve of his shirt. He rolled the lint into a ball and flicked it to the other side of the room.

There he sat with his fingers interlaced beneath his chin.

'I had a look at it,' he announced.

Did he mean the Ballet Shoe Factory?

'Beautiful old building. Lots of great spaces.'

I nodded enthusiastically. 'Maybe a Performing Arts Centre?'

He smiled. 'Maybe.'

My cheeks twitched.

'Do you smoke?' He opened a box on his desk and extracted an enormous cigar. As I shook my head he lit it with a big cedar match. The aroma of new wood mixed with the smoky tang of the flaming match.

'Is it yours?' he asked.

'The Ballet Shoe Factory?'

He nodded.

'Sort of.'

'Uhm, kinda vague.'

As he gazed thoughtfully at me I gave him a laboured explanation of the provisional status of my inheritance.

A lock of dark, curly hair loosened on Howard's brow.

'Who *is* this Shady Green?'

'He's probably no one. My grandfather could be a bit weird.'

'So who's living there now?'

'Must be deros.'

He raised an eyebrow. 'Have you seen them?'

'I think they're pretty hard to pin down. Elusive.'

Howard Starr blew a pensive ring of smoke.

The office on campus might be free but Howard's hold on it was tenuous. The prospect of a bayside setting and a long-term place of residence at the Ballet Shoe Factory had their appeal. The occupancy arrangement with the vice-chancellor was not working out. Only the week before Howard had been summoned to the vice-chancellor's office atop the Administration Building. There, surrounded by impressive shelving of Hansards and Law Reports, and without a single witness, the silver-haired, straight-backed vice-chancellor, the embodiment of bureaucratic steel, had given Howard fair warning his time was all but up. 'Can't keep on,' the vice-chancellor had said. And he meant the demonstrations: the War of course and now Child Care. 'Occupied the Council's chambers for five days last week. Longhaired hooligans. What would they know? Child Care. Hooey. Not on. Has to stop. Little bastards barricaded me in my own office. Broke some of the windows. Not bloody on,' fumed the vice-chancellor through a spray of spit.

Howard had listened nervously. Watergate, Contragate, Cash for Questions those modern political messes hadn't yet hit the news but he knew what he was involved in, what he was sitting on: the lit powder keg underneath his arse. The story he didn't want to emerge was this: Howard Starr aka the Maestro, on-campus funster, the Pied Piper of freshmen and women, the man with his own eponymous club El Maestro, complete with acolytes and a stall on orientation day for new recruits. The El Maestro in the sequinned suit of lights, fighting cape and matador's montera that showed up at every demonstration of any size or note or political significance to make merry, run riot, poke fun, in short do anything that belittled or degraded a cause. El Maestro didn't do any of this out of principle. He did it because he was on the payroll of the vice-chancellor.

The vice-chancellor was a law unto himself, who had done as he liked for as long as he liked. But with recent appointments to the university administration this had begun to change. His untrammelled power had begun to be questioned. This, and the rumour that the university paper had got hold of material that linked the administration with the activities of El Maestro had clearly rattled him. An ordinary man would have broken the arrangement then and there but he just wanted the job done. He wanted Howard's side of the arrangement honoured.

The patrician vice-chancellor put the fear of god into Howard. 'You're wasting my time, my money. What you're doing is ineffectual,' he yelled. He wanted El Maestro to quit prancing about in his bullfighter's suit of lights on the periphery of the action just gibing and cracking jokes. The university chief wanted Howard right in the middle of it all, breaking it up. Howard suggested there might be a modicum of danger in what he proposed. 'Stuff and nonsense. Crap. These malingerers couldn't beat time. They're gutless Peaceniks for Chrissakes.'

The free accommodation would clearly not continue without a further price. Howard could handle, even enjoyed, the comic, festive, playful persona he'd created, and apart from the odd negative reaction, generally speaking, protesters, organisers and bystanders, could see the funny side. Some even regarded his presence as an acknowledgement of the protest's relative importance. If El Maestro wasn't there it somehow wasn't hitting the mark. Howard was disruptive. A howling heckler from the sidelines, but he never stopped the demonstration running its course. The mission, as Howard saw it, was to be a thorough distraction and that was all. He was not there to break up the demonstration; there were state and federal police who could do that. In a disorderly and entertaining way he had made whatever purpose the demonstration had somewhat more difficult, not impossible to achieve. This was never the vice-chancellor's understanding.

A pin-dropping quiet had descended upon the storeroom. Howard was looking at me, and I at him, and I'd lost track of whose turn it was to speak. The question/answer question/answer routine needed a circuit breaker of some kind. A discarded scrunched-up piece of paper blew in the open door, and the harsh stiffness of its edges scratched on the bare concrete floor. The ball of paper twirled at the base of my chair, caught in an eddy going round and round like a mini-tornado. I stretched my feet to interrupt its orbit and it promptly circumscribed a wider orbit beyond my reach. How could I have had the gall to front up at a real-life impresario's office? Desperately I tried to put together a couple of coherent sentences about this vague idea of a Performing Arts Centre that I'd mentioned to him on the phone. Instead I sat clueless and pathetically thankful for the merciful distraction of an eddying piece of trash.

Howard saw before him not some slight and gormless boy but a youthful would-be Medici. Gauche and certainly unremarkable in every other way this Michel White kid had something Howard really needed: commercial premises. Michel's inexperience and youth should make things easier to manipulate. Howard leant across the desk. 'Do you know much about Hollywood?'

'Not a lot,' I confessed.

'Let me run a few ideas past you and see what you think.'

For thirty minutes Howard Starr sold me the idea I had so casually, inanely and incompletely pitched to him. It would be where Hollywood and Vine met downtown Williamstown. In time it could be its own Grauman's Chinese Theatre with famous alumnis' hands dunked in cement out the front. Not only the Performing Arts it could be a commercial blockbuster to boot. Throw in a soda fountain/ ice cream parlour and an entertainment precinct of some sort. It would be a mecca for young actors and performers from all over the city, and maybe the country. A place to learn, perform, hang out and get discovered in a vast commissary of up-and-coming talent. Australia had its National Institute for Dramatic Art, but this would aim at younger performers, tapping every government, corporate and artistic heartstring it could find.

I came for a smokescreen and left with a fully-fledged technicolour master plan to make it big in show business.

SIX
HOMEWARD BOUND

Shady Green leant alongside a primary school fence: Wil-liamstown Primary School State School No 8106. The school, he had attended as a boy and which had given him the moniker, Shady Green, just behind where the bicycle sheds used to be, in the shade of a large gum tree.

'You like your shade don't you, Georgie Green? Always taking yurself off for a doze in the shade. Hidin' out in the gloom and the dark. You're a bit of a Shady Green,' one of the kids had yelled back, and they'd all agreed that 'Shady' summed Georgie Green up best. No one needed to add that with skin a deep mocca in colour Shady was a moniker very well-suited to him.

Shady's coppery eyes took in what he wore; what a sight he thought he must be: dressed as though he was going to some wintry place, in a thick shirt, a jacket and a heavy pair of shoes. Melbourne was certainly a long way south but it was still summer.

Children came out to play. They poured from every direction and all parts of the school. The playground teemed with boys and girls running and shouting. Shady placed his bag at his feet and watched with concentrated interest. The sun came out from between the clouds. Perspiration trickled into his eyes from his matted, curly hair. Uncomfortably hot, Shady removed his coat and laid it over the fence.

The children kept a distance. Some looked his way, though, none ventured near. Eventually a person, who he presumed was a teacher, came across. She stood tall and her face had no friendliness in it. 'Can I help you?' she asked, and as she did, she frowned. The woman was quite young and verged on pretty. 'No, I'm just fine,' replied Shady. She seemed momentarily confounded. Shady adjusted his hat for the sun—the effect of the adjustment was to obscure his eyes. This may have been disturbing, this lack of eye contact. Shady curled up the brim of his hat, so that the teacher and he for a few moments could look into each other's eyes. The temptation to ring the police, Shady believed, was the subject of debate in her head. He knew it was mischievous of him to remain, when he had come to this realization. The teacher averted her gaze, and Shady scanned the black asphalted playground. Boys playing kick to kick, others marbles on chalked outlines, and in groups of three, girls skipping rope, one at either end counting, and the skipping girl, her eyes cast down for fear of tripping. The air was rent with shouting.

'Play-lunch?' asked Shady.

There was a whistle on a loop of string around the teacher's neck. It wouldn't take too much for her to blow it. He wondered what the whistle would sound like. Would it be a screeching sort of whistle or something almost Pied Piperish and tuneful? The woman gave the appearance of someone who was acutely aware of her responsibilities. Shady thought the whistle would screech and although his hearing was not as sharp as it used to be, he inwardly braced himself. As if she'd been cued, the teacher raised the whistle to her thin, heat-cracked lips and blew. The whistle merely warbled in the gusting breeze. Shady heard the pea wobbling in the whistle's throat. 'Jim Wilson you stop that right now,' the teacher yelled to a boy who had pinned another boy under his armpit.

The whistle and the shouting forced Shady a half-step back. A wave of dizziness made him unsteady on his feet. The teacher seemed to comprehend this unsteadiness and loss of balance as a sign of something else. 'Look I don't think it's a good idea standing here at the fence like this.' She crossed her arms, a not totally convincing figure of authority.

Shady thought it might help if he made conversation. Should he say he'd just come down from Brisbane? Or would that just make her more uneasy? After all until he went up there, he thought Queenslanders were a very strange lot. No, he wouldn't mention that.

'Used to go to school here,' he said.

The teacher's face brightened. She was relieved, if not relaxed, just a hen looking after her chicks. 'Oh really,' she looked interested in a superficial way. 'And when would that have been?'

Shady looked back in the direction of the railway line where he heard a train passing distantly. It was a lifetime ago. 'The year Comedy King won the Cup was my last,' and the teacher made an oval-shape with her mouth in vague, but unlikely, recognition of the name of the winning horse. He could not, however, recall the year. '19… something…'

The dizziness was passing, his legs felt steadier beneath him. He knew he shouldn't delay the journey any longer.

'Do you want something?' asked the young woman.

'Oh no,' said Shady, 'I've got everything I need.'

Shady removed his coat from the fence and ran it

through the handles of the duffel bag. He picked the bag up and carried it by the handles over his shoulder like a swagman. 'I'll be saying good-day to ya,' he said, and with a dip of the lid of his slouch hat, and without waiting for any acknowledgement from the teacher, he turned and continued down Parker Street.

By the time Shady had walked one hundred yards the bag weighed heavily on his aching arms. Sweat spooled in cool patches on his shirt, his armpits seemingly drains to any moisture his body held, the sweat tickling as it ran in its own dizzying way down his back into the cleft of his buttocks. His thirst was fierce.

He recalled that the Steampacket Hotel couldn't be far from where he stood. When he reached the intersection of Parker and Cecil Streets, he turned right in a south-easterly direction for a short distance, and then left into Cole Street. He would make an attempt to find that hotel or if he came upon one sooner, a milk bar. Shady stopped for a moment in the shade of a tree and removed his hat, marvelling at how the heat dissipated so rapidly, and at how cool his head, slick with sweat, felt to the breeze. With his hat he fanned his face.

Memory had served him well. The Steampacket Hotel stood on the next corner. For a few long moments, Shady hesitated at the Public Bar entrance, as if his long-dead stepfather could be on the other side of the door. He pushed the door open and entered. The bar was much smaller and more inviting than he recalled from the times he'd been sent to fetch his stepfather home. There were two men at the bar, one with a newspaper and the other man clutching a drink that he revolved slowly through the fingers of both hands. The barman tended to the slops-tray beneath the draught beer taps. Shady spotted Carlton Draught as one of the beers on tap. A thickset man in a white short-sleeved shirt behind the bar, who looked too well-fed for a barman, Shady figured for the owner.

'What can I do you for?' asked the barman that Shady surmised was the owner. The voice was friendly but businesslike and the man did not smile.

With an outstretched finger Shady pointed at the Carlton Draught tap.

'Pot or glass, mate?'

Oh, that's right, thought Shady these southerners have different names for it. 'Not a big one.'

'A glass would be what you're after,' the barman suggested.

'A glass then, thanks.'

The barman grabbed a 7 oz. glass and flicked the tap on. When the glass had filled, the barman shut the flow of beer off with the back of his hand.

Unsure of the cost Shady set a pile of coins down on the bar.

From the pile of coins the barman took what he needed. 'You from around here?' he asked, while he rang up the change.

'Brisbane,' said Shady.

Shady took a long pull on the beer, the foam of the beer's head clinging to the groove beneath his nose. The beer went down his gullet in a series of icy gulps. His hand shook as he replaced the empty glass on the bar.

'Another?' The barman motioned his head at the empty glass.

The widely spaced foam lines ringing Shady's empty glass marked the beer's quick descent. He nodded at the barman.

'Nothing better than an ice-cold beer on a real hot day,'

said the barman as he placed a fresh, foaming beer on the cloth on the bar in front of Shady. The barman helped himself to the remains of the small pile of coins.

Shady gave the barman a weak grin as if he had been right in what he had said. He took a sip of the newly poured beer. The beer tasted good, quite different from the Castlemaine XXXX he drank in Queensland, which Tick Tock thought unworthy of a genuine drinking man.

'Brisbane, eh?' the barman inquired.

The barman's tone suggested that he thought Brisbane was a long way from The Steampacket.

'I used to be from around here.'

The man gave Shady a good close look. 'Is that so?'

Another wave of nausea swept over him. Clutching the beer and on unsteady legs he searched for a dark, cool corner of the bar. As Shady shuffled away into the Lounge, a man who'd been sitting at the bar just along from him exchanged a few words with the barman. Shady thought one of the words exchanged might have been *police*, but it also might have been *please*. He told himself he should have nothing to fear after all these years, yet, he was uneasy. The past dragged behind like an anchor. When he found a quiet position in a corner nook of the Lounge and taken off his hat—the Public Bar and Lounge were separated by a common counter—the barman said something to the man sitting at the bar, who turned to look at Shady. The man's gaze was hard and fixed.

On the table was a copy of the *Williamstown Advertiser*. On the front page was a story of a steamer forced to discharge cargo at Port Melbourne for fear of running over a sewerage main if she continued up the Yarra to Victoria Dock. A crowd of 'many hundreds' had reportedly watched the drama from the Williamstown side. Shady turned the page. The Mechanics Institute and the Empire were all going strong—large advertisements featuring both of them. Then a story that stopped him dead:

'Ballet Shoe Factory Owner Dies.'

```
Local identity of many years, Valencia
Fiorentino, known more familiarly around
the district as Tick Tock, has passed
on after a brief battle with illness.
The new owner of the Ballet Shoe Factory
is cloaked in mystery. The family of Mr
Fiorentino has indicated that a search
for the rightful owner is underway.
Speculation surrounds the final will and
testament. Sources suggest that members
of the family may contest any outcome.
Those same sources believe that devel-
opers could be looking at the property
as a substantial development opportu-
nity. It seems that the Ballet Shoe
Factory will continue as an object of
interest for some time to come.
```

Shady reeled back against the wooden wainscoting of the bar nook. His hands slowly released their hold on the newspaper. Leaning forward he dared to re-read the headline. A veil of blackness had replaced the sickening sense of vertigo. His hand instinctively reached inside his shirt for the rosary beads, as if the news could have shattered them, made them disappear like they had for all those years since they fell from the army uniform of Tick Tock's beloved eldest son Patrick to the floor of the New Guinea jungle. But they were still there, warmed by his chest. Now it was too late. His great friend was gone and, so too, the chance to help square up what had started all those years ago in the network of drains and tunnels that ran beneath the leafy boulevards of Williamstown.

SEVEN
A DAY AT THE RACES

Over time the tunnel that they called the 'Cave,' had come to resemble a work of art, an Aladdin's cave of sorts. Newly polished copper pots clustered in corners, and in that part of the Cave George described as 'the kitchen,' old carpets lay strewn to blunt the coldness of the concrete in the mornings. George vowed that the carpets were Persian, found at the tip and washed at the creek's edge until hunters on horseback with golden cutlasses emerged in vivid dark blues and shades of red. One such carpet George had suspended from the ceiling—George called it the partition, dividing as it did territory that was George's and that which was Val's—and above which was written: *One Man's Rubbish Is Another Man's Treasure*. For George there could be no finer epitaph.

With the dyes he'd extracted from the vegetables and weeds and porous stones from the bank of Kororoit Creek, George had transformed the bleak grey of the tunnel into a spectacle of colours and designs. In one corner of the tunnel was a replica of a fireplace. It remained perpetually 'lit'. The hearth was painted in fiery yellows and oranges. Flames leapt impressionistically from the wall. At any time of day or night, with a lamp for light, George could be found standing upon old packing crates with what passed for a paintbrush in his hand. Like Michel Angelo he had decided to paint the ceiling. He had in mind the Sistine Chapel and had so informed Val of the challenge that lay ahead of him.

From his mattress Val appraised, in reasonable comfort, the progress of the painting that George insisted on calling a fresco. Privately Val wished he had painted an azure sky, one billowing with clouds, or trees shaking in the wind their leaves fluttering to the ground or even a colourful queue at the Empire cinema waiting expectantly for tickets to a double feature starring Charlie Chaplin. Not this vast canvas of black, alleviated only by pinpricks of gold—stars shining through a night firmament—and a complex technicolour border that was the painting's frieze. Nevertheless it made a change from bricks and mortar; a distraction from this infernal counting of bricks. A habit Val had fallen into to pass the time of day and sometimes night. This tracing of a line of bricks from the base of one side of the Cave as it curved over his head to the base of the other side of the tunnel. He was pretty sure, it measured two hundred and eighty-six bricks. But with that many bricks it was almost impossible to believe he hadn't counted one brick twice.

Fresco—yet another word with which Val was not familiar. He supposed George got it out of one of the books that he had beside his bed. George referred to it as the library. At last count there were thirty-five in the pile. The source of the books seemed to be school fetes and bazaars where they sold for sixpence. A sum that even George could afford from what he got from selling the occasional catch of fish, not destined for their bellies, to the Williamstown Fish Co-op. *The Arabian Nights* lay open on its spine on George's mattress. His favourite stories were 'Aladdin's Wonderful Lamp,' 'Ali Baba and the Forty Thieves' and

'The Seven Voyages of Sinbad The Sailor.' He knew these stories by heart.

Dark paint ran along George's forearm and dripped on the concrete. Armed with a brush more used to painting the outside of a weatherboard house George leaned back to appraise his work: 'What's that look like to you?'

The swirling lines meant nothing to Val. They could have been as easily words or human figures. Although if they were meant to be human they were gothic and grotesque. In the future they would be described as graffiti. 'Can't you paint something people might recognize?'

A barely audible groan descended from the ceiling. George climbed down the ladder. Once down he untied the lamp from where it hung on the uppermost step. With the slyest of grins he rubbed the lamp genie-like with the elbow of his shirtsleeve.

'You don't believe that rubbish?' asked Val.

A teardrop of gold paint glinting on the lamp caught George's attention. First with his finger and then with his shirtsleeve, he tried, unsuccessfully, to wipe it clean. 'Don't you wish for things?'

Val knew better than to get into a discussion on magic or the stars or anything of the kind. Too often he'd been dragged down this impenetrable hole of philosophical claptrap.

If George's mind was in the clutches of *The Arabian Nights*, Val's was in the thrall of another classic, *The Adventures of Tom Sawyer* that he had snuck from George's pile. Spurred by Huckleberry Finn's coming back from the dead—his appearance at his own funeral, a scene that was for him the highlight of the book—Val had been planning his own adventure. A visit to a world that he missed: thoroughbred horse racing.

'Why don't we go to the races?' Val knew this suggestion would take George by surprise.

'Isn't that taking a bit of a chance?' George inquired.

Val turned where he sat and from behind his back, amidst the bedclothes, produced a black trilby hat. 'Not with this,' and as he spoke he produced another hat, pretty much identical to the first, if a little more flattened in the bonce, 'and this.' As if to prove his point Val tugged one of the hats down tight over his head, partially covering his forehead—gangstersterish, mostly mouth and nose.

'You look like Squizzy Taylor without the gun,' George observed.

Not quite done with, Val reached beneath the blankets and raised for inspection a couple tawdry old suits, one brown and the other a shade of deep burgundy. 'Which one do you want? They're both the same size.'

If Val had expected a scolding from George on the dangers of wandering about 'above ground' it was not forthcoming. 'I see you've been busy,' said George.

The young men were foreign to the discomfiture of a suit and both suits were a little worse for wear in the seat. They didn't need to be Sherlock Holmes to know that the incumbent had been, if not lazy, somewhat disposed to the sitting position.

'I suppose you're wondrin' where the suits are from?'

George replied as quick as a shot. 'For a bloke who's as prone as you to protest his innocence on matters of the law, I imagine you've got that covered.'

Val smiled. 'Sometimes George you're cleverer than you look. But ole Reg Cuthbertson won't be needing these no more. The Missus left them on the front verandah for the church collection. She's well rid of that no-hoper anyway. Couldn't wait to give his stuff away.'

'So now we're taking from the Church?' George said.

'We're saving the church the time and trouble of finding poor beggars just like us to give it to.' Val waved his arms over the suits in a form of absolution almost ownership.

'And you expect me to go out in public in this sort of get-up?'

'Well you don't want to be recognised, do ya?' With that Val drew the hat lower and put on the jacket. Reg Cuthbertson had been a bigger man. The shoulders sagged. The sleeves hung long over his fingers. 'Not too bad,' Val said as he rolled the sleeves up one large fold's worth of cloth. In truth, he felt like Frank Heinz at the local mens wear shop, keener for a sale than a decent fit.

'You are hardly inconspicuous...'

'...but I'm not recognisable.'

'Quite so,' said George, 'but hardly an ideal outfit for two supposed villains, on the run, who've for some time kept contact with the outside world to a minimum.'

'Look, you'll have a good time. You can have a bet,' said Val, manifestly excited by that prospect.

'With what?' inquired George his serene brown eyes disputing the likelihood of any such thing happening. Gambling and drink were the devil's work. That wasn't written in the stars. His mother had told him. She'd learnt that from George's stepfather who did both with gusto.

Of course, money wasn't any longer a problem for Val. Every night in the tunnel, right before he went to sleep, Val secretly removed the great wads of bank notes he kept in the pockets of his jacket. He'd count each note one by one with the care of a bank teller, whispering the accumulating number, savouring every moment as the total went higher and higher in his head. How he longed to tell his hoped-for bride-to-be, Maisy, of his good fortune. 'I can give you a lend.'

George raised his eyebrows. 'To bet on a horse, you mean?'

Put like that it didn't sound like much of an idea. And whether Val won or lost, he had so much money it hardly mattered. 'Just come out for the day, then. You'll enjoy yourself. Everyone does.'

There was nothing that Val loved more than the races. And one of the things he loved the most about the races was having a bet. That had been reason enough to take a job as a lookout at the SP bookmakers. The SPs weren't fussed about his age. Nor were the cops. The whole operation was illegal.

It seemed that all of Williamstown and many parts of Melbourne had come to the races that day. From early morning the trains had been arriving at Williamstown Beach Station with ladies in their finery and the gentlemen in top hats. Nobody seemed to mind that there were not enough buggies to ferry everyone from the station to the track. The colourful crowd snaked across the dunes, the women's heels sinking in the soft sandy soil. Spirits were high.

With their suit jackets slung over their shoulders George and Val negotiated a subterranean path to the vicinity of the track. Val had wanted to stroll in the sunshine. George refused. He would not 'perambulate about the countryside' in a suit. The suit was for the track and not much 'anywhere's else'.

On the far side of Kororoit Creek the two young men emerged cautiously from a drain opening. The grandstand and the noise of racegoers rose to greet them. The two young men melted in with the crowd, pressing for entry through the gate.

'That wasn't so bad, was it?' said Val once inside the track, one hand patting his suit jacket to confirm the thick wad of notes inside.

'What you see in all of this I don't know,' replied George.

Val's enthusiasm was undeterred. 'I'll show you where I used to work.'

'I thought ya worked at Flemington. Isn't that where it all happened?'

Val's face tightened in a grimace. 'Not so loud,' he spoke in a whisper, 'someone might hear. I rode at Willi' too.'

Despite his mother's deepest misgivings George liked a beer. It was a question of taste and not even his stepfather had put him off. Two years older than Val, George did the honours and joined the queue at a bar opposite the main betting ring. Val waited just inside the door. George returned with two draught beers. 'Better here than the Steampacket,' said George and Val agreed with a nod of his head. 'Nah, can't go there, too dangerous there.' The people from Cavenagh's Tote, Maisy's dad, and some of the horsetrainers for whom he'd ridden trackwork before he got too big went there. He'd also have to keep an eye out for them at the track.

'My mother would have me whipped if she saw me now,' George said as he raised his glass for another deep sip. 'Put me across her knee,' she'd say and he snorted the foam off the top of his beer at the preposterousness and familiarity of the proposition.

In no mood for thinking about his family and how worried they'd be about his own whereabouts Val took a final gulp of his beer and said, 'Time for a bet.'

The betting ring was bursting with punters. It was five minutes to start-time in the first. Casting his eyes from the top to the bottom of the roll call of horses' names on the bookie's blackboard Val made his pick. How could he go past Time and Tide, the beaten favourite in the race he'd made so much money on?

'What do you want?' he asked George.

'I told you I don't have the money to waste.'

'I'll put it on for you.'

'What if it loses?'

Val hesitated. 'You can just owe me.'

'But I don't want to owe ya.'

'Then don't owe me.'

'But if I lose I will.'

'Not if I say you don't.'

'What you say won't matter. Borrowing and owing money isn't like that.'

Forgetting himself and not just a little annoyed with George for his infernal arguing and not being able to accept a gift for what it was, an unthinking Val in the full view of George took a huge clip of money from inside his jacket. 'Suit yourself, I'm on Tide and Tide.'

Leaving George's side Val made his way through the crowded betting ring to the bookmakers' stands. He was relying on the hat and the suit to hide his age. The crowded ring was full of suits. His pulse raced with the prospect of a bet. Not the rails bookmakers he would place his bet with one of the lesser-known bookies. The line of betting boards beside each bookmaker pronounced the odds. It seemed the best he'd get would be 5-1, not bad for the quality of the horse.

From the corner of his eye he noticed a man in a dark navy suit who appeared to be looking at him and not the odds. Something told him not to look, not to make eye contact. Up to the bookie Val strode and placed his bet—ten pounds to win on number 5, Time and Tide. The bookie wrote the ticket and the bookie's clerk snaffled the ten pounds into the big white bookie's bag. As he did a voice behind him roared, 'Eh, you little thief.' Val couldn't help himself and turned. Barrelling through the crowd was Big

Jim Cavenagh, the bookmaker, his face a deep red, his eyes popping with anger. Val turned and ran.

From a short distance away George watched Val fly out of the betting ring, followed by a large man struggling to keep up. George took off after them. He'd guessed what had happened. Val had never given him all the details of the fateful day at the track, but it took no effort of imagination to know that the man in pursuit was the wronged bookmaker.

If he had to he'd deck Jim Cavenagh. He'd decked bigger. 'Hey lard arse,' he called out to the big man. At first Jim Cavenagh didn't hear. When George repeated the cry Jim Cavenagh gave him a surly look that seemed to say, this is none of your business whoever you are, and continued lumbering after Val.

Not a man to make a fuss, not a man to get riled for any reason George would have preferred Jim Cavenagh to have just run out of puff, and for the fleeing Val to have made good his escape. But Jim Cavenagh seemed as determined as any man had ever been to catch a lad and wring his skinny neck.

The yelling and the fast flash of suits scything through the crowd had caught the attention of many racegoers and, in particular, the men in white coats that manned the turnstiles to the gate, the nearest point of exit. It was only a matter of seconds before the police were involved.

While the men in white coats didn't know who was in the right, there was a natural unwillingness to allow a man to flee past them. They barred the exit. Val saw that they meant business and drew up short a few yards from the turnstiles. By running on the diagonal George had caught up to him. Still fifty yards adrift Jim Cavenagh was muscling his way through the throng.

'Give 'em a fiver,' yelled George.

'What?'

'A fiver. Give 'em a fiver.'

'For what?'

'To let you through.'

Safety for the cost of a single fiver of which he had dozens in his pocket. The blank expression on Val's face was a portrait of indecision.

'It's only money for the love of god,' yelled George into a face that registered not just indecision but also anger.

'What have they done to deserve it?'

The men in white coats came slowly towards Val. 'What's all the commotion,' one of them said even-handedly.

George approached the men in white coats with a broad smile on his face. 'A misunderstanding is all. A daughter. My mate's done nothing but the father won't hear a word of it.'

'Ah,' said one of the men in white coats, 'I know what it's like I've a daughter myself.' The man in the white coat turned to the other man in a white coat. 'Horace, we've a bit of a domestic on our hands if we don't let the lad through.'

George clicked his fingers at Val. 'The fiver to grease the wheels. You can afford it,' he said knowingly.

With a fiver to share the men in white coats shepherded the young men through the turnstiles, and then stood like soldiers to brave the onslaught of the heaving, angry fat man.

EIGHT
LEN DOES HIS DUTY

Len wasn't much for talking. After the 'Ho ho ho,' routine, Len would kick off his shoes (no lace-ups for him) turn on the TV at the far dark end of the living room, and settle his chubby bottom into the squeaky leather of the Jason, adjusting the controls until he had the settings just perfect and his outstretched limbs exactly where they'd been the night before.

Len communicated most effectively by deed. Talking was for him largely a waste of time. If it were worth doing he'd already be doing it, and if it wasn't worth doing it certainly wasn't worth talking about. The final part of a series of school sex education evenings—The Trilogy of Self-awareness—would have loomed as a trial for him, and it was on tonight. The third part of the Trilogy was aimed at those who had more or less got the gist of the first two parts and might already, inadvisedly, be putting some of the information into actual practice.

All Len had to do was turn up with me at the designated time and place: 7.30 p.m. at the school canteen. What Len had done was have a few drinks up at the local golf club so that by the time he'd got home, he was, as my mother would observe, 'Half-charged'.

I could tell he'd upset her for not being as dead sober as he ought to be. Mother bore a look of quiet suffering and disappointment, her face stiff and pained and braced for the worst, when she farewelled us at the front door, touching me lightly on the shoulder and saying, 'It'll be all right.' In her mind I was going to the equivalent of an R Rated Film. The final part of the Trilogy was for her a controlled experiment. In a clinical sense I would be exposed to things normally regarded as unhealthy or impure and certainly off-limits. Such things that, if handled badly, could do untold damage to my formative mental and emotional states. I might walk out of the Trilogy tonight and my future could be completely warped; that's the look she had on her face.

The canteen was full because we were late. The auditorium filled from the back to the front, because that's what Australian men do, and besides all the dads took one look at the big drop-down film projection screen on the raised floor at the front and made the quick-fire decision, that whatever would show on the screen could be witheringly big and confronting and hopelessly discomfiting at close range, shoulder to shoulder with your little man next to you and some stranger and his offshoot adding to the discomfort on the other side, and all of you staring at the same screen and whatever anatomical shock might be on it.

If that were the general expectation then Father Nate Evans would not disappoint. Father Nate, ('Call me Nate') blessed with lush seal-grey hair still dark at the roots, swept back rocker-like, distinctly over his shirt-collar by at least an inch, struck a dashing figure in his black trousers and his gleaming stark white shirt which, in itself, was a perfect counterpoint to the glow of his tanned ruddy distinguished face. Father Nate strut the stage like a great commercial evangelist, except Father Nate was preaching not salvation but 'Oh Lordy' about the ins and outs of sex, in a detail both excruciating and pornographic.

Father Nate took to the task with a disconcerting gusto, mixing medical and anatomical facts with the popular lore of what might only be found with credibility in the Letters Section to *Penthouse Magazine*. Boys should not be discouraged if their PEE-NESS was a bit big and unwieldy for the woman. Father Nate at this point was not proclaiming chastity or the exercise of judgement or quality control of any kind, (although there was some mention of that later for the many goggle-eyed in the audience who were on a different trajectory); there were creams and jellies and appliances that could all help get the job done. 'Don't WORR-EE. We're not all built the same. OK?' Dads all squirmed and shifted in their seats and probably wondered if Father Nate may have been speaking about stuff a bit closer to home than was appropriate for his own clerical circumstances so to speak. I mean with what practical authority did he speak?

Len swore under his breath. I couldn't be sure what he said but it sounded like, 'Bullshit.' No one looked at him including me and I hoped the grog wouldn't prise his lips open for more of whatever he did say. I didn't fancy the undivided attention of Father Nate and God forbid the prospect of role-playing couldn't be totally ruled out of the question? Oh Dear Christ, the ramifications were appalling and hideous. A massively enlarged shot of a vagina flashed on the projection screen and the male audience shrank back like it was an alien power. It wasn't even a real vagina but a model of one, rubbery and surreal and an awful thing to look at. 'Pervert,' Len said quite distinctly. I looked across at him and his eyes were narrowed and his face bright red.

The night did not get any better.

Afterwards, Mother stayed up for us. Len shut the door with a bang and threw his keys scuttling across the sideboard in the dining room. He went into the kitchen, yanked open the fridge door and pulled out a large can of Melbourne Bitter that he filled to the brim with a big frothy head. My mother waited in the living room. Downing the beer in one continuous drinking motion, his Adam's apple bobbing as he gulped, he then refilled the glass and dropped down into the Jason with the beer in hand. 'Waste of bloody time.'

'Don't let him hear.'

Mother meant me but I'd already said a perfunctory good night, cleared off down the hall and out of sight into a position where I could hear everything they said quite distinctly.

'What's wrong?' she asked.

'Preverts.'

'What happened?'

'What ya watchin'?'

She turned to the TV as if she needed reminding and as if it in turn needed an explanation. Graham Kennedy (Gra-Gra), the King of Australian television, a charming naughty smile playing on his lips, was holding a well-known brand of washing liquid up to the camera for a close-up endorsement. The studio audience screamed with laughter at Gra-Gra's every gag and strained expression of exaggerated belief in the advertised product. Shiny, transparent bubbles of washing liquid floated off unscripted about the set.

Len laughed at Gra-Gra and took another sip of the cold amber liquid.

My mother sat forward on her chair. 'How'd it go?'

'Genitals in ya face.'

'Sorry, Len?'

Len, somewhat out of sorts, fiddled with the controls of the Jason. 'Do we have to talk about it? Look I went, right? What more do you want? A blow by bloody blow.'

'How is he?'

'He's all right'

'Have you asked him?'

'Jesus, what is this?

'I'm just asking if he's all right?'

Standing there in the hallway, I felt all right. I didn't think I was mentally damaged.

'What did they do?'

'Preverts.'

'Len,' her voice a little shocked, 'not in the house'.

Len snorted with laughter at the TV.

Mother reduced the distance between them to keep their voices lower. 'Who? Who's the…pre…the pervert?'

'That whisky priest.'

'Father Nathaniel?'

'Him. Whisky Priest. Something not right about him.'

Len didn't trust Father Nate and it didn't matter that he came legitimated both by church and state. 'Should pull him out,' and then he belched.

'The school?'

'Yes.'

My mother was terrified. The prospect of being ripped out of a school that had taken no small amount of effort to get into was not something she cared to think about.

'Look the kid's hardly Steve McQueen. He'll be the least of our worries,' said Len. He was more interested in Gra-Gra.

NINE
TWO GIRLS AND A TRAIN

The crack about Steve McQueen hurt a bit. I didn't need reminding that looks weren't my strength. I knew I wasn't Steve McQueen. Riding on the train to school with Kenny Roberts everyday drove that realisation home with the subtlety of a nail gun.

When I first saw Kenny it was like 'game over' for girls and me. Kenny was the same age as me but a good six feet two. Broad-shouldered, his blue school jacket always looked a size too small, so he had taken to carrying it over his shoulder like a towel. On one occasion Kenny bent to pick up his bag and the act of stretching tore his shirt in half. It opened up right across his back to reveal muscles and tendons that I never knew existed. Competing with the likes of Kenny or anyone like him was not something I'd have bet real money on. At least that's what I thought right up until the train trip to school this morning.

On the train we travelled in packs as if we had assigned seats. Brenda held court with Sharon, Jenny and Raelene; Kenny was close by, recounting to Jerome and his little brother Ray how on the weekend he'd helped his uncle geld a horse.

Brenda was a year older than any of us in her final year of school. She was also the sorriest-looking girl for who the description plain did not do justice. Her appearance was masculine and doughy and although it would be a little unfair to describe her as fat that was the general impression. But Brenda had clearly had enough of Kenny and his unrelenting eyewitness account of gelding horses and the inevitable fistfuls of horse testicles involved.

'What the hell's that, Kenny?'

Kenny stopped pontificating on the merits of gelding horses. His beautiful head peered perplexed and arrogant in Brenda's general direction.

'That,' she said, and pointed at Kenny's crotch. Kenny could see where she pointed but refused to look directly because occasionally he was the butt of minor jokes.

'There, you moron. There! What's that?'

Kenny knew he had to take a closer look and by this time everyone on both sides of the train was interested. His eyes followed her finger that pointed directly between his wide splayed legs. He looked and saw nothing. The relief was evident on his face. He gave her a snarl but saved on the wisecracks. Whatever he said she could no doubt top. Kenny began to talk to the boys again, 'As I was saying'— but he was interrupted by an insistent Brenda, who now was laughing, as were Sharon, Raelene and Jenny who had pretty much the same perspective of things as her. Kenny stopped talking again and was clearly uncomfortable that others understood whereas he still did not.

'There you, imbecile. Are you blind as well as epically stupid?' Brenda screamed. 'There! There!' She pointed and finally Kenny saw what it was. Basking in the early morning sunshine that cut a band of light across the seat and Kenny's trousers, were a couple of long, golden, glistening pubic hairs snaking through his flies. Kenny's embarrassment was acute, but he made no attempt to conceal the source of amusement. His slow, angry mind couldn't even admit the obvious. He couldn't put his hand down there and fix it up. He would not do it. Reddened with anger he was visibly and very obviously trying to think of something funny or hurtful to deflect the attention.

Brenda laughed. 'Well you're not just going to leave them like that are you, handsome? It's disgusting. Yuck.'

Kenny finally had his cue. 'Talk of disgusting. Look at you.' Pointing at his crotch and the offending hair. 'This is the closest you'll ever get so why don't you make the most of it.' Jerome and Ray laughed reflexively yet cautiously. Kenny displayed a vacant temporary look of triumph that didn't convince in its fixed, nervy expression. He took the few moments of silence to hurriedly tuck in the offending hairs.

'Handsome, I wouldn't do it with you if you were the last man on Earth,' Brenda declared. She convulsed with laughter at the ludicrous idea of sex with Kenny. This from a girl so unfortunate in appearance, that I would have thought her chances of getting any self-respecting boy were only marginally less than mine of finding a Miss Dead Right.

'Yes, you would,' said Kenny, softly almost a plea, 'you know you would.' His big, dumb, brown eyes were wet with the insult and the hurt that his looks didn't make up for his stupidity, even to the ugliest girl in the country.

I tried not to laugh with Kenny sitting so close. What struck me was that looks could be so…well overlooked. Did girls, generally, have this more broad-minded approach to the other sex? I mightn't be Steve McQueen but I wasn't stupid like Kenny. If I could just find a girl who could split the difference on looks and brains then the quest for

Miss Dead Right might not be in vain. And the very next morning, on the train to school, although I didn't know her name at the time, I met Vivian.

When the red, heavy metal doors of the Red Rattler's carriages swung wide open, we all charged for cover from the wild summery shower that lashed the platform. Heads down, eyes on the deep puddles, bags in protection shouldered high on our backs, we shuffled as quickly as we could in the direction of shelter, indifferent to the jostling and the grumbling of those around us.

An exquisite pair of coppery-brown calves shuffled in front of me. Shortened, muscled staccato steps that fell just shy of the heels of the slow-moving logjam of commuters ahead. I bunched up behind her. She was not quite my height. A heavy driving rain prevented me looking up. The roofed area of the platform was full. The way forward was an impasse but only those ahead could see, and all the rest, most with heads bowed, bumped like a slow motion, collapsing concertina into each other. I bumped into the girl and she in turn into another in front of her. Exaggerated moans and groans and 'Sorrys' rang out. Each person turned to the one nearest in the little people wreck. And so the girl turned to me, who was amongst the last and had run up her back. I said, 'Sorry,' again and she simply smiled, her mouth shut but a strange mysterious smile had come over her face, an enigmatic look brought about by virtue of the length of fringe that fell to her eyebrows. A thick, auburn waterfall of hair that made her seem shy and reclusive, as if she was in a cave looking out and had seen something she was not sure of.

The rain tumbled down and we squeezed and pressed to within the limits of the platform roof, everyone adjusting their stance to face the track and the awaited connecting train. I formed a part of the outer layer of human protection from the rain. The toes of my unpolished shoes extended just beyond the roofline. I watched the rain splash on my shoes and run off. The body of the girl pressed behind me. I did not know what part of her I could feel, but the longer we stood there motionless the more convinced I became that it was her breasts. I stood as rigid as a mannequin intensely aware of what could be in my back, and of the dark, hooded eyes that for no other choice could only be upon me and absorbing me in microscopic detail. Was there dandruff upon my dark blue jacket? I mean I didn't have a major problem. At worst it would only ever be a light shower of fine flakes, and it was invariably only after I used that damn cheap shampoo Mother got in those damn big supermarket bottles because it was on special. The girl was probably counting each and every flake right now in their discrete constellations—my own little disgusting Milky Ways. I would have loved to brush the jacket clean but I couldn't take the chance; they might not be there. I tried to spot them on my shoulder without moving my head. It was hard to see that laterally. My eyes strained to confirm their presence. Those things were still in my back but on no account would I move and having moved maybe know, and identify their shape. Did I feel them move? I was sure I had. And yet again? Or was it something sharper like the edge of her schoolbag? Perhaps she was sizing me up. I instinctively straightened and lifted the back of my heels off the ground for that extra half-inch. Maybe I should get those shoe 'lifts' advertised in the men's magazines the local barber stocked. If only Mother had been an inch or two taller, I wouldn't be subjected to this additional stress. Gerry said height came from the mother's side. The eyes were x-rays in my back. I could feel their imagined heat. Where else could they be? What could she be examining now? Surely she'd got over the dandruff even if it were there. What now? What other inadequacy or imperfection had she found? Why did we have to meet like this?

For a few brief agonizing seconds I contemplated reneging on my vow never to do anything like *that* again. Where *that again* was having a rush of courage at the St Michael's dance and abandoning the safety of the perimeter of the church hall and the companionship of my mates, and waltzing up to Linda X—universally recognized as a spunk—with false derring-do and confidence and asking her to dance. She didn't say no or at least I didn't hear her. Linda X looked at me with the eyes of a heroin-addict, remote unconnected, almost disbelief that I'd asked her. Her convent education and the presence of the nice women from the ladies auxiliary, patrolling the hall, compelled her to dance with someone who so hopelessly failed to meet her expectations. Her revulsion and sense of romantic mismatch could not have been conveyed any better than if she'd fainted. The surrounding clique of girls sniggered at her predicament. Linda X didn't dance, she swayed, any real motion almost undetectable. She was energised to the point she was not quite still. But that's as far as she got. Linda X kept her face turned to her friends in a masque of unbearable boredom. I quite literally cannot even type her full name: Linda X will have to do. I cannot shame the page it would be written on to do that. I wished like Christ I'd never asked Linda X to dance.

If I went out on a limb there was just too big a chance the girl would simply turn her back as if I was some kind of joke. I would not take that chance ever again. I would die celibate and emotionally marooned rather than do *that again*.

A blue Harris train screeched its arrival. The waiting

crowd huddled tighter as the column of air displaced by the train pressed it back. Then the whole platform of commuters surged for the limited seats on the train. I grabbed the silver knob of the double sliding train doors and wrenched them open. I headed straight for the window seat on the far side of the carriage, hoping she'd follow. But she was gone.

TEN

HYPNOSIS?

If Len hadn't drunk so much on the night of The Trilogy I think he might have asked a few questions about Shady Green. Through the open venetian blinds of the lounge room window I could see him working on the car in the driveway.

The Fairmont had its bonnet up and motor idling. I might be able to leave the house without being quizzed. Len was fiddling with the carburettor. Every now and then the engine would rev hard and he'd grunt in acknowledgement. As the motor revved hard one more time, I sidled behind him with the full intention of not saying a word. Len pulled his head out from beneath the bonnet at precisely the moment I attempted to squeeze past. As he wiped oil from his hands with a cloth, he fixed me with his eyes.

'You'd tell me if you know about this Shady Green, wouldn't you? We'd look like mugs if you don't. Maybe worse.'

Should I mention my meeting with Howard to him?

'Son, you've got to be careful. There's a lot of money involved. When it comes to money people can be very unforgiving.'

Len's face was world-weary and evidenced an exasperation that I would not tell him all that I knew. He swiped sweat from his brow with the clean under part of the cloth he'd folded in half, and leant on the front fender gazing into the heart of the engine in what might have been a search for inspiration. He turned his head to me while still leaning on the fender. 'And the fact you're not saying anything makes me think you do know more than you're letting on.'

'What if he does…exist?' I said.

'Does he?'

'It's not that simple.'

'How simple is it?'

'Someone's been living down at the Ballet Shoe Factory.'

'I've seen the mess down there. Is it him? This Shady Green?'

'I don't know. It might just be deros. It probably is just deros.'

'There is such a person as Shady Green, isn't there?'

I rubbed my hand up the nape of my neck to indicate some thinking might be in progress. 'I can't remember.'

Len finally punctured a long pause. 'You don't remember? What don't you remember?'

'That's the thing. I can't remember what I think I know. It's like a secret that won't reveal itself. I try to force it out but that doesn't work. Sometimes some of Tick Tock's actual words pop into my head…like…'

Len stepped back from the car. 'Like what? What words?'

'Shady Green. I know he mentioned the name Shady Green.'

'Sure?'

I nodded slowly almost reluctantly.

'What about Shady Green?'

'It's not that clear. I just know he's said things and when

he has he's sworn me to secrecy, but that's the only part of it that I can remember; that I must keep it a secret.'

Len became impatient. 'Is that it?'

I shrugged probably more nonchalantly than was warranted under the circumstances. 'Sometimes I think that maybe I was hypnotised or something. That might be why I can't remember the secret parts of what he said.'

'Hypnotised? By whom? Tick Tock?'

Len straightened up and threw the oily cloth on top of the engine.

'Tell me. Are you saying Tick Tock might have hypnotised you with a secret about this Shady Green?'

I shrugged my shoulders again. 'I don't know.' I'd already said too much.

'Bullshit.'

Swearing meant he was angry. When he didn't understand, like when he struggled to fix something, he got angry. Ordinarily, for a solution, Len had to look no further than his pudgy hands and a brain which instinctively saw every problem with those hands wrapped around it. The line about hypnotism had thrown him. You could no more hypnotise Len than get him to put on womens' clothes.

'Well I don't know how to explain it. That's how it feels. It's in here somewhere,' I tapped my head conclusively, 'but it won't come out.'

'Son, you're stretching me. You really are and you know it.'

'Not actually hypnotise, that's not what I mean. I'm just trying to explain the feeling of knowing something and not knowing what that something is. Like someone told me a long time ago. Not recent. Like you've had a dream but unlike most dreams you've woken up because of it. All of a sudden you're awake and what woke you up isn't there anymore. You're awake because it was as real as if it had actually happened.'

Disbelief showed on his face. I wished I'd said anything other than 'hypnotise'. 'People are searching high and low for this Shady Green character,' he said.

'Dad, does it really matter? I mean I could just be imagining it? The mess at the Ballet Shoe Factory is probably deros.'

'My view, son, is this: I don't think Tick Tock was off his rocker, senile, in dementia, whatever it is some choose to call him. Yes he was eccentric but eccentric isn't crazy. I know crazy and he wasn't. I don't understand why he wrote the will the way he did to confuse us. I don't understand that. I do think this Shady Green was real. Maybe he's not around anymore, but I'm sure at some point he was. Maybe Tick Tock owed him something, a favour, a war buddy, I don't know. I do know two things. The first is I'm flying to Brisbane tomorrow to hopefully meet a few of his old friends who might know something, and second, is that if people think this family is hiding something so it can get rich at their expense, then, that's something this family doesn't need. Do you understand?'

The way I saw it I had no choice but to develop this Performing Arts Centre idea. Even if Shady Green didn't turn up, I still couldn't pretend I would donate the Ballet Shoe Factory to the public good or divide the spoils amongst the relatives, as Len and Mother wanted me to at least contemplate. But I did want to do *some* good, because if I didn't, both mortal and immortal forces might array against me, and I was just too mindful of my shortcomings and too uncertain of where I stood on the scoreboard of eternal salvation to have a charge of avarice hanging over me. I didn't want to wear that hunted look of guilt that Nigel and Priscilla probably had to endure, peering over my shoulder to identify the whispering snide remarks that explained the clothes I wore, or the new black panel van I drove and the spectacular blonde in the Jackie O shades, who struggled to find the strength, the willingness or perhaps the aptitude to shut the side passenger door properly. I wanted to be rich *and* happy. And the very thought of being rich did something chemically to me like the release of endorphins, that made me feel better, even if, it was only fleeting and superficial.

ELEVEN
MYRA MAKES HER CLAIM

'Your father's gone to Brisbane.'

The statement was maternal and imperial. She could have been a US 5-Star general, informing his president that one of the country's finest officers had unfortunately been called upon to deal with a skirmish on a remote hitherto before forgotten protectorate—for which there were ongoing political, economic and legal responsibilities—rather than the issues at home, which were after all, what really mattered.

'What do you think he'll find up there, Mister?'

In this sort of mood you had to choose your words with the care of a Queen's Counsel.

'Shady Green?'

'And what are the chances of that? Tell me.'

'One of his old mates might know something.'

'And which one might that be?'

I had countenanced the possibility of no reply. Sometimes this worked like a bushfire hitting a firebreak. Not today, it wouldn't.

'I haven't got all day,' she said.

'Any one of his mates up there might know about Shady Green,' I ventured.

'I don't even remember Tick Tock mentioning this Shady Green character,' she countered.

When Tick Tock went for his annual trip to Brisbane, Mother would almost fret. She'd send long letters in the hope that he'd tell her something insightful about what he did up there. 'I don't know what he could be doing all that time. I mean it's not as if he's going to the beach every day,' she'd say to Len. Occasionally, he would send a letter saying how nice and warm it was and how he'd eaten a whole barramundi the size of which you'd never seen in Melbourne. She'd keep sending him letters as though he was on a vacation when, in reality, he was living somewhere else for three months. Once she suggested that we all go up with him for a holiday. Len said it wasn't his idea of a holiday and if she really wanted to know what Tick Tock did when he was up there, why didn't she ask him when he got back? She said she did, and what he told her didn't amount to anything.

Mother folded her arms across her chest. 'Is your father wasting his time? Can you tell me that? Or do I have to put you under hypnosis?'

I knew the hypnotherapy allusion had been a mistake.

'I don't think he's wasting his time.'

'You don't, eh?'

'Well…'

What should I say? Tick Tock spent three months a year for close to twenty years, in another city, in another state. For all we knew he could have had a second family up there. After three months in Brisbane, he didn't steam up the hallway to regale the family with a load of stories. He would no sooner be back home than he would be on his way out to the chook pens, to see if the chickens had been looked after properly while he'd been away. How many eggs are they laying? Are they on their feed? The family would stand around the chook pens as he fussed with the chickens. He would cluck and talk to the chickens as if no one else was there and as if he had never been away. The sun did him good and he came back, and that was—that.

The doorbell rang.

Mother glared at me as I began to circle around the kitchen table by way of intended exit through the dining room door.

'I don't suppose you're getting it?' she asked.

'It won't be for me.'

'See who it is.'

I obediently trod down the hall and opened the front door to—Aunt Myra.

'Oh, Michel.'

My appearance seemed to come as something of a surprise. I think I made her feel uncomfortable.

'Mother. You're after Mother?' I asked helpfully.

Myra fussed with the bag that she was carrying over her wrist and looked past my shoulder down the dark barrel of the hallway. 'Yes,' she answered finally, adding to the impression that speaking to me was a struggle.

'She's in the kitchen,' I volunteered.

Myra came in with her shoes thumping on the carpet. Mother was already on her way to find out who it was, wiping her hands upon her apron as she went. They met in the passage where the light was dimmest and three porcelain swallows speared like a slips field up the wall. There was a faintly hollow sound to their voices when they spoke.

'Late for a visit,' Mother said with a final drying flourish of her hands upon the apron.

It wasn't.

'Oh,' said Myra surprised at the archness of the comment. 'Are you in the middle of something?' She was still a full three paces from Mother and advancing. There would be no stopping the visit. 'Just on the way back from the chemist's,' she said, and held up a bag of pharmaceutical goods wound around her wrist. 'Thought I'd drop in for a cuppa.'

My mother's face deepened in colour. She turned without a word and Myra followed her into the kitchen. While Mother filled the kettle with water, Myra arranged herself upon a kitchen stool.

Myra sighed as if in mild pain. 'Just got Alf's medication. They've increased the dose, poor thing.' Myra's great chest went up and down as she spoke.

'Really,' said Mother. The prospect of general chit-chat didn't loom large.

Uncle Alf had a thyroid condition that Len had officially declared as a pretext not to work and likely to last a lifetime.

'He's not much of a one for shocks. Over-activates the thyroid, you know.'

Mother turned the kettle on and Myra resettled herself precariously upon the stool at the island bench that separated both women. Mother fetched a matching pair of our better porcelain cups and saucers down from the cupboard, although, she might have thought about a couple of cheap mugs, which Myra would have accurately taken as a slight.

Myra took out her cigarettes and put them on the bench. 'All this Ballet Shoe Factory business is very odd. Don't you think?'

'One or two sugars?' Mother must have hoped she would dare to light up. There was nothing that aggravated Len more than cigarette smoke in the house. He'd given up, so could everybody else. If he asked who'd been smoking in the house, she'd be delighted to tell him.

'Ah two, thank you. But odd, don't you think?'

'Odd?' Mother was not to be drawn easily on this.

Myra, unperturbed, 'The Ballet Shoe Factory…business.'

'Biscuit?'

'Ah, don't mind if I do. Ooh Milk Arrowroot.' Myra would masticate the biscuit to powder and wash it down with a loud slurp. For a finale, she'd rub the tops of her fingers together preying mantis-like to rid them of crumbs, then inspect her lap for any debris, and finally dab her lips dry and spotlessly clean with a pristine, white handkerchief she had permanently tucked up the long sleeve of her blouse.

Mother sat down with her finger crooked and tensed in the delicate handle of the cup.

Myra advanced on a related front. 'I hear Len's gone to Brisbane.'

'Last night,' Mother replied frostily.

Myra took a slurp of tea.

Mother eyed Myra over the gilded rim of her cup.

They both replaced their respective cups in their respective saucers simultaneously, with a little clink that filled the room.

'Don't know what they expect to find up there. Do you, Marg?'

Marg? This was very friendly and sounded peculiar coming out of a mouth that never called my mother anything. 'Any prospects of Alf getting back to work?'

Myra acted surprised. 'Oh no, dear no.'

Mother persisted. 'The pills, all the medication, that's not doing him any good?'

'Oh yes, but he's still far too sick for work. Dearie me, far too ill for that.' Myra bent down to take a mouthful of tea as if to give herself time to think.

'Mmm,' Mother added purposely and uncomfortably to

the silence.

Mother and Myra barely tolerated each other. Together, they acted like lionesses disputing territory. And Mother had never forgiven her and Uncle Alf for opting out of any financial contribution to Maisy's funeral arrangements because 'Now was not a good time for them.'

Mother having formed a view was rarely of a mind to change. Mother hated dogs because they shat on her lawn, 'Just look at it,' she'd say, about a parallel set of turds on the front lawn as if a crime had been recently committed. But Mother loved cats because they buried their shit out of sight—'You won't find our cats committing that sort of abomination on Mrs Murray's property.' There was no need to swear or curse and if you did, 'You'll got a good box around the ears and your mouth rinsed out with soap.' Swearing revealed how uncouth you were, and in turn, your parents. She would not be her children's collateral damage. Mother loved her country, although, I never heard her say it. In 1942 as a member of the Women's Auxiliary Air Force, she went up in a single-engine, open-topped fighter plane in helmet and goggles. Mother would tell you about the experience 25 years later with the same breathtaking astonishment she felt on that day. She had not hesitated to go up in that plane, nevertheless, she still did not believe in women airline pilots. If airlines had to use them, she'd say, then surely the pilots should keep it to themselves and not announce their presence over the plane's internal address system and frighten all the passengers. Sport was good. She loathed all opposition sporting teams from school grade football to Test Cricket with unbridled energy and passion. Len called her a 'good hater.' She loved the Essendon Football Club as if it had been founded by Christ. She called all Essendon's star players Saint This and Saint That. She would scream out at a match if anyone looked like touching Essendon's captain, Ken Fraser, 'Get your hands off him you thug.' To her there was a villain in every opposition side. She made sure she found at least one, and they fed her hunger to oppose like blood to ticks. So Mother taking a liking to Myra was no longer an available option.

But if Mother had an abiding dislike for Aunt Myra and a wrath for opposition sporting teams, she hit real pay dirt with the Japanese. An anger not just on behalf of Tick Tock and the three years he spent at the mercy of the Japanese Imperial Army in the savage confines of a Java Prisoner of War camp, wasting away to a skeletal 80 pounds, surviving on rat cunning and a stolen egg every other day from the kitchen; but a wrath also on behalf of her brother Pat, her beloved eldest brother whose face shone youthfully from a framed photograph of him resplendent in his private first class khaki infantry uniform, hung in pride of place above the mantelpiece in our living room. Pat, more boy than man, gazed out of the photo with a naked innocence and youth that never diminished. Pat went to War, never to return, three years of continuous duty, never the prospect of leave as the enemy poured down through the jungles of New Guinea and bombed the Australian mainland at Darwin. Pat, cut down by the single shot of a Japanese sniper as he fixed rations for a campfire meal, in the early dusk of April 17 1945, in a War which would officially end just weeks later. Uncle Pat peered from the photo with the wry makings of a smile, the absolute image of Tick Tock his southern Italian heritage highlighted in the brown of his eyes and the open honest expression upon his face. He peered with absolutely no knowledge of what was to come, of which, I was so minutely and acutely aware that to look at him for long was impossible, without wishing I could have told him to be ever wary of trigger-happy enemy soldiers, who might hide in treetops waiting for the approaching dark and the opportunity to sight an unsuspecting soldier in the crosshairs of their rifles. Uncle Pat keeled over on his kit as if he was suddenly taken by tiredness and sleep. No soldier there mentioned they heard a shot, but I suppose they did. He, apparently, made no sound as he fell softly to the earth his precious rosary beads spilling from his pocket.

The busloads of Japanese tourists, their wallets and money-belts bulging with appreciating yen had begun to arrive. The signs of Japanese emergence from the disgrace of war and unconditional surrender could be observed most ubiquitously on the Made In Japan impress that seemed to be on the underside of all the best-priced electronic equipment. Mother would turn these appliances over as if they were rocks in the backyard and a slug might come crawling out from under any of them. A small tour group of Japanese, never mind a busload, was a wicked affront. 'Look at them,' she'd say as if we'd all forgotten what they did in the jungles of New Guinea and the POW camps of Java, let alone the epic monstrosities of the Burma Railway. For all she knew, one of these skinny, sallow-skinned, almond-eyed, baseball-hat-wearing tourists pointing a new expensive Minolta at her Melbourne Cricket Ground could be a blood relative to the ignoble, craven, inhuman creature who shot her brother Pat from the canopy of a remote jungle rainforest.

Myra dabbed at her lips with a handkerchief smeared with lipstick.

'Would you like a top-up?' asked Mother.

'No, no, bad for the bones I'm told. Sucks the calcium right out of them. Leaves them all as brittle as bread sticks.'

Myra laughed nervously. 'Probably a bit late for all of us. Can't worry about everything, can we?'

Mother did her best to conjure a smile.

Violence of some kind emanated from the TV in the living room. 'Can you turn that thing down,' Mother called out.

I did as I was told.

'When's he back?'

'Len?'

Myra nodded, crumbs of Milk Arrowroot biscuit caught in the corners of her mouth.

'Wednesday.'

'Does he really expect to find anything up there? I mean really?'

'That's why he went.'

'None of us believe this Shady Green nonsense.'

'Who's us?' Mother's eyebrows curved aloft with curiosity.

Myra was a little taken aback. 'The family...most of us, anyway.'

Mother held her tongue. 'Why wouldn't you believe in this Shady Green?'

Myra straightened herself upon the stool. 'Um, well it's hard to say it to his own flesh and blood, but the old fellow was a bit funny in the head...understandable after all he'd been through with the War and all...and Patrick...and I mean he never did come back the same.'

Hardly.

But was Tick Tock out of his mind? Anybody who spent so much time with chickens was bound to be thought of as odd, but mental? Could the old papers from the Ballet Shoe Factory that I'd stashed in the cavity of the garage wall shed any light on how mad he might have been? And with Mother otherwise preoccupied with Myra and Malcolm on a sleepover, no better time had presented itself for reading them without interruption.

TWELVE
ON A BED OF BAMBOO

I retrieved the two bundles of papers from the garage wall. In the privacy of my bedroom, beneath the almost life-sized posters of a holy trinity of rock guitarists I placed the papers side by side on my bed. One bundle of papers was twisted and torn with only a fragment of the title page remaining, caught in the string. The other bundle seemed to be intact and was headed Java 1943-1945, and signed Valencia J. Fiorentino at the bottom. I untied the string that bound this bundle of papers together.

May 13 1943
I sleep on a bed made of bamboo. It is knotted and rutted and makes sleeping difficult. The huts are packed tight with POWs. If I stretch my feet either to the left or right, I will touch the limbs of another fellow. If a fellow accidentally touches another's ulcerated limb—an ulcer is such a thing as I have never seen that eats the flesh and exposes the bone, an ugly gaping crippling wound—he will awake screaming. This happened to Matthews last night. Matthews suffers from dementia. I do my best to steer clear of him as he draws too much attention from the Nips. Today he woke

up screaming and tore out of the camp wearing only his Jap-happy—a sort of floppy pair of underpants with not much material either front or back—and was last seen canoeing down the river with Nips on both banks screaming at him to stop, but unwilling to waste a bullet on him. Generally speaking, dying by the gun around here runs a distant third to malnutrition and dysentery.

May 16 1943

Matthews was found and returned to the camp today. The Nips put him in the isolation hut with the 'trouble-makers'. I could hear him yabbering to himself in a language no one really understood. When the Nips let him out to go to the latrines, he fell right through the flimsy wooden cubicle into the mess below. A couple of our boys had to get down in there with him to get him out. Afterwards, all three of them fought for space beneath the solitary tap in the camp that stands only two feet six inches off the ground, making for a mad scramble to get clean, surrounded by Nips, who kept their distance from the stink and filth of it all, but wary, lest Matthews made another break for it.

May 29 1943

Something is up with the Nips. Maybe we are moving camp again? Copped a beating from Nip guard, Sato, for improper salutations, in that, I did not hold for sufficient length of time. A blow to the back of my leg is a cause of some concern. I've seen the way these ulcers start. Two men passed on today—Jeffries and Phillips. Jeffries had been virtually in a coma for a month. Both had dysentery and ulcers and beriberi and malaria and whatever else. When we carted Phillips out, he had balls the size of grapefruits. Sato pointed them out to another Nip as apparently something of a record.

June 5 1943

Still on orderly duties in the hospital. It has rained solid for a week. The camp is a quagmire—everywhere is mud. The attap can't keep the rain out of the huts. My blanket is sodden and I have the chills. I have no doubt a bout of malaria is on its way again. Within the hut, the water has risen to just beneath the level of the bamboo platform arrangement on which we sleep. My canvas boots are ruined and my feet swollen and full of sores. I assisted on three leg amputations, both with the minimum amount of anaesthetic that the Docs were surprised was sufficient for the task. Another two men passed on—Satterley and Grimshaw. They knew it was coming. Grimshaw told me he couldn't go soon enough—he said he wasn't going to stand in the way of dying. I don't think I hate the Nips. I just want to kill them. I miss Maisy and the children but I do not wish I were home. I wish I were being useful fighting Nips or Germans. One can die of uselessness. This is I think what happened to Grimshaw.

June 14 1943

Mercifully, the rain has stopped. The camp is a cesspool—the latrines have overflowed—one picks where one walks carefully. The Nips are on edge. Sato dragged three men out of parade and beat them senseless. Salutations were the problem, the men too slow to give them. Matthews re-admitted to hospital today and to my care. Just lay on his bed all day nice and quiet. Took his medicine. No problem at all. When I saw him come in I thought we'd all be in for a time of it. Big yellow lizard eyes that never seem to blink. Follow me everywhere. He's a bit spooky but otherwise he's as good as gold. If he makes a run for it I'm not chasing him. I've told the docs.

June 17 1943

The heat after the rains is terrific, the mozzies are everywhere. I think every man now has had a bout of malaria and the quinine is in short supply. The docs give me more than my fair share seeing that I am needed at the hospital. We no longer complain about the bitterness of the quinine; the shivers and aches and pains of M are much worse. I stole a couple of eggs from the kitchen. If you pick a time in the middle of the day, not too close to mealtimes, the Nips are scarce and no one is preparing what passes for food.

June 24 1943

No one has said anything but the rations are less. We are down to just a couple of portions of that damnable rice per day. Beriberi is rampant. No meat or eggs for a week. Our officers seem to be holding up all right. I saw them with their shirts off down the river—they bathe separately to us—hardly a rib in sight!

June 30 1943

Close call today. Got caught going into the kitchen trying to steal eggs. I have successfully been pilfering for the last week or so and got a bit over-confident. Nip asked me where I was going. On the spot, I said, that the hospital needed a pan from the kitchen for boiling water. The Nip waved me away with a gesture that seemed to indicate that I might be a purveyor of disease and shouldn't be anywhere near the kitchen. Heaven forbid you wouldn't want the Nips to catch anything!

July 2 1943

A letter out of the blue from Maisy through the Red Cross. Amazes all of us that any of this stuff still gets through even if everything is 9 months late. Maisy says everyone is fine. Margaret and her sisters are all in the war effort—specifically what, has been blacked out, by Nips or our people, I don't know. No mention of the boys. No mention of what Pat is up to. The girls are going to the dances in St Kilda. I'll bet that's where that damn Billy Henson and his Hawaiian band are playing. Flies around the honeypot for my girls. Maisy too flighty and shouldn't be letting the girls, particularly Margaret, be going to places like that. All of us in the camps have heard about how the Americans are behaving in our towns with our girls. It would be too much to expect a letter from Shady.

July 4 1943

Patrick's birthday. If I am to be honest I miss that boy more than anyone, although, I miss them all. He is, I know, my spitting image. I wonder what work he has found? An apprentice fitter and turner at the dockyards would be good. I wonder if that private welding school's still around. Oxywelding: that's a skill that would keep him going in the future. If this War drags on he will be of an age to join up. I dread that thought. Fortunately he is still too young. I tended to a lad today who looked no older than Pat. This is no place for boys—it is a hell. How thankful I am that Pat is safe and sound with Maisy and the girls.

July 7 1943

Matthews did a strange thing today. After I gave him a wash he held my hand and wouldn't let go. Not threatening like. Just held my hand softly yet firm enough that he meant me to know he wanted to hold on. I asked him if he was all right. But he didn't say anything. Big ghost eyes that he has make me almost shiver.

*****

The front door slammed shut. I heard Myra's shoes going down the front footpath. There was the sound of steps running up the passage. I braced for Mother's appearance. The steps went quickly past. I could hear drawers opening and closing, and then the sound of what must have been a chair dragged along the floor. Shortly after, there was the crash of something quite heavy, and for a few moments I couldn't think what this could be. I didn't hear the silver fasteners of the old, brown leather suitcase ping open, the one Mother kept on top of the wardrobe full of Maisy's old belongings. I didn't see her riffling through the bundles of old documents and faded black and white 6" x 3" photographs, searching for evidence of this Shady Green.

I retied the sheaves of paper into a single parcel and stowed it for greater convenience inside my guitar case. I would show it to Mother and Len when I'd finished reading them. Although, I did wonder how much Mother would want to relive the War. I remember when she told us the story of Tick Tock returning home. She couldn't finish the story so engulfed was she with tears. Perhaps, she might wish I'd never found Tick Tock's papers.

Len said don't. Mother said it would be all right. I said, 'Go on Mother tell us, please tell us.' So Mother did. She told of how Tick Tock and the survivors of 10/28th Battalion (Infantry) went straight from the transport ships at Station Pier to the Veterans' Rehabilitation Hospital ('The Rehab') at Heidelberg for convalescence and demobbing. Maisy had been notified by telegram of his admission. 'But,' said Mother, 'the whole family couldn't visit him so your grandmother just took the eldest, me.' 'Did you want to go?' Esther had asked. 'Of course I wanted to go. I hadn't seen Tick Tock in almost four years.' Maisy and Mother had put on their prettiest dresses, ones they had made themselves with the help of Mrs Yule down the road. When they arrived at the 'The Rehab', the Head Sister warned Maisy and Mother that after what he had been through, he might not look the same; they might not recognise him at all.

Mother said Tick Tock was one of many in a ward divided into two long lines of single cast iron beds. None of them weighed more than six stone. Their heads were little more than skulls. The Head Sister told Maisy and Mother not to show any surprise; they must act as if the men looked normal. She led them to the open doorway of a ward and pointed him out.

Tick Tock was propped up on pillows, staring vacantly down at the tight, white linen sheet that covered him. Maisy and Mother approached him slowly to make it easier for him to recognise them as they neared, but he did not. Not until they stood right beside the bed and Maisy had placed a hand on one of his frail, withered arms did he look up. His eyes widened in recognition. He summoned a thin smile with a mouth that partially opened to frame Maisy's name, although, he made no audible sound beyond the suck of his dried lips. Maisy had replied, 'Yes…and Maggie.' Mother said she wanted to cry but she knew she mustn't. She said she wanted to cry all the more because she knew something Tick Tock didn't. She knew Pat was dead. The eldest boy made in his father's likeness was buried in the Military Cemetery at Rabaul. The boy who had become the man of the family when Tick Tock had gone to War. The boy who had stood on the safety of Spencer Street Station platform, when the family had farewelled their father to War. The eldest son, who in the very brief time available to him would grow to be a man in his father's absence. His spitting image that his father had envisioned grown up taller than himself as he lay awake in his prison hut. The sweat pouring off what was left of his body as he literally melted in the suffocating tropical heat. Pat, his father knew, would do his best to look after and keep safe his mother and his sisters until the rightful head of the family returned from doing his duty. Never once did it occur to him that Pat would forge his father's signature and sign up. Never once did it occur to him that he would be anywhere other than at home. Maisy had asked Mother, should they tell him then, in the hospital? Perhaps, Mother said, they could tell him later, after he was released and in the comfort of his own home? But how could they wait? asked Maisy, he was certain to ask. How's Pat? How's Pat been? Where's Pat? And he would have asked, knowing the answer would be that Pat was fine. Pat had been grand. Pat had been the real man of the house while he was away. Pat had been everything a father could possibly want of a son. Tick Tock would ask all these questions in earnest, but it would be with a smile because the answer was sure to be good. 'Val,' Maisy said, and although the affection between them was rarely apparent, she took his bony hand in hers, 'I've got to tell you something.' Maisy and Mother began to cry and soon Tick Tock was weeping silently for the boy he loved and was gone.

And when Mother told us we all cried too because we had never seen Mother cry like this.

THIRTEEN
YESTERNIGHT

Still in a state of shock Shady sat slumped on the seawall that ringed the Strand. It was inconceivable that Tick Tock was dead. For two hours he had walked the streets of Williamstown like a man who had lost his bearings. Dare it be said, like a man who'd lost his mind.

Shady had stuck to the treeline of the wide, old streets where the trees sprouted roots through the bitumen of the roads, cracking and breaking open whole thoroughfares. Few cars had gone past. The temperature had risen. It was as if it was too hot to travel. Delirious with heat and exhaustion Shady eventually fell to the ground, the pale, blue sky spinning above him. Crouching on all fours like an upturned beetle fighting to regain a lost sense of equilibrium, he struggled to his feet. When his eyes finally refocused he saw the seawall and the Royal Victorian Motor Yacht Club and realised that he had come a little too far north.

A swarm of March flies roused him to walk. With the wind now in the north it was like they had waited in squadrons on the northern outskirts of Melbourne for the all-clear to take off. Madly, he swatted away at them. Indomitable creatures that, for reasons beyond him, could survive a man's punch thrown full-blooded in anger. He staggered across the Strand, the seawall his destination of temporary respite.

The Nelson Place shops appeared quite prosperous, cars parked out front nose-to-tail for the length of the high Victorian terraced block. Seniors' Butchers, Elsums' Bakery, Dr Coutt's surgery and McCulloch's grocery were all still there. A steady stream of people went in and out. In the midst of all the shops was a patch of darkness that Shady knew to be the arched pathway through to the lane at the back, and the Ballet Shoe Factory a short distance along.

Shady figured that Tick Tock, when he was a lookout for the SP bookmakers Cavanaghs, would have stood just inside the dark interior of the archway, where it formed its covered passage to the lane. Tick Tock's skinny, young neck would have craned around the corner, going in and out like a gobbling turkey, trying to spy any police coming, and if there were, he would have raced up the passage waving his arms at a fellow lookout, perched on the fence of the Cavanagh's Tote, whose job it was to relay the warning.

Shady sat slumped upon the seawall, his head in his lap, his arms braced for support. A little further along, a young man and a young woman, clad only in swimmers, sat huddled together, wrapped in beach towels for warmth from the freshening breeze. The sound of heavy machinery from the Naval dockyards momentarily shifted Shady's gaze. In dry dock was a naval destroyer. From beneath the vessel the bright light of welding equipment sparkled. Sensing that he had recovered sufficiently to resume his journey Shady stepped down from the seawall to recross the road.

The passage was not as dim as Shady remembered. Light shone through from the far end. He took small, slow steps that scuffed like sandpaper underfoot. The breeze funnelled coolly around him. His steps sounded loud and enclosed as he passed under the archway and into the lane.

The Ballet Shoe Factory rose before him, quite as beautiful as it did all those years ago—gleaming white, sunlight glinting from the white points of its steepling roof, each sparkle a 'bling' of virtual sound.

Shady heard the cackling of hens. He peered over the back fence looking for signs of life—for the Tick Tock he knew could not be there. The backyard was empty. But he could not stop himself calling out, 'Tick Tock are you there?' Perhaps he had not read of his death? Perhaps that had been an hallucination.

A boy came out of the chook pens, dressed for an occasion in a blue coat and tie. The boy crossed the backyard in the direction of the salon without looking his way. From the back door, a man in a dark suit appeared and called out to the boy, 'We'll be late for Tick Tock's funeral if you don't hurry.'

Shady felt the muscles in his arms slacken in their grip upon the fence.

'Couldn't forget to feed the chooks,' the boy replied, rubbing his hands down the sides of his trousers and hastening after the man.

'Last time you'll be doing that,' the man said, 'they're going tomorrow.'

Both man and boy disappeared from sight around a corner of the Ballet Shoe Factory.

Shady sank to his knees upon the cobblestones. A desperate sadness came over him and he fell as if into a coma. Neither the rough edges of the cobblestones nor the sniffing noses of the dogs that roamed the lane roused him to any sense of consciousness. It was only the light of a full, bright moon, appearing from behind clouds that finally stirred him to life. How long Shady had remained like this, he didn't know, but night had descended and the changeable Melbourne weather was living up to its reputation: a cool change had arrived from the south. Shady pulled his jacket about him. It seemed unimaginable that Tick Tock could be dead, and he cursed himself out loud for waiting so long to make the journey.

No lights glowed within the Ballet Shoe Factory. After he knocked on the front door, without receiving any answer, he went around the side and tapped on the kitchen window.

Rain began to fall.

When he turned the handle of the kitchen door, it opened. As Shady moved quietly through the Ballet Shoe Factory, he called out for Tick Tock. But the only sounds were his heavy breathing and that of the grandfather clock ticking time in the hallway. Upstairs was where he was headed, a little distanced from any unexpected arrivals like the boy and the man. If he heard them coming he'd have a better chance of leaving without being discovered.

Quite out of breath he reached the landing at the top of the stairs. With a faltering step Shady lurched through the open doorway ahead into a sitting room. Shaking with cold he found himself in a high-ceilinged room where the furniture was covered in white sheets. Moonlight shone through windows shorn of drapes, and, before him, was an empty fireplace.

A fire for warmth was what he needed, so Shady, with the aid of a fireplace poker, ripped back the carpet and prised up the floorboards. He was destroying what he loved but somehow it made no difference. As he broke across his thigh, what he thought might be the last plank of wood he'd need, he noticed, jutting out from beneath the tacked-down carpet, two bundled sheaves of papers tied with string, yellowed with age, virtually indistinguishable in colour from the faded newspaper that lined the floorboards. Shady untied the string of the topmost bundle of papers and squinted at the large writing on the first page—A Strapper's Tale. The writing was as revealing as a signature, he'd seen it in letters and postcards—Tick Tock's neat up-and-down lettering the words almost as well-formed as newspaper print.

Struggling to read the writing in the dimness of the room, he took the bundle of papers over to the window and examined it under the light of the moon. As he flicked through the pages and saw his name repeated over and over and finally the mention of a little blue Navy bag, he snapped. His instinct was to destroy what should never have been written. Grasping the bundle in both hands he twisted it this way and that manically trying to tear it in two, but only managing to rip most of the title page free. He dropped the bundle and crushed the single partially loose sheet into a ball of paper that he fed into the fire. The paper ignited. Flames licked and eventually incinerated the fine dark print of Tick Tock's hand.

Shady stood transfixed before the blazing fire clutching the sheaves of paper, wondering if he was capable of destroying them. After great hesitation he came to the realization that he could neither burn nor read them. So many words and thoughts, and whilst they were painful for him, they might not be for others. What they would be for others he didn't know. Yet, they were not his to destroy. The words were Tick Tock's. He would leave it for others to judge. And so he put A Strapper's Tale and the other bundle of papers— which he presumed to be more of the same—somewhere safe, high atop the pediment of a large sideboard.

The fire soon warmed the room. Shady crept beneath a heavy curl of carpet. His eyes grew heavy. The moon hung in the window and the Milky Way spread out in the great black beyond. Shady dreamt of his mother and Yesternight.

'Yesternight is a place and not a time, Georgie. It is nothing like 'Yesterday'. Nothing like it at all', she said. 'In Yesternight every person is a star. Some people are big stars like Alpha Centauri and, others, while just as important, are little stars like our Sun.' George didn't know that the Sun was a star and he certainly didn't think it was small. His mother had assured him that the Sun was most certainly a star although compared to an Alpha Centauri it had barely grown up at all. 'But do you know the most amazing thing?' she said. And George asked what? And his mother told him in a whisper as if it was a secret, 'They all speak to each other.' George asked how she knew. 'It stands to reason,' she replied. 'All those stars flying about for millions of years and so few of them crashing into each other. That's because they talk.' To prove the point she took George outside into the backyard. She told him to shut his eyes and listen hard. At first he heard nothing, and then to his amazement he could hear beautiful voices coming from far far away. But the voices were in a language he didn't understand. 'Of course, they don't speak English, silly, they don't come from Earth. They come from Yesternight. It's the language of Yesternight. The language of the stars.' Whether George's mother knew that the Sacred Heart choir practiced of a Tuesday and Thursday night and had a fondness for Latin one will never know.

FOURTEEN
POACHING EGGS

Mother and Malcolm were up the street getting pies for lunch. Barring fire Esther wouldn't get out of bed for at least an hour. And Len would take his time down the tip. Besides, there was no reason why he'd climb the stairs to my room when all he had to do was yell. So I opened my guitar case and took out the bundle of Tick Tock's papers and resumed reading where I'd left off.

July 15 1943

The heat today is unbearable. After the rains, the heat seems to rise from the very earth one stands on and very nearly sleeps upon. At night the air is as still and thick as custard. A death's head spider has taken up residence in the webbing of my mosquito net. Some of the soldiers—Dillon and Phillips, the most notable—have taken to feeding him grasshoppers and various other bugs. When I return after a day in the hospital, I search for him in the netting. He is always there as the netting catches a feast of bugs. Sometimes I talk to the spider, and when I do, I call him Shady. Dillon, I know, thinks this is a form of madness. He asked me today why I called him Shady. I told him a lie, saying it was on account of his colour, quite dark.

July 23 1943

It is many years since I picked up a pen for anything other than writing the odd cheque; not since the letters to Mrs Gorham's boys and their thankful mothers and fathers. The ones who didn't realize she was dead. Maisy didn't know any better. She just sent them back 'Return To Sender'. But not the ones I intercepted. I suppose a lot of what I wrote was just palaver. I remember one from the mother of a boy called Harold. Shady had told me about Harold. Harold used to sit next to Shady in one of the high-backed wooden chairs in the kitchen. Harold was a simple boy from the country. Dimboola, I think. In the letter his mother wrote to say that Harold had passed on in the fighting at Villers-Bretoneux. I replied to the mother—for a time I kept a copy of the letter, now lost, so I could use similar words for other letters—that Harold had been much liked by the boys and a favourite of Mrs Gorham. I wrote that he had been full of kindness and never idle. Cutting wood and getting coal from the cellar had not seemed like chores for him. That Mrs Gorham called him one of her stars. I hope this pleased her.

August 8 1943

Lent my bed netting to Matthews. He is perilously close to death but survives on little food or sleep. Rarely is it that I catch him with his eyes shut. Spent a wretched night without the netting, hiding from mozzies under a damp cold blanket. Miserable. Woke up when the night was at its darkest and thought a bout of the M was coming. Probably just the mind playing its little tricks with me having lent my netting. I definitely have something of the writing bug. And I now find it frustrating that I am too tired from a day in the hospital to write. If I can, I will write of the times Shady and I spent in the drains.

August 18 1943

Sato told us—an arrogant smile on his face—that Darwin, Brisbane and Sydney had been bombed. One of the Docs has a secret little wireless and says this is rubbish. Still I worry for Maisy and the kids. I had never thought it would come to this. At least in Melbourne they're almost as far south as it is possible to go. Not like Shady up north in Brisbane. How I'd like to hear what he's up to. But he's about as likely to write as sing an opera. I am still not to make a beginning of writing the story of Shady and me in the drains and tunnels of Williamstown—but I am more actively thinking about it. The days in the hospital are becoming longer.

August 22 1943

Very busy in the hospital. Men are dying regular now. A new cemetery has been dug. Dillon and his men have taken it upon themselves to make proper wooden crosses for the graves. We all went down the cemetery today for a ceremony to commemorate our dead lads. I am convinced that the way I am staying in some state of health, or, at least, staying alive, is the eggs I pinch from the kitchen. I have had a number of close calls—one with Sato that had me shaking. I daren't get caught. But I must get my eggs. I wonder who is looking after the chickens back at home? Probably Pat, though, I forgot to mention the chickens before I left. The boy knows how important the chickens are to me. I am sure he will look after them.

August 31 1943

There is a rumour that we are to be moved to Thailand to build a railway. In one sense, we are all happy to go, just for the sake of any sort of change. We hear stories of the

railway but no one knows if they are true. I can only hope
for the best. I have started my story that I am calling, A
Strapper's Tale. I passed Matthews today and his eyes were
shut. First thing I thought is he must be dead. Then his eyes
sprung open. He has not said a word in weeks although for
a moment today I thought he might say something. His lips
moved a little.

September 1 1943
I had been stealing an egg a day. I have cut this back to every
other day so as not to draw unnecessary attention to my rel-
atively good state of health. A couple of times, I have given
one of the eggs to good men of the likes of Dillon. This is
a little dangerous as they wonder how I come by them—
not imagining I would be so brazen as to enter the kitchen
and steal—and ask for more on behalf of other mates. On
this score, they will have to take their own chances. If Sato
caught me with a haul, I think he would kill me. He does
not like me. He is cunning and knows that I fare better than
most and wonders why. My mind may be playing tricks,
but on some days it is as if he is following me. I think I will
go without my extra eggs for a few more days.

September 25 1943
Disaster! I was caught red-handed in the kitchen by a Nip.
Peering through the wire-door I'd seen no one inside; nor
when I crossed the threshold of the doorway was there any
detectable sound of someone in there. The eggs were not in
their usual place and so I was forced to root around in the
semi-darkness until I stumbled over what was the sleeping
figure of the Nip on a little pile of hessian, he'd made as a
pillow for his head.

Malcolm burst into the room. 'Whatcha reading? Not one of those magazines, is it?'

'Nothing you'd be interested in,' I replied, scrambling to gather together the pages of the diary and wondering how he'd got home so quickly.

When he saw it was just print he lost interest. 'Pies are hot.'

The rest of Tick Tock's journal would have to wait for another day.

FIFTEEN
GERRY LEADS THE WAY

Mrs Nelson told me that Gerry was up at the cricket club. It was mid-week so it could only have been training. There were a couple of senior players practising in the nets. The batsman smashed a delivery straight back at a big-bellied bowler who was too slow to get down to it. The ball rocketed under his outstretched arm. He stood with his hands on his hips and watched the ball speed towards me. He raised his hand in the air as a signal for me to stop the ball and return it. I fielded the ball and threw it wildly back beyond his reach. A single word was uttered, which I couldn't hear, but I'm sure it wasn't, 'Thanks.'

I drifted past the nets on my way to the cricket sheds. The cricket sheds were on a small embankment between the old and new ovals. The new oval was built upon the old rubbish tip and had a raised looked to it. If someone was standing on the other side of the oval, it was impossible to see them from head to toe because the oval curved in a convex way. In that sense it was like the MCG, although, it attracted a lot more seagulls. The balmy afternoon heat drew an unpleasant scent from the soil as if a vast body was interred within it.

As I got closer to the sheds I could hear the laughing of

older boys. Big booming laughs as if the funniest thing in the world had just happened.

I wanted to tell Gerry that Len had gone to Brisbane to find this Shady Green; that if they didn't find him soon they would have to give up and I would officially inherit the Ballet Shoe Factory.

The doors to the cricket sheds, or as the president of the Beau Vista Cricket Club called them, The Pavilion, were shut, but the voices within carried almost undiminished through the ventilation grates set high in the walls. I pushed the door open slowly. A few bags of cricket kit were piled in the middle of the concrete floor. The talking stopped. In a corner of the room, Gerry sat in his cricket 'creams' with a couple of older boys, each at least seventeen or eighteen. The silence continued, until one of them laughed and said, 'It's not them. It's only some runt.'

They all laughed except for Gerry.

Gerry stared in my direction without an acknowledgement that he knew me. I recognised the other boys as first grade players.

'Gerry…,' I said.

I would have said more, but it occurred to me that what I wanted to talk about, might sound out of place in here, where deep voices had sounded and the smell of eucalyptus oil hung manly and heavy.

Gerry stood up and placed something on the bench next to him that made a soft clink on the hard wood: a can of Victoria Bitter.

'Do you know him?' one of the boys asked.

'Yeah,' Gerry said somewhat reluctantly.

'He's a bit of a runt, isn't he, Gerry?'

The way he said it was neither menacing nor friendly.

The largest boy took a big slurp from his can of Victoria

Bitter. 'What are you doing here, runt?' he asked.

'He's going,' said Gerry.

Gerry took a few steps towards me.

'He came here for a reason. What did you come here for, runt?' asked the largest boy.

I hesitated.

'To tell Gerry something,' I said.

'Tell Gerry what? We're all friends. Aren't we, Gerry?'

'Not here,' said Gerry as if he knew it could be embarrassing.

The largest boy took a final great suck of his can, and after crushing it in one hand, threw it accurately into a large, plastic rubbish bin on the other side of the shed.

'Come over here,' he said.

For the first time I noticed he hadn't called me runt.

I looked at Gerry who stared impassively back.

'Don't ask Gerry for permission. You're not asking Gerry for the OK, are you?' the boy insisted.

'Don't, Bruce,' said Gerry.

'Don't "Don't Bruce" me,' said the boy who was apparently called Bruce.

'Now what is this you came all this way to see Gerry for?' asked the one called Bruce.

Gerry wriggled his neck at an irritation in the collar of his cream shirt.

'The Ballet Shoe Factory,' I said quietly.

'What?' Bruce said.

'The Ballet Shoe Factory,' I repeated just as quietly as before.

'Piddles, did you hear that?' Bruce said to the other boy.

Piddles was very fair-skinned with short, white hair, nearly albino. I suspected if he stood up he was quite tall.

Gerry walked towards the door. 'I'm going.'

'Come on, Gerry,' said Piddles, 'we want to know more about the ballet. Don't we, Bruce?'

'See ya Saturday,' said Gerry as he pushed through the shed doors to the outside.

Both the other boys laughed and I followed Gerry out.

Gerry walked briskly across the oval.

I ran after him. 'What's wrong?' I asked.

Gerry didn't slow down.

I tagged after him like a little brother. 'The old man will kill you if he knows you've been drinking,' I said just for something to say.

Gerry stopped and turned. 'He'd be a lot more upset if he thought I was hanging out with a homo?'

'Howard?'

'How many homos do you know?'

'How do you know he's a homo?'

'Forget about it…all right? I don't want anything to do with it. It sounds so ridiculous…Ballet Shoe Factory.'

'What's ridiculous about it?'

'Listen to yourself. I don't know how you can even say it…Ballet Codpiece Factory or whatever it is,' Gerry said.

'Who cares what it's called? It's worth a bomb,' I said.

'It's not yours anyway.'

'Len can't find any Shady Green. Nobody can. It'll be like winning Tatts.'

'What about all the burnt ash? What about the painting? Have you told anybody about the painting?' Gerry flicked hair out of his eyes. 'You haven't have you?' he almost accused.

'Why would I?'

'I don't want to know about it. You and your homo accomplice can have it all to yourselves. You're just like that Nigel and Priscilla stealing money from old man Nordith.

No better than them. I hope you'll be happy.'

I wanted to say that I didn't want it all to myself; that I was no Nigel or Priscilla. But it was too late.

Before Gerry had a chance to reply, two girls on horses clopped into view. They reined their horses in tight and steered them into an empty paddock just up ahead. Gerry grinned and made an adjustment to the way his 'creams' fitted about his groin. I inwardly groaned.

One of them was reasonable looking with a nice, shapely figure that would've looked better in an old, tight, stressed pair of Levi's, and not the blue and white checked slacks she wore, that reminded me of Wilbur's wife in *Mister Ed*. The other girl was big, fat and plain. I wanted to cross the street and put a bit of distance between us and an encounter I could do without.

'Don't you dare,' threatened Gerry, all too aware of my backwardness and cowardice. 'Here's your chance,' he said quite seriously.

Reluctantly I took another look at the girls as they dismounted the horses. What could I be missing?

The huge, hideous one glared at us. 'What you starin' at, eh?' She held a fistful of straw to the horse's mouth. Her riding companion adjusted the saddle of her horse while she looked over her shoulder in our direction.

'Come down and check out the horses. Won't bite ya?' yelled the fat girl with a knowing glance at her companion.

'Come on,' said Gerry.

Under my breath. 'No way.'

'Jesus what is wrong with you?' he said. 'They'll go like dunny doors.'

Observing our indecision, the fat one bellowed, 'I betcha you both have got tiny little ones,' she said and held up two fingers about two inches apart. 'Don't you, Kay?' She looked at the other girl. 'Really tiny little ones,' her fingers now only an inch apart and narrowing.

'You slut,' said Gerry, not loud enough to be heard by the girls. 'You are one hell of a slut aren't you, girl,' he spoke with admiration as if he was watching a dirty movie and was compelled to engage with it, to somehow heighten the reality. 'I've got a good mind to drop these strides and prove you wrong you…' and his hands went to his belt as if to undo it. This was an alarming prospect, as the girls might have been more of a mind to cheer, and ask to see mine, so I spun around and scurried off.

From behind me, I heard, 'Jesus you shit me. Your chance of a bloody lifetime and you run away.' Gerry was stalking after me and by continually looking behind at the girls had encouraged them to remount their horses. I bounded up the street with the aim of making the safety of the family home. Gerry was as mad as hell and muttering about how both of them would bang, and he'd take the fat one if that were the problem. By continually rounding on the two trailing riders Gerry ensured the girls would follow, and whilst I couldn't bear to look, I knew they were there from the hard clopping sound of horses' hooves on the bitumen.

'What's wrong with you?' he insisted.

There was indeed plenty wrong with me. 'But they're sluts? Aren't they?' I asked.

Gerry was incredulous. 'Yes I told you.' He said it like what more do you want, but all I could see were the slides of the sex night with Len, and a cankerous, weeping cock paying the price of not waiting for Miss Dead Right. He said I'd blown it and I tended to agree. 'When d'you reckon you'll ever get one?' he yelled. Picking a point in the future when I seriously thought I was a chance was better left in the hands of a clairvoyant.

Going home was not the smartest idea. Then they would know where I lived. Of course, I hadn't imagined for a second that we had been worth following all the way home, even by fat, ugly girls. When I'd managed to drag Gerry around to the back of the house and out of sight, I could hear the girls out the front of the house yelling with all get-out to, 'Come out, come out wherever you are,' as if it was a game of hide-and-seek. Gerry said it still wasn't too late, then all of a sudden, we heard Len telling the girls to get lost or he'd call the police.

Gerry and I agreed we had no interest in telling Len how it all got started, and we'd make ourselves scarce, by going for a sunbake and swim down at the salt pans. We gathered Malcolm on the strength of a promise to collect Gerry's little brother Brian along the way.

The sun was still well above the horizon in a sky low with accumulating cloud. Salty patches of the bay's briny water dried on our skins as we climbed the high continuous dune that shielded the beach from the abandoned salt pans. We were all naked, carrying our clothes in little bundles. In the privacy of the salt pans we hung our clothes out to dry on gnarled, desiccated scrub. Gerry hung his creams as a sort of shade over a bush, and we sat beneath the bush, partially protected from the sun.

'Bit like *Lord of the Flies*?' I said.

Gerry squinted. 'More like *Lawrence of Arabia*.'

The salt pans were a vast, white, crystalline reflective surface almost too bright to look at.

'They kept their pants on in *Lawrence of Arabia*,' said Malcolm knowledgeably, pretty much summing up for him the real difference between the two movies.

Brian who had only seen *Lord of the Flies* made the point, 'They weren't totally naked. I mean they had undies on, didn't they Ger'?'

'The big old-fashioned ones,' said Malcolm. 'Not the coloured ones, the jocks like Gerry and us wear now.'

We all instinctively looked around at the assortment of underwear including Gerry's lime green jocks that hung suspended like nesting birds on the branches above us.

Brian didn't want to be left out. 'Dad still wears the big white ones with the hole at the front. I saw them on the clothes-line yesterday.' The way he said it, it could have been the one and only pair his father had.

'Dad's got some too. Hasn't he, Michel?' asked Malcolm on reflection.

'You mean the special ones he's got in case he has an accident and has to go to hospital,' I said sarcastically.

Malcolm quite seriously, 'Actually I think he's got some of both. Do you think he's got some of both, Michel?'

'Probably,' I said absent-mindedly.

'Jesus do we have to talk about jocks and undies?' asked Gerry. He splintered a dry twig and poked the fine point of it in his mouth and sucked thoughtfully. 'What about that girl, whatshername? Joan?'

'No. Apparently her name's Vivian.'

'Apparently?'

'That's what Brenda said.'

'Brenda? Haven't you spoken to her? I mean you all but fell over her at Newport station, right?'

'Not yet. I'm working up to it.'

'Jesus, working up to it? Doing what?'

Malcolm sparked up. 'Probably is Joan. Michel it would be Joan. You know how much you love Joan.'

My obsession with Joan the waitress at the Motel

Montague in Narooma rose like a burning pyre with me lying sacrificially across it. We went to Narooma for summer holidays as reliably as we went to Sunday Mass. I would do almost anything to get out of going again this year.

'Forget Joan.'

'It's all over with Joan?' Gerry baited.

'All over,' I said quietly.

'That's right,' said Malcolm as he remembered a pertinent fact. 'Michel found out she was married. Didn't you?'

'Married, eh?' said Gerry. 'You're ahead of me there.'

A pair of jocks mercifully fluttered down upon Malcolm's head. 'Oh God, disgusting. These are disgusting. Whose are these?' Malcolm snatched the offending yellow jocks from his head and held them accusingly in front of him.

Brian laughed.

'These your shit-catchers? These things.' Malcolm threw the jocks as far as he could out onto the shiny, white expanse of the salt pan.

Brian continued to laugh and this annoyed Malcolm who chased him out from under the bush. They screamed as the soles of their bare feet eventually registered the searing heat of the salt pan. Brian zigzagged into the distance with Malcolm and his outstretched hands very close behind.

Gerry drew a line in the fine sand with his big toe. 'So what about this other one, Vivian? What are you really doing about her?' To demonstrate the not unpredictable direction in which he was heading, he leant back a little and scooped from between his legs enough genitalia for a Doberman's dinner.

I turned away. 'Do you have to…I mean what is that if not…homosexual.'

'Nothing homosexual about all this, mate. Let me assure you.'

'Jesus,' I felt giddy.

'Just need a scratch that's all. Know what I mean?'

'Give it a break,' I said.

'I don't know why you go to all the bother you do with girls. It's sort of lost on me.' Gerry seemed to be tucking the offending equipment away. 'I mean what's the point of all this chasing and fantasizing.'

I rested my head on my knees. Down there, of course, was something limp and lifeless: the open-cut of its circumcised head pointing to the ground as symbolically as disappointment itself. I shut my eyes and behind closed lids squeezed very tight.

'There's a party on.' I murmured, my head still between my legs.

'What? I can't hear when you're talking to your dick.'

I raised my head. 'There's a party.'

'Whose?'

'Brenda's.'

'Not exactly good-looking.'

'She's where you'd draw the line?'

Gerry laughed.

That Brenda had invited Vivian was reason enough for me to put in an appearance. 'She's got plenty of friends.'

'Ugly attracts ugly.'

'All of them can't be.'

'Ugly's a powerful thing.'

My backside was getting very uncomfortable on a crack in the hard salt pan. I jiggled into a different position.

'Getting toey, eh?' Gerry smiled. 'Give us a look at it.'

'Piss off,' I said, and hoped like hell the damn thing didn't do anything of its own volition.

'When's the party?' Gerry asked.

'Tomorrow night.'

'You reckon those fancy private school girls might take a fancy to me?' he asked.

Before I had a chance to respond, Gerry stood up, the thing between his legs hung like a stevedore's hook, and I didn't know where to look or how to answer.

SIXTEEN

JOHN CARSON AND KILLER PAY BEAU VISTA A VISIT

Kids queued to be served by me at the tuck shop. I had become a minor celebrity. Each of the little morons would stand at the counter with their right hand inside their jacket as they placed an order in abominable French. I'd oblige by saying, *'Excusez moi?'* The orders were largely incomprehensible.

John Carson piped up from his usual non-serving position at the back of the tuck shop. 'If you get any more popular Froggie we may well have to enlist you in the French Foreign Legion.' John Carson's sidekick Richard 'Killer' Speck—so named after the Chicago serial killer of the time—giggled as he turned a page of *Portnoy's Complaint*, apparently able to listen to John Carson and pick up the nuances of whatever debauch was taking place on the page.

As I served and Killer read, John Carson maintained a running commentary from the shadows. 'Charles, we're thinking of taking a run your way. Aren't we, Killer?' Killer rocked his head up and down without raising his eyes from *Portnoy's*. *Portnoy's* was his bible. His book of revelations.

His daily running sheet. He went nowhere without it.

I looked across to Killer, who leant on the front counter with the book between his elbows, oblivious to any customers.

John Carson continued, 'We're thinking Saturday would be good. How's that suit you, Charles?'

I shrugged my shoulders, as I threw a packet of chips at an offensive pseudo-French-speaking prat from third form.

John Carson, in a more authentic French accent than most, responded, 'You do not seem, how can I say this, Froggie, overwhelmed at the prospect of our visit to your humble shores.'

I cringed at the thought of what John Carson and Killer Speck would make of my little Beau Vista world.

'Will we need passports, Charles? Do you have a passport, Killer?'

'No,' replied Killer.

'You must tell us, Froggie. We would hate for there to be, how shall I say, an international incident.'

I rubbed at a meat pie stain on my shirt that I hadn't previously noticed. 'Bugger me,' I said, straining to remove the stain with a tuck shop towel.

'Now now,' said John Carson, 'and I know that Killer here will agree with me one hundred per cent, that this fine boys' establishment is no place for that sort of language or expression of interest. We can accommodate many personal requests in Le Tuck Shop, but buggering will not be one of them.'

Killer sniggered, and I kept on rubbing the stain and wondering how serious he was about coming to Beau Vista.

'Is my French not good enough for you? Is that it Charles? Are we too much of the *je – ne – sais – pas*, the peasant for you, Froggie?'

I threw the towel at John Carson and laughed. 'You are

so juvenile.'

John Carson threw his hands up in the air in mock horror. 'Killer, what is this expletive? This form of abuse? This horrific word-crime —joo - be - nile?'

Killer put the book down. 'I think the peasants are revolting.'

John Carson clapped his hands together. 'As usual Killer you have it in one. Froggie is indeed revolting. His manners are appalling. His manners are the manners of the Frog. When he should be leaping about like any good Frog at the chance of visitors, he deigns to turn them away.'

Killer unwrapped a bar of chocolate and took a bite as if it was his lunch. 'Doesn't make any sense to me. Should be open arms. Begging us to come.'

'*Absolument*,' intoned John Carson, '*begging* Froggie, not any of this damnable *buggering*.' He wagged his finger at me to not be so naughty. 'Don't panic, Charles. We won't come when you are all packing down to your vittles and grits and whatever else it is that you eat. We'll come when it suits. So when on Saturday would that be?'

'Whose car's that?' asked Malcolm.

In the drive way was a white Datsun 1600. Getting out of the car was John Carson. Inside at the wheel was Killer Speck, who by dint of having to repeat Year 11 was the first boy in his year to get a driver's licence and a car that he was allowed to park at school.

'Shit,' I said.

'What did you say?' asked Mother.

'He said shit,' said Malcolm.

'I didn't ask you to repeat it,' said Mother.

'You wanted to know,' said Malcolm.

'They're boys I know,' I said, and stood to go outside.

'Boys from where?' asked Mother.

'Boys from school.'

Mother looked interested. She made her way to the window. 'Haven't met any of your friends from school. Not St Sebastian's, anyway.' Mother was keen to meet them. 'Did you know they were coming over?'

I couldn't say I'd hoped they wouldn't come. 'They said they might.'

John Carson strode up the driveway looking very unlike his usual self in jeans. He was made for a uniform of some type. Killer stayed in the car. I reached John Carson before he got to the front door. 'I see the peasants are doing rather well,' he said in reference to the house.

I was about to usher him back to the vicinity of the car, when Mother appeared over my shoulder. 'Who's this, Michel?'

John Carson introduced himself without any hesitation. 'John Carson, Mrs White, a pleasure to meet you.'

Mother was not the most easy-going of people, but she had taken an instant liking to John Carson. 'And a pleasure to meet you, John.' She smiled broadly.

'You have a wonderful place here, Mrs White,' John Carson enthused. 'And the views too. You would never tire of them, I'll bet.'

Mother looked across the bay in a good impression of seeing it for the first time. 'No, we don't. It's the reason we built here.'

John Carson stepped back from the front door to notionally frame the overall perspective of the house. 'You built it as well?' he said. He could have been appraising some kind of architectural miracle.

'Well yes...we got an architect...'

'Ah,' John Carson said, in such a way that it conveyed he

now understood the house's touch of class.

Mother beamed and didn't finish her sentence.

Malcolm poked his head between Mother and me. 'Whose that in the car?'

'That's Richard Speck,' said John Carson.

Mother's brow lifted in low-level recognition, which was sort of what I'd expect at the mention of a serial killer, if only in name, sitting in our driveway.

'Where are you boys off to, then?' she asked quite amiably.

What? Mother would just let me drive off with them? She didn't even inquire about who had the driving licence.

'Just passing through, Mrs White. Mentioned to Michel that we might drop in after we saw Kenny.'

'Kenny Roberts?'

'Almost killed himself.'

'Has something happened to Kenny Roberts?'

'Sprained his neck mucking about on the train,' I said.

'Got his head caught between the ceiling of the carriage and the overhead handrails doing chin-ups. For a while he just hung there. Almost a goner.'

One of Mother's hands clasped her neck. 'Oh my goodness. I didn't know.' She looked at me. 'Did you?'

'It's not one of those things that you miss, Mother,' I replied.

'But you didn't say anything...'

'Mother he was just showing off.' Immediately following the pubic hair incident Kenny thought he'd try and break the record for chin-ups, as if that might partially erase the humiliation. But his head was too big. After a few sets he got it stuck between the handrail and the ceiling of the carriage. The only thing that prevented Kenny from hanging himself was the two bodies of Jerome and Ray hurriedly wedged beneath him. At Newport station the train was held up while the conductor wriggled Kenny loose with the help of a can of oil that he rubbed over his hair and face and neck. 'Besides no time seemed like the right time to talk about something like that.' I looked around for Malcolm as an excuse.

John Carson offered helpfully, 'Some people think he did it on purpose. The Brothers want to keep it hush-hush. Not good for the schools reputation and what not.'

'What kill himself?' asked Mother, almost speechless.

Mother was taking all this rather badly, which was not lost on John Carson. 'He'll make a full recovery, Mrs White. Apart from this awful abrasion he's got here,' he wrapped his hand around his throat by way of illustration, 'all he got out of it was a sprained neck.'

Malcolm's continued presence had gone mainly unnoticed. 'Has Kenny broken his neck?' he inquired.

Mother ushered him away. 'What are you doing here? Why aren't you playing in the backyard like you usually are?'

Malcolm's expression said, What? Are you weird or something? Obligingly he wandered off.

John Carson put on a face of adult concern. 'Not really a conversation for a young boy. Never know what sort of impression it could be having. Hate to be giving him ideas.'

'Mother it was an accident,' I insisted.

'Unrequited love,' said John Carson.

'Sorry?' asked Mother.

I had told John Carson about Kenny and Brenda and the incident of the pubic hair.

'A girl, Mrs White. A heartless hussy had been leading poor Kenny on. He was trying to impress but to no avail.'

A spark of anger flickered in her eyes, 'Do you know who the girl …?'

I had to step in. 'Mother, Kenny's got a whole lot of girls

running after him. It's not just one…'

'But John was just saying…' and the sentence dissolved in thought.

John Carson was making it up as he went. Kenny's pride had taken a hit but the suggestion he was smitten with Brenda was pure fabrication. Mother bore the look of a dilemma. 'Do you think it's such a good idea going to this party?'

'Mother, I told Brenda I was going.' Mother was a stickler for social niceties. If I said I was going, I was going.

Her face continued to cloud over as indecision roiled. Mother gazed at John Carson for a few seconds of deliberation. 'Are you going to this party, John?'

John Carson's eyes registered surprise. '*Michel* hasn't mentioned a party. I don't think so anyway…'

'Mother, it's Brenda's party. She invited the kids from the train.'

'I suppose people like Kenny Roberts are going? Like some sort of hero coming back from the dead,' Mother said with a subdued sense of outrage.

'Mother I don't know if Kenny is going.' The last time I saw Kenny he was hanging by his chin from the overhead handrails. It took some effort of imagination to visualize him jigging under the bright strobing lights of some makeshift disco.

'I know Brenda's mother.' Everyone knew everyone in Beau Vista. 'I'll ring her. Would you like to go, John?' Mother gave John Carson a smile of hopeless anticipation.

A look of cultivated uncertainty spread on John Carson's face. 'Well, I was going to the pictures with Richard,' he said, as he turned to the Datsun and Killer, thrumming the dashboard with his fingers, 'but sure – '

'That does it. I'll call Brenda's mum right now and fix it up. To have someone at that party who's a bit grown up and responsible won't hurt one little bit.'

Mother gazed appreciatively at the departing John Carson as if he was the representation of a boy I could be if only I put my mind to it. 'Michel will ring with the party's address and the details,' she called out.

I followed John Carson down the driveway.

Killer had his arm out the window adjusting the rear-view mirror to watch two girls walking on the sea wall across the road.

John Carson took a voluble sniff of air. 'Froggie, I think something's passed away in the general vicinity. Killer?'

Killer took his own sniff. 'Without a doubt,' he confirmed.

A southerly was strengthening and with it the stench of seaweed washed up overnight. Beau Vista beach couldn't be trusted. I could tell the house had impressed John Carson, and the car, too, that the raised Roller-Door had revealed. Then the stinking beach had to bring me crashing back to Earth.

'Phew, that is one killer stink, Charles. How can you possibly live here?' John Carson clamped two fingers either side of his nose. 'Killer get us out of here before it's too late.'

As the white Datsun 1600 sped away down the esplanade, John Carson hung his head out the window and screamed, 'And don't forget Brenda's address…' and whatever else he said after that was lost on the putrescent breeze.

SEVENTEEN
STARRY STARRY NiGHT

Shady felt uncomfortable living in the Ballet Shoe Factory, even if only for a few nights. The boy had visited twice and spent most of his time in the chook pens; once by himself and the other time with a tall shifty-looking youth, who had a fondness for scratching his groin.

On the first occasion he had almost been caught. Boys' voices had floated to him, as if through the open window of the upstairs living room. When he'd realised that the voices were inside and coming from the top landing of the stairs, he had time only to crawl out onto the gabled roof. After they left, he discovered that the painting had been moved and Tick Tock's journals had gone.

Shady didn't regret not having read what Tick Tock had written. He couldn't read the words without seeing his face or hearing Tick Tock talk, and he had not come all this way to read the ancient words of a dead man. But he was glad that he had not burnt the journals. A cursory glance at A Strapper's Tale had given him a good guide to what lay inside. Not the other journal's horror of the POW camps but something much worse: the revelation of secrets never meant to be written down, secrets that could only be spoken of between the closest of friends. And then there was that other matter. Shady knew how Tick Tock had come into the money for the Ballet Shoe Factory; for him it had been no different to getting a good tip at the races; he didn't need any convincing that it was all fair and square. Something he didn't approve of; not something he'd condemn. But he knew that for Tick Tock the money would always be tainted.

Shady also knew he hadn't made it any easier by occasionally taunting Tick Tock for being so apparently well off. 'I don't know why you hang out with an old derelict like me, you're a rich man.' And the fact that Shady was obsessed with the Ballet Shoe Factory meant that he was forever talking about it, which acted as a permanent reminder and source of embarrassment for Tick Tock, although this had not been his intention.

When the boy came the second time, on this occasion alone, he spoke to himself in Japanese. Tick Tock was the only man he knew who spoke some Japanese. This speaking to himself in Japanese struck Shady as more than coincidence, and he looked for signs of a resemblance to Tick Tock and saw none. The boy was pale and could they be freckles spotting his cheeks? It was hard for Shady to imagine any relative of Tick Tock with anything other than perfect olive skin.

Shady supposed there was bound to be a search for him as a major beneficiary of Tick Tock's will. What would he do with all this? he thought, as he looked up at the vast gabled roof that towered above him. How wonderful it would be if another Mrs Gorham should come along. The Ballet Shoe Factory was far too big and grand for him. What would his mother have made of it all? She would have thanked the stars: each and every one of them. And

Yesternight, no doubt, would have had another great story to tell, something like: 'In Yesternight the moons and satellites of Mars and Jupiter have come together in the most astonishing display of planetary power to bestow on one of Man's own an extraordinary blessing, the most beautiful object the townspeople of Williamstown had ever seen, the Ballet Shoe Factory. What a wonder it is…' He'd certainly come a long way since the time in the drains with Tick Tock all those years ago.

Yes, he could see as good as any rat down in the drains. He had gotten—what was the word? —acclimatised. The subterranean world of drains and tunnels had become his home. And when Tick Tock, or should he say Val, as he was more generally known back then, had entered his kingdom, on the run from the Cavenaghs, George had resolutely gone about the task of foraging for food for two with the same enthusiasm he'd had in merely providing for himself. He rose early with the sun. A sun he couldn't see until he climbed the rungs of an iron ladder and pushed aside a manhole cover. He broached the surface of the earth every day at the same time as if he'd been awakened by a primal alarm.

Shady remembered the morning not long after Tick Tock had joined him in the drains. Indifferent to whether it was early or late, he was busily occupied on the far side of the Cave some twenty yards from where Tick Tock had apparently lain in feigned sleep. With a tack in his mouth he hammered at the underside of a rectangular wooden box open-ended on one side. The hammer and the tacks that he was using for the task he'd scavenged from Mrs Gorham's. The wood he'd found washed up on the banks of the creek.

Tick Tock twisted and turned on a mattress that caved in the middle to a V. Eventually he raised a sleepy head above the horizon of old blankets. Gazing with blurred eyes he called across the considerable width of the Cave, 'Can't you do whatever that is, somewhere else?'

Undeterred George thumped a stave of pinewood more firmly into place with the hard underside of the palm of his hand. 'This,' he declared, holding up the wooden contraption, 'is for your benefit too.'

Reluctantly, Tick Tock trudged over to where George sat splay-legged on the bare concrete floor of the Cave. In George's hands was an object about the size and shape of a shoebox. 'For my benefit?'

Holding it aloft George appraised it in the lamp-lit tunnel. 'Not perfect,' he said, peering through the open end, 'but it'll do.'

Tick Tock did not have the faintest idea what it was.

'Rabbits.'

'Rabbits?'

With a sharp pointed stick George propped the box up on an angle of around forty-five degrees, making an opening that could comfortably fit over anything that approximated the size of a rabbit. Pulling on a piece of string that he had tied to one end of the pointed stick the box dropped with a clatter over an imaginary prey. 'You said you were sick of fish.'

The previous night on the banks of Kororoit Creek, in fading light, Tick Tock had said no more to fish. More precisely what he had said was 'I've had a gutful of stinking fish.'

George had seemed genuinely surprised. 'I thought you loved fish. I thought you came from a long line of Sicilian fishermen.' Tick Tock had a tendency to talk up a maritime heritage and a grandfather on his father's side, the captain of a Sicilian fishing fleet. 'Do you want to help me or not?'

Tick Tock rubbed sleep from his eyes. 'Catch rabbits?'

'What else, do you fancy? Venison, duck, pheasant? Perhaps start dinners with some imported caviar from the store down on the Strand.'

Later that sunny morning the hunter and his companion set off with their contraption: two solitary figures upon the tidal flatlands where in the rusty sun-glazed shallows of the creek pelicans pecked for fish in their own reflections and along the creek bank where the white mangroves met the saltmarsh and the water pooled, seagulls sorted rubbish. Not so obviously, rabbits alert to the hawks and falcons that could sweep down from the sky, nibbled cautiously nearby on thick tufts of grassy vegetation.

George led the way; Tick Tock on his coat-tails, mapping precisely George's trodden path, all too aware that this was snake country too. George's speed defied his bow-legged-ness. He'd stand astride an object of interest as if he had a horse beneath him. A flattened clump of prickly pear, a smooth dark flinty stone suitable for skimming water and faint paw prints in the sandy soil were all matters that stopped George in his tracks.

The sun perched high above them. They'd been laying their trap since dawn with no success and without a break. A fanning breeze had done its best to ward off the simmering heat. Their lips were parched from the salty air. A repeated licking of lips had done nothing to moisten the parchness. Nevertheless the thought of rabbit for dinner had helped keep them going.

Squatting on a gentle rise George was laying the trap in yet another attempt. Tick Tock stretched out on his side taking now only a distracted interest. With a faraway look in his eyes, George guessed that he was thinking about Maisy and the Cavenaghs and the money.

George motioned for Tick Tock to hold the string. 'Tighter,' he whispered.

A shot rang out, and then another. Tick Tock ducked and involuntarily pulled the string. The trap dropped over empty space.

George glared at Tick Tock. Undeterred by the gunfire he crawled to where the trap had fallen and reset it.

Shots continued to ring out. Finally, Tick Tock realized what it was: the Commonwealth rifle range. As if to explain his actions and speaking breathlessly and so close to the ground that his lips touched the sandy soil he said, 'Never been this close. Never heard them firing like that before.'

Although the firing was not in their direction, and the sound quite distant, no more than whistling pings, Tick Tock reflexively hunched his shoulders at every shot. 'I'll bet old Fritz is regrettin' starting this War.'

George settled himself back in beside Tick Tock. 'They'd have their hands full.' It seemed to make no difference to him if the volleys of shots continued or stopped.

'Sure would. Our boys'd be givin' 'em a right bit of hurry up.'

George muttered something to himself that seemed to indicate he was assessing the merits of resetting the trap further up the incline.

Tick Tock lifted his head so as better to see the terrain that George was appraising. 'Do you believe that stuff about the mustard gas?'

Scratching his head George replied, 'I'd believe anything when it came to war.'

'They reckon Tommy Flay copped a dose.'

George looked over his shoulder. 'I don't know any Tommy Flay.'

'Well that's what I heard.'

'Can't always believe what you hear.'

'Seen him too.' Tick Tock was keen to impress George with first hand information. 'Bandages wound round his head. Good as blind.'

'Wouldn't be much use out here huntin' rabbits, would he?'

'I guess not.' Wouldn't be much good for a lot of things, thought Tick Tock. 'They reckon he almost got a VC for what he done.'

He turned and looked at Tick Tock and for a moment Tick Tock was convinced he was going to say something else, but all he did was give a nod at the ground and say, 'This is good.'

For almost six hours they had hunted rabbit with nothing to show for it. There had been the odd one putting in an appearance, just none with the inclination to put its head beneath a contraption that had a habit of wavering in the wind and occasionally collapsing. With the day mostly over, and having laid traps across most of the obvious vantage points that the tidal flatlands afforded, their patience finally paid off.

When the rabbit's face appeared at the entrance to the burrow, George was squinting at one of the creased photographs of the Ballet Shoe Factory that he carried in his back pocket.

Tick Tock nudged him. 'There.'

George tucked the photos back into his pocket. 'Got the string?'

Tick Tock tightened his hold upon the string. The string pulled taut.

'Careful. Don't frighten him.'

The rabbit nuzzled the well-grazed patch of turf just beyond the dark arch of the burrow.

'Come on, you can do better than that,' said Tick Tock to the rabbit.

The shade of the box cast a shadow down the slope and away from the sniffing long whiskers of the rabbit. Tick Tock maintained a tight hold of the string. A breeze rustled the grass and the box wavered.

The two young men stretched lower to the ground flatter than lizards. They could have been brothers. Both with thick dark thatches of hair and skin by its nature olive and inclined to brown but by dint of time in the drains now a sallow colour that did not seem quite healthy.

The rabbit took a step forward and sniffed, raising its head in the direction of where the two boys lay. George nodded. Tick Tock jerked the string and the box snapped shut over its prey.

Suddenly Shady awoke. He thought he'd heard a voice. The man's? The boy's? he didn't know but a voice all the same. He sat upright and peered around him. He readied himself to hide. The voice must have been in his head. There was nobody about.

Shady slowly raised himself and went downstairs carrying over his shoulder a long ribband of torn-up carpet. He planned to sleep in the backyard just as he used to do. It would be easier to escape if he was out there. Soon he was lying on his back, his hand behind his head, looking up at the stars. Fifty years ago he would have heard the clopping of Clydesdales' hooves from the dairy just up the road; the tinkling of milk bottles, and the clucking sound only a tongue can make in the cheek of a man to get a horse going.

But tonight a perfect stillness and quiet had descended, a sense of solitude that Shady had not felt since his time in the drains. He turned to the Ballet Shoe Factory as if its presence commanded his attention. 'There, there,' he said in reassurance, 'you are still my Taj Mahal'. And the leaves atop the elm tree seemed to awake and answered with a shivering, soft, indistinct whisper not unlike the voice of his mother, when she would tuck him in at night and say, 'Shhh, my sweet Georgie, rest assured, the stars shine silvery bright tonight. It is starlit in Yesternight.' Yes that voice never really went away.

EIGHTEEN
THROUGH THE FIRE STOOD MISS DEAD RIGHT

The Wilkinsons' house at 144 Queen Street burnt to the ground. I would have liked to report, that the neighbourhood united as one, in a valiant effort to save the meticulously kept home of the profoundly deaf and mute Wilkinson Family, but by the time anyone noticed that the little double-fronted weatherboard was on fire, it was already well on its way to a conflagration.

From pretty much the outset—at least until after somebody had established that the Beau Vista Fire Brigade had been called—Mother and the local ladies had congregated in a kind of avian gaggle on the front fence of the Town Clerk's house, a few houses along from the Wilkinsons' on the other side of the street. In unguarded voices that rose above the general commotion of the fire, and the occasional explosive pop of a paint tin in the Wilkinsons' carless garage, each of the women, in turn, wondered how ever they could not have noticed the fire taking such a hold. 'Plurry hell,' said Dot Frogett, 'what if it'd been one of us?' And with that thought the line of women simultaneously shuddered, their shoulders visibly shaking, as if for a few seconds they'd been caught in one of those vibrating paint-mixers you see in a hardware store.

The spectators on the other side of the road, down from the fire, were told to go back inside their houses; there was a danger the powerlines would fall. Mrs Van der Hoop, one of the intensely disliked Dutch family that lived directly opposite the Wilkinsons, yelled out, 'We always miss out on the excitement,' and with that she reluctantly led her family back into their house. Dot Frogett said, 'Damn Dutch,' and Fi Stewart and the Town Clerk's wife and some of the other women exchanged a knowing look. The Wilkinsons were standing right there in the flickering shadows of burning light, and saved from the insensitivity and the heartlessness of the Dutch woman's remark only by the completeness of their inability to hear, and Mrs Van der Hoop's annihilated version of English.

After an hour of watching the fire Malcolm had left my side to join a game of British bulldog in the Stewart's front yard. I was about to join him when the conversation turned to ballet.

'Is your Esther still doing her Belly?' Fi Stewart asked.

Mother strained to understand. Then it dawned on her: Ballet. 'Not as much. She's been a bit browned-off from all the exams.' She returned her gaze to the fire. 'I hope they can save something.'

'My Jackie can't get enough of it. Throws her leg up on the furniture at the drop of a hat,' continued Fi Stewart.

Mother gave no indication of any intention to respond.

There was a ballet barre in the salon of the Ballet Shoe Factory. When Esther was younger she'd continually pester Mother and Len to visit Tick Tock. She'd barely have said hello to her grandfather and she'd be in the salon with her back arched and a leg thrust at the ceiling in an arabesque.

'But you're right about those exams. Worse than school. The poor little thing spends half her time doing the splits. Honest to god you need to be double-jointed. Alastair and I can't bear to watch it looks that painful.'

Len, sick of making the trip to the Ballet Shoe Factory whenever Esther wanted to practise, had installed a ballet barre in our garage. Occasionally she'd ask me to be her *premier danseur*, as if this was an accolade. I'd stand behind her, holding her by the ankle, as she pivoted and dipped one way and then another, occasionally wondering, if I could tip her on her head and get away with it as an accident.

'Belly belly belly that's all she talks about. I've never even been to one,' said Fi Stewart.

'I like the ballet,' mused Mother. She stared into the heart of the fire its flames reflecting on her gently perspiring face. 'I don't go often.'

'And the cost of it all! Alastair wants to know who I'm running around with, with all the bills. Got her a tutu. Just a plurry tutu. Barely covers the little thing. That excited when she saw it. Wore it all weekend. Wanted to wear it to school. I said, "Jackie, love, you can't go wearing a tutu to school. The teachers'll think we're all a bit silly in the head or run out of money or something."'

The fire raged across the road.

A tutu would melt in this heat.

Mother brushed her hair from her face. The wind had strengthened. 'Do you think we should stand a little further up the street?'

The ladies shuffled sideways a few yards. From my sitting position on the nature strip I edged my way over so I was still close enough to hear what they said.

'That girl over there with her back to us,' Mother said,

and pointed to make it clear whom she meant, 'I hear she's very good. She's at the Australian Ballet School.'

The fire lit her auburn highlights like sparks in darkness. It was Vivian with a hand like a visor shielding her eyes against the brightness of the blaze. And no more than three paces from her amongst the throng were Gerry and his new 'love' Ruth.

The fire crackled and burned and another fire engine could be heard coming in the distance, its red light flashing as it took a straight line up Queen Street.

'Plurry Alastair just keeps going on about the codpieces. He calls them protuberances. Honestly it's the longest word in the English language he knows. Goes on and on about it, and he's never been either.'

'Mrs Gavan's girl, isn't it?' said Mother.

Fi Stewart gazed at Vivian in non-recognition. 'Are they new?'

Then Mother saw Gerry. 'And that damned Gerry.'

The fire engine reinforcements arrived as the gum tree in the front garden of the Wilkinsons' cracked ominously and seemed as if it might explode. One of the men said it was on account of all the eucalyptus resin and sap, and they had better stand further back in case it really did explode. There was no telling how far that stuff could fly.

Everyone was obliged to move even further up the street.

'She's on a scholarship.' said Mother resettling on the town clerk's fence bordering the Stewarts'.

Was Vivian some sort of rising ballet star? With the Ballet Shoe Factory inheritance imminent no better segue in history had been created for even a social moron like me to say something impressive to her.

'Your father's property, God bless him,' she blessed herself, 'had something to do with the ballet, didn't it?'

asked Dot Froggett.

'Ballet Shoe Factory.'

'That'd be worth a pretty penny,' went Dot Froggett, and Fi Stewart who knew the value of a quid, nodded in agreement.

'Who knows,' said Mother.

'Oh it would,' insisted Dot Froggett, 'where it is and everything. But I do hear that that part of Williamstown is going to rack and ruin with those blasted Housing Commission flats they've put up in Nelson Place.'

From where I was sitting Mother seemed to take a deep breath. 'I don't think it's as bad as that.'

'Mark my words, Margaret, if it isn't yet it's only a matter of time. You'll have derelicts and vagrants crawling all over it.'

To a gossip like Dot Froggett I had no doubt that Mother would not let her know that derelicts were apparently already a problem.

Oh God! Philip Wilkinson had gone up to Vivian. It was virtually inconceivable that mousey Philip Wilkinson with his unfortunate circumstances would have the courage to speak to anyone like her.

Rudolf Nureyev. Something about Rudolf Nureyev. No better leave that one alone: not sure of the pronounciation. Hate to crash and burn on that one. Capsize on the rocks of some linguistic technicality. Play it safe. Margot Fonteyn. That was a good one. Play that one like a trump card in euchre after I've regaled her with a bit of Ballet Shoe Factory history. What ballets would I throw in? Margot Fonteyn's got to be dancing in something. Can't just say her name. *Swan Lake*. No, boring. Any idiot knows *Swan Lake*. Even Gerry's probably heard of *Swan Lake*. Got to do better than that. *The Nutcracker Suite*. Geez who dreams these names up. *Firebird. Giselle.* There's something about that one that rings a distant bell: *pointe* shoes. I know a bit about *pointe* shoes. Right up on their tippy toes. Always impressed me that.

The light from the fire shone like the brightest of halos into a night sky that was almost as perfect as that of a planetarium, more blue than black, the Southern Cross as visible as it would ever be in a great violet blanket pinpricked by stars.

Philip Wilkinson was definitely talking to Vivian. But not in a way that I could. His whole body was animated. For a few moments I thought all the sign language and the accompanying flurry of fingers might have been directed at his mother and father. No, he was talking to her. She stood calmly in profile, and gave no sense of dismay or wonder that Philip should be doing anything other than what he was doing. She responded, her hands and fingers flying, if anything, faster than Philip's.

How could I, for whom appearance meant so much, have missed something so profoundly obvious as this— deformity? Could this beautiful girl be so flawed? Was it possible to want something that fell so far short of perfect? When would Gerry notice?

I got to my feet, threading my way through the crowd with the ready-made pretext to talk to Gerry, but really to discover that perhaps my fear was wrong, that this beautiful girl wasn't deaf and dumb at all, she just knew sign language, and no need as such because no one that good-looking could possibly have that sort of thing wrong with her.

I sauntered as casually as I could up to Gerry and Ruth.

Before I could say a word Gerry said, 'Obviously the spastics got out.'

I wanted to say that the Wilkinsons weren't spastics, they

were deaf and dumb, and that anyway it wasn't their fault, and they certainly didn't pose a threat to anyone. But I didn't do anything other than turn my head ever so slightly to see if Philip Wilkinson and the girl had overheard the comment.

'They can't hear,' Gerry said, meaning the Wilkinsons.

'Philip can,' I said.

'Since when did that little weed matter?'

I would have liked to say that Philip Wilkinson was a sort of friend, but to do that would have attracted a kind of death sentence by association.

Gerry turned to Ruth. 'You haven't said hello to Ruth.'

I hadn't said hello to Ruth because I found it impossible to talk to Ruth without looking at her breasts. I said hello to Ruth and reflexively my eyes dropped to her breasts, as I was certain they would. No sooner did I raise my eyes than they lowered again, and so on, until I picked a line of sight far enough above her head that even tits that big weren't within my peripheral vision. An obvious pervert, I was not. If I wanted to look at tits we had a stash of *Man* magazines wrapped in plastic hidden down at the salt pans.

Gerry pulled a loose cigarette from his top pocket and lit up, which in the circumstances seemed like a very odd thing to do. I supposed with a real fire already ablaze around us what possible difference could it make?

'Wonder where they'll go now. Maybe the Kew Cottages,' Gerry wondered.

The Kew Cottages was an institution for the mentally handicapped. I went there once on a school excursion and a mongoloid boy reached over the fence and grabbed my arm. It took all the self-control I could muster not to scream. I was acutely aware of the strength of the genuinely insane, knowing that once I was in their clutches, it would take a superhuman effort to save myself.

'Philip could come in with us for a while. We've got room.'

'*Philip*?' he mocked, as if this was a familiarity he was unaware of. 'What? You kidding?'

'No-one's offered…yet.'

'Jesus H. Christ, make sure they don't.'

'It's not contagious.'

'How do you know, hot-shot?' Gerry was looking over my shoulder with this odd, mischievous expression. 'You won't believe who's here.'

I knew who was there. Had Gerry seen the hand-signals?

'Look,' he insisted. 'It's your girlfriend?'

Ruth turned to face the object of Gerry's attention. 'Is that your girlfriend?' She didn't say this with any great confidence.

In ordinary circumstances, more precisely, up until less than two minutes ago, I would have said something quite self-serving to indicate that there was at least a scintilla of truth in the assumption that such a gorgeous-looking girl could be my girlfriend. 'No,' was my reluctant, abject denial.

'You haven't even looked,' barked Gerry. 'It's her.'

When I turned Philip Wilkinson was still with Vivian. She whispered in Philip's ear and he nodded in apparent agreement.

'What's she doing with him?' asked Gerry in a distracted, not altogether inquiring way.

In the next moment Gerry dashed across the road into the front garden of the Wilkinsons'. The movement was so quick and unexpected nobody fighting the fire seemed to notice. Gerry trawled like a looter through charred sodden pulp along the fence line. 'Hey,' he yelled, and from the wreckage, he extracted an old cricket ball in triumph. 'One of ours, I'll bet.' There was a history of 'lost' balls on old man Wilkinson's property.

Philip took Gerry's brief absence as an opportunity to escort Vivian the short distance to where Ruth and I stood alone. His plain, honest face seemed to indicate that he thought he was doing something good. 'Vivian says she knows you.'

For a few dreadful, mind-shattering moments I was incapable of uttering a word. Philip waited calmly and patiently for a response he must have been sure would come in time. Vivian looked at me with a curiosity and a shyness that were not inconsistent with the imminent betrayal of a minor secret, a little confession of a personal kind.

'Yes, the train,' I said.

'We get the train together,' added Vivian in a soft, hollow, breathy voice in which the words seemed to fall away and not quite finish. Perhaps I had been mistaken and she was not some deaf mute. Or was she reading my lips? The voice was, however, not quite normal.

Tossing the warm, misshapen ball from one hand to the other Gerry said, 'Catch,' and threw the ball in my direction. The ball hit the palm of my hand with a slapping sound and fell to the pavement. 'Weak as,' said Gerry. 'And who have we got here?' he inquired with a hint of trouble coming.

Philip blinked a couple of times as if to clear his eyes and make them bigger and better to take in what he saw.

Gerry bent down and picked up the vulcanised ball and showed it to Philip. 'Your crazy old man wouldn't give this back to us. Now look what's happened to it, eh?'

'Sorry,' said Philip.

'Sorry won't make it better,' Gerry said. 'Will it?'

Philip blinked.

A series of small explosions erupted from the back of the burning house, more paint tins.

'I'm sorry about your house,' I said.

'Is this your house?' asked Ruth.

Philip shifted his gaze to the blaze and nodded.

Gerry couldn't help himself. 'What did you do? Forget to turn off a kettle or something?'

'Gerry!' said a startled Ruth.

'Only joking, geez,' said Gerry.

Philip said he had to go and Vivian without a further word left with him. They went and stood with the elder Wilkinsons.

Gerry watched them like a hawk. 'What's she doing hanging out with him?'

Any anger I had at Gerry for ruining the opportunity to meet Vivian properly for the first time, was overwhelmed by the fear that he would see her fingers and hands twirling and waving about.

'Spoke kind of funny. Don't you think?' he said to Ruth.

Ruth shrugged her shoulders. 'Bit hard to hear. She spoke quite softly.'

'Didn't you think?' he said to me.

I looked away. 'She didn't say a lot.'

'Don't crack the shits with me,' he said.

The fire was eventually quelled and the house reduced to a smouldering ruin. The crowd dispersed and I didn't even see Philip and Vivian leave. Gerry told me that he and Ruth were going to the pictures. He put his arms around Ruth's shoulder, and from behind her head gave me a big, exaggerated wink.

'Be seeing ya,' Gerry said, and with that he swaggered up the street.

At that moment I would have loved to knock him

sideways into the path of a departing fire engine. He was my best friend in the world and I hated him at that moment as much as I have ever hated anyone. But finding out that Vivian was a ballet dancer gave me heart. Turning the Ballet Shoe Factory into a Performing Arts Centre was not only the right thing to do. It could also transform my romantic fortunes.

With the excitement of the fire it had taken some time for Malcolm to finally fall asleep that night. I tiptoed across the carpet of our bedroom and gently released the catches of my guitar case. Using a torch for light I shuffled the sheaves of Tick Tock's diary to find where I'd left off and began to read.

Sept 25 1943
…I don't know who had the larger shock, the guard or I. He jumped to his feet and began laying into me. I kept upright and simply took the beating as best I could. It must, then, have dawned upon him, that both he and I were in trouble, as by rights, he had no business sleeping in the kitchen. In broken English, he said, 'No talky.' I could smell his sweat and fear. I repeated the words, 'No talky,' twice, so there would be no chance of a misunderstanding. To make sure, I took a precious bar of chocolate from my pocket and handed it to him. This seemed to reassure him. He ushered me from the kitchen and through the door with a final, 'No talky,' sounding in my ears. That night, back in my hut, on my gnarly bed of bamboo, the fellows played cards and discussed things of no consequence. Not for a moment did I consider telling them of my close call or my pact with the Nip. This is an odd sensation, that one of the enemy and I share a secret.

October 12 1943

The secret weighs heavy with me. How can I trust the enemy? If he should tell Sato my fate will be sealed. My mind twists and turns on this matter. I do not know how an enemy mind works—how a Nip thinks. I recall the fear in his eyes, and console myself with the notion that he is after all a man like me, and, perhaps, he thinks much the same. Matthews may be dying. The Docs aren't sure. Physically he looks no worse. His urge to escape seems to have gone entirely. But we think if the Nips make him go back to work he will make a run for it and that will be the end of him.

October 14 1943

Docs all stood around Matthews' bed today and said he had to go. That he was good enough to work. The Nips said he and others like him were staying in hospital too long. Matthews grabbed my hand. The Docs reluctantly agreed to discharge him tomorrow. But I know that if he is discharged he will die an awful death on a work gang. At least the weeks in hospital have been peaceful for him. Later on the nightshift Matthews finally spoke. Only three words but they were plain enough—Please help me. And so I did.

October 15 1943

They found Matthews, dead in bed, as I knew they would. The trace of a scarey smile split his face.

October 19 1943

The Ballet Shoe Factory seems a world away. I miss sitting in the salon or out in the chook pens, tending to the chooks and thinking about the old days with Shady and all his stories of Mrs Gorham and those boys of hers. How he'd go on about her. How as long as they were honest and law abiding she took them in. Got them work up at the new power station in Newport or the gas works or just pulling weeds out of the gardens of the fancy properties on the Strand. She wouldn't let them go to 'seed'. A miracle-worker he called that woman. Look no further than me, he'd say, with no hint of a smile upon his face.

October 23 1943
We leave for Thailand today. I feel relief. My secret bargain hangs heavier with time, not only because of Sato and the risk that he finds out, but also the need to withold from my fellows, any kind of knowledge. The sensation I have is one of betrayal, an uncleanliness of spirit. How I wish to be of real use, to be in the Middle East, at Tobruk or El Alamein. This I wish for more than anything—other than to see the children and, especially, Pat, to hear the sound of his voice, to touch the warm olive skin of his forearm, to stare into his eyes and see what he sees.

Who knows what Thailand will bring? The tales of the railway make the weaker men quiet and fearful of their prospects. Some men are happy to die where they are. They have given up hope. I cannot think this way even if I wanted to.

The more I read of Tick Tock's diary the more I could imagine Tick Tock in his attap hut on his hard bamboo bed, an image of him far removed from the Tick Tock I knew. The Tick Tock who took fastidious care of his appearance, and was always turned out well, who even Maisy conceded was as neat as a pin. The Tick Tock, who, when he went down the street, got himself up smartly in a brown pork pie hat that he dimpled in the middle with a chop of his hand, and perched high on his bonce with a slight tilt to the left, his fine, silver hair showing beneath the brim. Not a tall man but with strong broad shoulders their span a perfect spirit level. Always in a white shirt that I guessed showed his olive skin to its best, and a creaseless dark green jacket which he hung with care in the small, mahogany wardrobe that faced his bed.

I could hear some movement in the kitchen downstairs, and afraid that I might be interrupted, skipped to the diary's last entries.

November 15 1944

The Nips are very jumpy. There is much rumour that the War is over. I haven't written in the journal for some time, as it takes all my remaining efforts to write A Strapper's Tale. I am no longer an orderly in the privileged spaces of a hospital. Pressed into working on a railway gang, my day begins in the dark and ends in the dark, and allows little time for writing. My greatest fear is the American B52s. The bombardments are regular and heavy and often wayward. There is a great scattering of both Nips and POWs when the far-off sound of planes is heard. Our American saviours will find nothing but bodies of both sides if they keep this up. I have learnt to count to ten in Japanese—ichi ni san shi…— courtesy of a young Japanese guard, curiously also named, Sato. This Sato The Younger has an interest in Australian words. Words like 'bloke' and 'bludger' and 'bastard' bring a smile to his face. He says these words repeatedly, even where it makes no sense. He called Dillon a 'bludger bastard bloke' for being late on parade. There was no malice in what he said or the way he said it. He looked at me for a sense of appreciation of his newly found mastery of the language.

January 15 1945

The spider continues to bring me solace. I have forgotten to mention that I took the spider with me from the camp in Java. He survived the journey in the confined space of an empty packet of Red Bull cigarettes with holes poked through it for air. Maybe he has formed an attachment to me, or at least to the mosquito netting, as he shows no inclination to leave. In the near delirium of tiredness after a day on the railway, I speak to the spider quite openly. I do not care that the fellows may think I am mad. If I look like my fellows—and not having seen a mirror for some weeks, the state of my looks is not something that I can judge—then we all look mad so sounding mad is not quite so strange. The malaria comes and goes. I am steeled for the aching shivers and hallucinations it brings.

January 21 1945

More talk of the War coming to an end. The Nips are looking disconsolate. Without the benefit of the Doc's wireless the War's outcome remains a mystery. It will come too late for many of the men who are still alive. I speak not for the dead. The men are dying in vast numbers—it is beyond counting. Those alive have the look of, if not the reality of, death. I am curiously without feeling anymore. I am beyond fear. Fear requires a certain energy which none of us has. The Nips seem to know this. A fellow beaten to the ground will now just lie there and silently hope the beating will bring him death, and the end of it all. That the War might be close to over bears only the remotest of happy thoughts. The fellows think the Nips will massacre us if their cause is lost. This, too, strikes no fear in the men. It is one of many possible bad outcomes. We are pretty much prepared for them all.

April 12 1945

The War is apparently over. The Nips want us to stay inside the camp but we are free to move around at will within the camp. Shady the Spider died today—maybe the news was too much for him. I'd been talking to Shady the Spider for some time about the progress of A Strapper's Tale (that I have nearly completed in my other journal), when I noticed he had not gone after a bug, caught in the netting near to him. I buried him with full honours in the cemetery. I asked Dillon and Samuels if they'd like to pay their respects. They were polite but said, 'No.'

NINETEEN
BRENDA'S PARTY GOES THE WAY OF A KNIFE

A little disc of Moon shimmered in the night sky, above a big, square, modern house at the far end of the residential court that on rough calculations corresponded to the address for the party, I had in my head. A cordon of V-8 Fords and Holdens traced a crescent in the street's gutters. The percussive thrum of rock music beat a low, pulsing, unerring bass line into the heart of the party. Gerry and I tracked the music as surely as a pilot would follow the directional fairy lights of an airport runway.

Out the front of the house, a couple of guys with hair to their shoulders and one with a beard he'd tugged to a point, fiddled with loose tobacco as part of what appeared to be the quite complex task of assembling several sheaths of cigarette papers. A Harley Davidson and a Norton rested on their stands in the driveway. As we passed, a volley of disconcerting laughter erupted.

My face still felt warm from the heat of the infrared sun lamp. With the lemon juice not really working on the freckles, I'd decided that if my face had an all-over tan this would fix the problem. I'd lock myself in the bathroom for a session. I had to be careful about the time of day because the light would shine through the crack under the door. The first time I did it I forgot the goggles. The light was so intense you really had to wear goggles. Otherwise it was like kneeling in front of the headlights of a car. I had been virtually blinded for hours. Maybe I had stood too close to the lamp. When I took the goggles off there were two large rings of white skin around my eyes—quite a spooky look. The first time I did it Mother asked what I'd done to myself. But I hadn't seen what she saw because skin takes a while to go pink. So in the bathroom mirror nothing had changed. Since then I've taken the risk of blinding myself and done it without the goggles.

Music ricocheted between the house and the side fence; Jimi Hendrix's guitar solo in 'All Along The Watchtower' tinkled psychedelically and the first toxic effects of a shared, skulled bottle of spumante fizzed ominously in my throat. Partygoers, illuminated by strobing disco lights, spilled from the garage up ahead in staccato silhouettes. The garage could have been an exploding box of fireworks.

Brenda burst from a swarming mass of bodies. She'd done something odd to her hair. A wild woolly bouffant of hair had been teased from a natural head of tight, spare, frizzy curls. Like a halo but this one was showing signs of deflating—an ominous, sagging telltale look of I Give Up. Brenda seemed blissfully unaware of any impending collapse. Her dress was phenomenally short. Thick, dark seams of eyeliner had begun to smear, so that she resembled a clown trying to smile. Apart from that she looked demure, sweet and happy.

Brenda took me by the hand and shouted, 'You can't stay here.' She led the way, cutting through the crowd, one hand in front of her like a cleaver. We took up a standing position at a trestle table full of grog, beyond the speakers and the stereo, and where a conversation was just possible.

'What have you done to your face?' she asked.

I'd checked in the mirror before I left for any 'goggle effect'. 'What's wrong with it?' Maybe it was the strobing lights mixing photo-chemically with the infrared beams that was doing it.

'You look…tanned.'

I patted my cheeks. I was quite impressed. This had been the general intention. But clearly I'd been too successful. 'Really?'

'Have you been playing cricket?'

I wish I'd thought of that: exposure to the real thing. 'Yeah, been in the field all day.'

'You must be thirsty as well, then. Grab a drink.'

Gerry grabbed a bottle of Southern Comfort, a container of orange juice and a couple of glasses. Brenda in that forward, slutty, meat market way of hers, gave Gerry an up-and-down appraisal. Gerry was more partial than most to a very short skirt, and if Brenda had a feature worthy of a second look, it would have been her legs.

'Who's your friend?' she asked.

'This is Gerry,' I said.

Gerry gave her a winning smile. He'd told Ruth it was a Sports Night, that she'd be bored out of her mind. For Gerry, two nights in a row with the same girl was a record he would not be setting soon.

'Gerald, eh?' she asked.

'Gerry,' he said.

'Where are you from Ger'?'

'Live down Maidstone Street,' he said.

'Not too far away,' she said meaningfully.

I panned the crowd for people I knew.

Someone resembling Kenny stood as one of a group in the far corner of the garage with his back to us.

'Is that Kenny?' I asked.

Brenda clapped her hand to her mouth. 'I couldn't believe it when he arrived. I really couldn't.' She tugged the hem of her skirt marginally lower.

As the strobe lights pulsed the figures within the crowd sharpened and dimmed. Kenny stood in profile, his head stiff and wooden, and in a very upright posture so that he looked very wide and tall. 'Is that a neck-brace he's wearing?' I asked.

Brenda gasped, as if somebody noticing had been a surprise. 'I know. It's awful isn't it?'

We all gazed at Kenny as the disco lights made him a shadow puppet on the back wall of the garage. A large saw hung on the wall such that when Kenny moved his head in the constraint of the neck-brace, it looked as if he was trying to decapitate himself. 'Oh my God he's coming over here,' she said.

'This is the guy who almost killed himself doing chin-ups,' I said nonchalantly to Gerry.

'What was that?' asked Gerry straining to hear.

Brenda slapped me on the hand in rebuke. 'You can't say that. It's just awful.'

I resisted the temptation to say that he could be the first man ever to be pushed over the edge on the strength of a couple of pubic hairs. Brenda's eyes filled with pain for Kenny, to have that magnificent head in a brace seemed almost a crime.

Kenny approached in slow, measured, mechanical steps. 'Hi,' he said.

Brenda was on the brink of tears, as if she had just witnessed an act of some courage. 'You wouldn't have met

Gerry,' said Brenda as she introduced Gerry to Kenny.

'Jesus, what happened to you, mate,' said Gerry. 'Fall off a horse or something.'

Brenda's fake eye lashes fluttered out of control. 'Kenny had a acc—', she began to say.

Kenny didn't take a backward step. 'Almost hung myself.'

'You what?' asked Gerry.

'Doing chin-ups.'

Gerry looked at me for some confirmation of the truth.

Kenny rubbed at his neck. 'Didn't do too good a job of it either.'

Brenda's face was like a chocolate sponge succumbing to tough humid conditions. Her mascara was thick and circled her eyes. Under the camouflage of the music, she sniffed back a running nose. She took a step forward and hugged Kenny, cradling her head on his barrel-chest, where there was just enough clearance to fit under his jaw that jutted out quite markedly by virtue of the brace. His arms hung limp, too embarrassed to respond. His overall posture was not too dissimilar to how he had hung from the handrail before Jerome and Ray had dived underneath him. He stared out across the crowd with an unstudied look.

Brenda suddenly let go of Kenny, took a step back and exclaimed, 'You pull yourself together Kenny Roberts… or…or… I don't know what I'll do,' and it was anyone's guess whether she would laugh or cry.

Kenny gave a cautious smile.

'Do you feel OK, Kenny?' I asked.

'The neck's real sore but that's about it.'

Kenny had been transformed. He was somehow indefinably different—a discrete member of an elite. He spoke in that same slow laconic drawl I would have traditionally ascribed to a mild intellectual dysfunction, except, what came out of his mouth now, wasn't so much slow and dull, as considered. Putting my profound distrust of the miraculous aside, I would have said Kenny appeared to have had a Lourdes or Fatima-type experience. This impression was reinforced by the brace on his neck that the more I looked at it, the more like a clerical collar it appeared. Everything Kenny said seemed to be invested with wisdom and a conviction and a ring of infallibility that no amount of reading or ordinary experience could have given him. I was convinced he'd seen a sign, been touched in a way.

'Don't you ever do that again, Kenny,' scolded Brenda, wagging her finger at him. 'Now let's go and find someone nice for you to meet.'

Kenny smiled in a kind and understanding way, and said there was no need.

Brenda thrust her finger at him almost angrily. 'Now Kenny Roberts, I'll be having none of that. It's just like a bike—you can damn well just get back on it.'

Kenny's face took on a vague but hopeless sense of appreciation for her good intentions. He reached out and took hold of one of her hands. He looked upon her hand as he might in a tarot reading and said, 'You may as well know. I'm becoming a priest. I'll go to a special school next year and after that a seminary.'

'Did you say you're becoming a priest, Kenny?' I asked.

Brenda almost swooned. The responsibility weighed heavy that an incident with a couple of pubic hairs could lead to this. 'Kenny Roberts, I'll wash your fucking mouth out with soap if you ever say anything so stupid ever again. Hear me!' Petrified by the distinct prospect of being lumbered with the ability to turn red-blooded boys into priests, Brenda muscled Kenny across the dance floor towards a circle of girls. 'Here he is, 'she screamed. The circle expanded and contracted, with Kenny and Brenda interlocked amongst them, and the centre of attention. Kenny's face shone, bemused perhaps at the no small irony that a near-death experience had proved to be the most potent erotic force he had ever hit upon.

John Carson and Killer Speck sidled into view at the entrance to the garage. I put Gerry in the viewing-line between them and me. John Carson made his way into the crowd like he knew where I'd be. This was a quality of John Carson that was unfailingly annoying. This ability to not miss anything that all too often was precisely the thing I'd hope he'd never notice.

John Carson's eyes twinkled at his quick success in locating me. 'Not trying to hide from us, are you, Froggie? Deep behind enemy lines.'

John Carson stared at Gerry as if he was Huckleberry Finn in the front row at the opera. 'Is the horse tied up out the front?' he asked. Fortunately, Gerry didn't hear what he said. His trademark pout flexed an aperture wide enough to insert a five-cent coin. It translated an unbearable—if often amusing—almost perfect superciliousness and misplaced superiority. Gerry, justifiably, seemed to take an instant dislike to him. When I introduced them they just nodded at each other. It was no better with Killer.

'Can't see any with two heads. Can you, Killer?' John Carson did a complete turn to identify any decent-looking girls that might have escaped his notice.

I gave John Carson a look of great vacuousness. 'I mean they're not my sisters.' John Carson thought of Beau Vista as a vast place of inbreeding, where I was accountable for everyone in the suburb like we were all part of the same family.

'How would you know, Froggie? I think there's some

resemblance, there and there, for instance.' He actually pointed to a couple of the less attractive girls. 'Killer?'

Killer despite a valiant attempt struggled to see any relevant visual connection. John Carson mentally shrugged it off. 'Killer's not himself today. Are you, Killer?'

Killer was working at a crick in his neck, rotating his head 180 degrees, exorcising some kind of pain that had his face all screwed up.

'The bolts coming loose?' Gerry asked.

John Carson resented anybody else trying to be a comedian. A sneer stretched on one side of his face as if partial paralysis was setting in. He stared at Gerry with empty, green eyes that saw no place on the planet for a boy with a rough haircut and a plaid shirt. Gerry offended him in a very fundamental way. John Carson was a snob, a paid-up member of the middle class, and there was no way Gerry Nelson would ever infiltrate that particular club. He was not only a snob there was something else basically wrong with John Carson. Youth had somehow passed him by. He was already in a state of advanced middle age. It's why the ladies at the tuck shop liked him so much: he was one of them. Even his hair in a soft outdoor light appeared flecked with grey. John Carson was more at home talking fascists than footy and hysterectomies than cartilage operations. A kind of aged bitterness, almost nastiness was never far away, as though he sensed he would never really shine, never really make it. It was as if his youth had been snatched from under him. Just to look at him in his middle-aged slacks and his cheap, striped polyester business shirt, and I could tell he wasn't quite right.

'Killer finished *Portnoy's* today,' John Carson declared. 'Hence the long face.' He described a long face in a rectangle of air. Gerry's eyes followed John Carson's finger.

'*Portnoy's*?' asked Gerry.

'It's a long story,' I said.

Killer did appear genuinely bereaved, he had the appearance of having lost something.

'I think it's time for a bit of Henry Miller. Maybe *Sexus*, and *The Tropic of Capricorn* after that,' said Killer.

'It will put *Portnoy's* in the shade,' said John Carson.

Killer said that reading Miller would be the equivalent of reaching the summit of a literary-Mount Everest, and he wasn't sure if he was up to it, not ready for the final assault—a lone mountaineer setting out from a Himalayan base camp in a sub-forty degrees Celsius blizzard, with only a parka, gym boots and a sleeping bag to protect him. 'I'm not sure I can do it,' he admitted, reluctantly.

'If you can't do it nobody can,' said John Carson.

Killer's eyes indicated agreement with John Carson. 'If I can't do it no one can,' he said it trance-like.

Brenda squeezed back through the crowd, appearing at John Carson's shoulder. He angled away as if he knew there was someone there he didn't want to meet. The John Carson pout was expressive of anticipated revulsion. Brenda had liberally reapplied lipstick and mascara, and contrived a facial masque that made her ashen and vampire-like. 'Are you keeping a secret from Aunty Brenda?' The words came out of a frightening red gash in her mouth. The whitened face peered directly into my blue, bloody eyes. 'Don't hold out on me, Michel!'

John Carson's face twitched.

I took a mouthful of the Southern Comfort and orange juice.

'Come on don't be bashful,' she urged. 'Is it true?'

'Yes come on, *Michel*,' parroted John Carson, 'tell us if it's true.' The pout was now a smirk. He thought a useful discovery about my secretive self was about to be revealed. He would be hoping that it was embarrassing or degrading or humiliating, fodder for the sausage factory of character assassination for which he was the past master.

Brenda seemed to notice John Carson and Killer for the first time. Addressing John Carson directly, and the party being for her after all, she asked, 'Do I know you?'

John Carson's smirk was fully fledged. 'Friends of Charl... Michel's,' he replied brightly as if the saying of it was enough to suggest it was true, 'from St Sebastian's.'

'Oh,' she said with a little hesitation, 'well you may already know.'

'Know what?' asked Killer.

John Carson raised his eyes at Killer in a deadpan attempt to shut him up.

Brenda's eyes darted from John Carson to Killer and back to me. 'Ballet Shoe Factory ring some sort of bell?' she inquired mischievously.

Gerry groaned.

'What's wrong?' asked Brenda.

'Nothing,' said Gerry, and he turned away from the conversation.

Brenda said, 'What's wrong with your friend?'

I shrugged.

'Ballet Shoe Factory, eh?' murmured John Carson thoughtfully. 'Are we talking the full codpiece here, Charles?' He rose balletically on his toes in a passable imitation of being '*en pointe*,' and completed a quite dainty twirl with his arms ballerina-like above his head as he forgot to call me by my real name.

Brenda stared at John Carson. 'He's not doing Ballet, Cooky. Sorry, I don't know who on Earth you are, but we think he's inherited the Ballet Shoe Factory down near the

beach at Williamstown that's worth a fortune.' She pronounced fortune with a long drawn out emphasis on the 'u'.

John Carson couldn't hide his disappointment. His
cheeks sagged and his eyes glazed and he couldn't think of a
riposte worth saying. The news didn't fit any notion of his
superiority.

'Is it?' insisted Brenda. 'Is it true?'

'Well,' I stammered, 'it's not totally true. I'm sort of
second-in-line.'

Brenda clapped her hands together. 'That's good enough
for me.' She'd little interest in the facts. It was simply
something else to celebrate. 'Richie Rich, eh?' Brenda
shot off to a ring of girls to give them confirmation of the
rumour. Her spectacular happiness for me contrasted with
the solemnity of John Carson as he digested this 'second-
in-line' dubiousness. I could tell he wanted to interrogate
me. He did not want to carry the burden any longer than he
must, that I might not be inferior to him in every respect.

'Can't stay,' said John Carson.

John Carson had wanted to know what a Beau Vista
party was like, and now he'd seen it in all its garage-glory,
he could return to Essendon armed with a few additional
demographics to assail me and my kind when I re-entered
his kingdom. The only thing he hadn't counted on was this
Ballet Shoe Factory piece of news, and he would get to the
bottom of that soon enough.

'You're going already? You just got here.'

'Froggie, this may be your idea of a good time but it's
not mine. Killer?'

Killer looked at John Carson with those black dead eyes
of his. 'Yeah the Datsun might get vandalised or something.'

John Carson beamed. 'Spot on, Killer. Or something.
Saw those bikies out the front. Hell, Charles what sort of

company are you keeping?' He turned to go. 'And tell your very nice mother, thank you for inviting us.' John Carson, sporting a wicked smile, led a murmuring Killer, who for all I knew was contemplating carnal activity with my mother, out through the crowd.

'Thank Christ for that,' said Gerry. 'What a dickhead.'

In the midst of the crowd Brenda was manoeuvring Kenny into the centre of a new group of girls.

'Is Brenda going out with anyone?' Gerry inquired.

'I thought you said she wasn't very attractive?'

Gerry's eyes roved the garage.

'Some of the average-looking ones are the best at it,' he said.

'I thought you thought she was fat?'

'I wouldn't say she's fat.'

'What would you say?'

'Her legs aren't bad.'

'Legs that important?'

'Of course legs are important. They've *got* to have legs.'

The Who *Live At Leeds* was playing, and we listened for Pete Townshend saying the word, 'Fuck,' the saying of which had become more important than listening to the song. Brenda returned wearing a schoolgirl's smile and a bottle of what passed for champagne. She touched Gerry's fingers when she handed him the bottle for a slug.

'I think our Kenny is going to be a very happy boy tonight,' she said, and winked at us.

Shafts of light in neat coloured squares lit a small patch of concrete floor that would do for a dance floor. Kenny, awkward and stiff-legged, straddled two of these coloured squares as if they were different countries and a step in the wrong direction might have long-term diplomatic conse-quences. He could have been cradling some priceless object from the Ming Dynasty, for all the care he took, in the hold he had upon the girl. The girl was petite and attractive, and given the not insignificant height differential between them, had adopted a lean that she balanced with a hand placed squarely in the small of Kenny's back. Kenny, who was bolt rigid from the neck up, sort of looked over the top of the girl's head. As he no doubt counted his 1-2-3's, 1-2-3's, modern dance movements currently beyond him, he revolved briefly in our direction, our eyes catching without him imparting any sense that he might be enjoying himself.

Brenda produced a smile of satisfaction that communicated Kenny might be on the path back. She turned to Gerry. 'Where do you go to school, Ger'?'

'Beau Vista Tech.'

'Tech?'

'Yeah. The sheltered workshop.'

Brenda didn't know if he was serious or not.

Gerry's eyes continued to scan the crowd like a scout for talent. 'There she is, again.' he said.

Both Brenda and I turned.

For my benefit he said, 'She following you?'

Brenda was a little taken back. 'Oh, that's the new girl. Sharon invited her. I forget her name…starts with a V.' She was trying to remember a name she'd already told me. 'What was it? Veronica? Valerie? Vanessa? Maybe it just had a 'v' sound in it like Yvonne, or Beverly.'

My heart raced. We stared at Vivian.

'Vivian,' said Gerry to put Brenda out of her misery.

Brenda looked suspiciously at Gerry. 'That's right. Do you know her?'

If Gerry said I was infatuated with her I would deny it with vehemence, ask where the toilets were, and with relieving myself as the pretext, walk straight up the drive way and go home.

Brenda, momentarily disconcerted by Gerry's unrestrained and unrelenting appraisal of Vivian, didn't give him a chance to answer. 'Do you think she's a spunk, Ger'?'

Gerry without taking his eyes off Vivian replied, 'Vivian? I'd say so.'

Brenda spun around. 'Apparently she's got a lisp.'

A tremor of unease, not quite a shiver, rippled over the surface of my skin. Deaf and dumb? Lisp? What was it? 'A speech impediment?' I asked as casually as I could.

'That's what a lisp is,' said Brenda, 'an impediment. It's not a help to anything—except maybe if you whistle.'

Vivian hovered in deformity between a lisp and outright deaf and dumbness. Visually she was perfect. I could never be too careful.

Brenda was tenacious and she would put an end to Gerry's drooling. 'You come with me, handsome. Let's put this record on.' She held up the cream jacket sleeve to the Stone's *Beggar's Banquet* and led him away.

The panic of aloneness and isolation gripped me in an icy instant.

Alone. Almost. And Vivian so near.

Where were all the other kids from the train? Who else was here that I knew? Jesus, Vivian would be looking at me like I was some big-time loser. A Michel-no-mates character. I had to get out of there.

Fortunately, I'd saved a couple of cigarettes from a small packet of Viscount. If I was smoking that was like putting up a busy or engaged sign. Observably, I would be occupied and not desperate for a friend to talk to. If I went outside it would be even better. Sometimes informal little huddles of smokers would gather and I'd be part of one of those.

Outside the garage the music played with the volume

only marginally contained by the aluminium sheeting of the garage. A spotlight recessed into the eaves of the house's roof shone like the midday sun. I shielded my eyes while fumbling in my top shirt pocket for a cigarette. The boundary fence was lit up and appeared quite new and yellow with pine. I went down the dark gap between the fence and the garage, stumbling over a pile of kindling wood. The cigarette glowed when I sucked and did the full drawback. Viscounts were cheap and nasty and after a couple of drags a wave of dizziness swept over me. I sat down on a makeshift seat of the kindling and held the cigarette at arm's length so the smoke would not go up my nose and make me feel worse. If I was to be sick this was the place for it. The spumante and the Southern Comfort and now the Viscount were an unknown combination.

The news of the lisp, if it was right, was almost a move in the right direction, on a scale of what was handicapped. I mean it wasn't as if she had plastic limbs. There might be something quite attractive and disarming, and dare I say it cute, in a sibilantly rich vocabulary, that made her forever sound like she was six years old. A lisp was not sufficient reason to give up. There had to be more wrong with her than that to abandon the quest.

Vivian had been standing in a cluster of girls, not a guy amongst them. Penetrating this type of arrangement would not be easy. I would need a special line to safely navigate my way to its core. It would have to be a line that had a general appeal, as every girl in the group would hear what I said. So that meant anything about ballet was out. I blew an inexpert smoke ring, a little cloud of smoke puffed along on the breeze. I couldn't speak a cliché when I knew it was a cliché. A cliché wouldn't work coming out of my mouth, in the same way it would coming out of Gerry's. So, 'What are you all up to tonight, girls?' would be suicidal. Likewise, 'Aren't we all looking radiant?' Actually, I could guess, more or less, what Gerry would say and it might not be quite clichéd. Something like, 'A bunch of good-looking girls and not a bloke in sight. What's going on?' That might work. They might even laugh. I repeated the line in my head a couple of times. Having smoked the Viscount down to the butt, I dropped it on the pebbled lawn and ground it underneath my shoe. The line might work, but it wouldn't work for me. It was too big a risk. I might be socially immolated if the line died en masse. Although, if I could isolate Vivian, then I would only have one look of derision, and one more stored humiliating memory to deal with. I could set them alongside Linda X in the mausoleum of humiliation.

As I stood to go back inside, no earthly idea what I'd do next, other than this inescapable fear, that I might throw caution to the winds and say something I would not have rehearsed and would regret forever, Vivian appeared around the side of the garage with one of the leather-jacketed bikies. I sat back down on the kindling in the dark and watched and listened.

Vivian appeared to hesitate when she understood where the guy wanted to go. He held out his hand and drew her behind him, stepping from the bright light of the backyard and the concreted driveway, into the gap between the garage and the fence. This was the time to make my presence known. I had to get up and walk out before anything happened. But I did not. I sat low and silent in that dark passage.

'Not here, John,' Vivian said.

The sound of her voice was odd and light and far away.

I strained to hear the lisp.

They kissed.

I hunched on the kindling, as low as I could go.

The kiss was long and soundless. I think all three of us had stopped breathing.

The moon shone full and yellow and timeless, and for a fleeting second I looked up, and wondered if that little humble Stars and Stripes that Neil Armstrong had planted up there was still standing, or, had it been obliterated by a meteorite travelling at 100,000 miles per hour, its fragmentary remains, only ever to be found, far off in the future under a newly-formed crater which if I was in charge of naming craters, I would have named, John.

'No,' Vivian said.

John took a half-step back.

Vivian straightened her top.

'Don't tell me you don't want it,' he said.

'Not here,' she said.

Vivian stepped away from the fence her shoes crackling on the white pebbles. She stood in the bright light of the driveway facing the gap in which I hid.

I sank lower on the bundle of kindling, and hoped desperately that I was no cat with luminous spooky eyes, peering like a little pair of stricken stationary headlights, in a place it had no right to be.

'Come on,' she said.

But John did not come.

'Suit yourself,' she said, and disappeared around the corner of the garage.

John exhaled and slumped against the fence, one hand pressed flat against the sappy wood.

'Bitch,' he hissed.

Then I heard the sound of a zip being ripped down and the twinkle of piss as John liberally doused the fence and the pebbles at his feet.

*****

I stayed down the side of the garage for a full half hour gathering myself. When I emerged the Stones were still on, and out the front of the garage a few kids were jigging about in a way that couldn't quite be described as dancing. The temptation was to go straight home, but where was Gerry? I decided to have a quick look inside the garage. No Gerry. No Brenda. The strobe lights had been switched off. It was dark and smoky. A figure at the back of the garage caught my attention: Vivian was sorting through the records and she was by herself.

I couldn't believe she was here after what I'd seen around the side of the garage. No planning was required. We were alone. It was dark. There was so little to lose. An opening line I knew would be good was forming on my lips as I walked towards her. My mouth began to open as she replaced a record in the pile. She turned, perhaps sensing my presence. Before she could say a word, even a syllable, a sound of any kind, a scream of '*Michel*,' soared above the music.

The horror in Brenda's eyes was made so much worse by the melting pancake of powder and paint, by degrees, sliding down her face. Brenda raced through the crowd—no obvious assistance forthcoming—shouldering people aside, and grabbed me by the arm. 'Come with me,' she commanded.

Brenda dragged me through the thinning crowd. Kids hastened down the driveway not quite at a run. She said, 'It's Gerry.' I briefly wondered what social outrage he might have committed.

Partially hidden behind a screen of spectators, lying on the nature strip, was someone in a pair of jeans and gym boots. The voice of Gerry could be heard quite clearly. 'Take the bloody knife out, will some one? Jesus!' Brenda led me to the end of the line of onlookers and said, 'There,' as if her manic behaviour finally had an explanation, and the sight of Gerry lying prostrate on the ground with a large silver-handled knife hanging out of his shoulder blade was all the explanation required.

'Don't just stand there,' said Gerry.

Cautiously, I moved towards Gerry. The prospect of removing the knife made me hesitate as I dropped to my knees.

I knew I should have done the St John Ambulance course. Mother had been on at me for years to do it. She said I'd regret it. If I'd done it I wouldn't be hesitating. I'd rip that big old knife out of Gerry without even this much thinking.

Brenda asked if I knew what I was doing. I said I knew a bit of first aid. This was not a complete lie. I was familiar with the first aid kit in the bathroom at home and the snake bite tourniquet, I used to gag Malcolm with, when he was playing his regular role as a kidnap victim. I told her I knew something about snake bite. Brenda's mouth opened wide. Gerry looked up at me and said, 'Forget the snake bite shit and just take the bloody knife out.' I reached for the knife and Brenda began to weep copiously. Gerry told her to go somewhere else. I told Gerry not to be mean. Gerry told me to get on with it and stop mucking around, as he was in a fair bit of pain. That's the last I remembered, as I fainted shortly thereafter. How was I to know that I had a thing called hemophobia.

TWENTY
CABARET

K enny had materialised through the crowd of bystanders at Brenda's party as a Clint Eastwood-type figure. There was such purpose of stride and steadfast expression upon his face that it was obvious that he would do something. Armed not only with his newly found wisdom and grace, he came with the knowledge of a senior volunteer in the St John Ambulance, and a lifetime as a decorated cub scout.

Kenny had taken one long look at Gerry and the knife in his shoulder, and torn the shirt from his own back and rolled it into a thick absorbent pad. Onlookers anticipating action had squeezed up behind the broad, bared back of Kenny. Gerry's eyes opened inordinately wide, not so much with pain, but with what Kenny might do next, with the thick piece of cloth that he was flexing with a repeated, violent snapping action. Uttering the prophetic words that were the master of understatement, 'This may hurt,' Kenny had no sooner withdrawn the knife in a single, lightning motion than he had staunched the flow of blood with his shirt as a dressing. Someone from the crowd asked more than rhetorically, 'Do you think he'll make it?' Kenny turned to the questioner and answered with all the seriousness of a surgeon on a medical soap opera, 'I think we can now safely say he's out of danger.' There was a little 'ooh' from the crowd.

The Melbourne *Herald* did Kenny justice. There he was on page 5 with a smiling mum and dad, bare-chested, pretending to tear in half a replica of the shirt that he had used to save Gerry.

Mother shoved the paper under Len's nose. 'That's where your son was last night.'

Len didn't need a newspaper to tell him that. The police had delivered me home early that morning with the advice that I appeared to have taken a turn for the worse, although, there didn't appear to be anything permanently wrong with me.

'I told you that Gerry-boy was trouble,' Mother declared.

Len picked up the paper and read a few lines. 'Says here the boy was attacked.'

'Len,' Mother said, 'trouble just follows that boy around like a sick mangy dog.'

'And Kenny Roberts, who would have thought it, a hero,' said Len undeterred.

Kenny wouldn't have photographed so damned well swinging from the handrail of the train carriage.

'Anyway,' said Mother swivelling in my direction, 'where were you when all this was going on, eh, Mister?'

I told them I'd been diagnosed as homophobic.

'What?' said Len as he raised his eyes from the paper in alarm.

'Hemophobic,' said Mother.

'Yes, hemophobic,' I rejoined. 'Faint at the sight of blood.'

Len considered this for a few seconds. 'Wouldn't do in a soldier, would it?'

Mother's preoccupation with the War didn't match Len's. 'Sorry?'

'Well they can hardly conscript the boy if they know he's going to faint at the first sight of blood, can they?' If Len added this frailty to a practical track record that had never looked promising since I'd rejected any interest in mowing the lawn, he now had all the evidence he needed to know, that me in the army would benefit only the Viet Cong. In a more real sense, he might have been thinking this revelation constituted a valid exemption from conscription. He didn't say. His eyes returned to the print of the newspaper, scouring it for more political outrage.

My mother handed me a letter that she had tucked in her apron. She must have only given it a cursory examination, figuring it was just another unsolicited swimming pool quote. 'Don't bother your father,' she said, quietly and out of earshot.

The letter was addressed to Michel White. I turned it over. The sender was Howard Starr. Up in my room I opened it.

It read,

Dear Robert

Thank you so much for sharing with me your good fortune and vision for the Ballet Shoe Factory.
I have had a few days further to consider the very special opportunity presented to us, and I would like to offer some additional thoughts, I have had in relation to the project.
To that end I would be pleased if you would accept an invitation for tea this Saturday afternoon.

The address is 164 Park Drive Parkville. Any time
around 3pm would be fine.
I look forward to seeing you there.
All the best,

Howard Starr

Gerry, as it happened, was also staying in Parkville, at the
Royal Melbourne Hospital, in the initial phase of recovery,
from the knife wound and multiple facial lacerations.
Mother, not without misgivings, had given her approval
'to pay that Gerry-boy a visit, but don't get it into your
head, Mister, that this means that it's all right to see him
whenever you feel like it.' This blessing had the distinct
benefit of saving me the time and creative effort to fake
another reason to be in Parkville for the invitation to tea
with Howard Starr.

Gerry was in the bed nearest the door, in a small ward
otherwise unoccupied, pretty much bandaged from the
chest up to where a type of bandana encircled his head.
Tubes flowed from his arm and down his throat as if he was
an integral part of a hydroponic watering system. Honestly,
it was a little difficult confronting his pain and near-death
experience in such close-up given the circumstances of our
last meeting. How did I know I would faint? It was bad
enough I had this incurable case of freckles and then they
told me about the hemophobia.

Mrs Nelson sat as near to Gerry as she could possibly
get, fighting back tears. Mr Nelson stood slumped in a far
corner of the ward too terrified to come any nearer to Gerry
and the reality of his injuries. When I came in the door,
Mrs Nelson said, 'Here's Michel,' as if my entrance had
been widely anticipated. Gerry looked at Mrs Nelson in

that despairing attitude of, 'Don't you ever tire of saying the absolutely bloody obvious'. Mr Nelson offered no acknowledgement that an additional human presence had entered the vicinity. He stared out the window in a private world of pain and disillusionment that his son had gotten himself into this perilous state of health, and dragged his family through the news pages of the Melbourne *Herald* into the bargain. Mrs Nelson suggested that I sit where she had been sitting. 'All the easier,' she said, 'to talk to Gerry.' After I initially refused her offer, she forcibly sat me down, the proximity to Gerry's injuries raising the spectre of another hemophobic attack.

The knife had punctured a lung preventing any actual conversation. I asked Gerry how he was, and he motioned for a miniature blackboard, that lay on the mobile tray that fitted over his bed, to be handed to him. He wrote: 'You FAINTED!' I whispered I was out for only a matter of seconds. Gerry wrote furiously, 'IF IT WASN'T FOR KENNY ID BE DEAD!' This was certainly salt for my wounded feelings.

I was summoning the courage to show Gerry the letter I had from Howard. Gerry looked pale and angry. My coming to see him might not have been the smartest thing to do. He might not appreciate my asking him for advice about the Ballet Shoe Factory. The homosexual-Howard Starr connection might send him right over the top. The last thing I wanted was Gerry rearing out of the bed with tubes and drip-fluids flying about, as he exhausted what little strength he had left to strangle me.

Gerry looked drowsy. His eyes were opening and closing. Before he dozed off I wanted him to know where I was going, just in case, there was a need for a search party. If it all went wrong, and I had blundered into a homosexual snake pit, there was something vaguely comforting in Gerry knowing where I was. I held Howard's letter open and flat against my chest for him to read, careful that no part of it could be seen by either Mr or Mrs Nelson. Gerry's eyes moved repeatedly across the page and back like the carriage of an old typewriter. He eventually looked up and then wrote: 'IT UPSETS ME THAT IN MY TIME OF NEED THE BEST YOU CAN DO IS FAINT. NOW WHILE EVERY BREATH I TAKE IS AN AGONISING REMINDER OF THE KNIFE YOU COULDN'T STAY CONSCIOUS LONG ENOUGH TO TAKE OUT YOU WANT ME TO CONSORT IN SOME PLAN WITH SOME POOFTER WHEN YOU KNOW THEY ARE THE PEOPLE I MOST DISLIKE ON THE PLANET EARTH.' Gerry executed the full stop with sufficient power to break the stick of chalk in half. I have corrected most of the spelling errors caused by the speed and vehemence with which he wrote. Mrs Nelson asked whatever was it that Gerry could be writing; Gerry was not a known writer of anything and particularly words of many syllables. Gerry had the good sense, and with no inconsiderable pain, erased the message with the sleeve of his cotton smock before Mrs Nelson could reach his side.

164 Park Drive was a three level terrace house a few short minutes walk from Gerry's hospital room. As I pushed open the front gate I looked up at the hospital, and in a moment of real paranoia, I imagined I saw Gerry's dad looking down at me from the tenth level of the hospital, and knowing exactly what I was up to. Before I had a chance to knock on the door, a voice called out from the basement, 'Down here.'

Howard stood dead centre of a hallway that was dark, musty and quiet. He told me to go to the end of the hallway and through an open door into what I could see was a type of bedsit arrangement: a couch, a dressing table, a couple of old chairs with rugs thrown over the back and a single roughly made bed, its turned down sheets depressingly grey, and its single pillow still rumpled with a deep, dimpled impression of a head in the middle of it.

I sat on one of the chairs and Howard went to the dressing table and turned the kettle on.

'Would you like tea?' he asked.

I nodded nervous agreement.

'Darjeeling, Earl Gray, Orange Pekoe…regular.'

I took a few moments to respond. 'Regular?'

'Regular,' Howard intoned in a low hollow voice, spooning tea into an elaborate porcelain pot.

I had just finished reading a biography on Oscar Wilde. I'd skipped past most of the literary accomplishments and dived into Wilde's arrest at the Sloane Hotel, and the gritty forensic examination of the circumstances in which he'd been exposed. 'Faecal' and 'inter-crural' and 'onanistic' had me running for the dictionary. Howard's room was precisely how I imagined Wilde's at the Sloane Hotel, right down to the dirty, unwashed sheets.

A standard lamp in a corner of the room threw a limited ring of dim, spooky light. Howard's room had only one small window that was covered in a lattice of metal bars. Other than the door there was no other way out.

'Sugar?'

I shook my head.

'Milk?'

I nodded.

Howard spooned a couple of heaps of 'regular' tea into the teapot and sat down with his legs crossed, waiting for the tea to draw.

One of my few recognised accomplishments from an early age was how to make a proper cup of tea. People had marvelled at my precocity. I would scald the pot and carefully measure out the tea: one spoonful for each person and one for the pot. Mother used to say I made the best cup of tea in the house. It remains unchallenged as the highest compliment she has ever paid me.

Howard passed me a cup of weak, milky tea. I loathed weak, milky tea.

'Too weak?' asked Howard.

'Perfect,' I replied.

I would drink it if it were bile.

The only sound in the room was the long, slow stirring of Howard's spoon.

Howard seemed content to sit and sip his tea.

Silences confounded me. They were there to be shattered. 'This your house?' I asked. A voice in my head replied, 'If it were my house why would I be living in the dungeon?'

Howard untangled his legs and stretched them in my direction.

'God, no,' he said, 'I wish.'

I took a mouthful of the disgusting tea and vowed to respect the silence.

The vice-chancellor had given Howard official notice he must move from the store room at the University. He must clear his things out by the end of the month. The role as Wizard was over and so was this fringe benefit. The ongoing childcare demonstrations had been a disaster for the University administration. Network news crews had staked out the campus all week while students staged sit-ins that eventually culminated in a full occupation of the Union Council chambers. The vice-chancellor had insisted that

Howard, as the Wizard, intervene and break it up. Howard
had approached the barricades with a sense of foreboding.
His crossover hippy-wizard appearance—high pointed
hat atop a fluffy curly head of hair and loud authoritative
ranting—had gotten him past the front line of younger
students. The scattered heckling as he had legged it over the
barricades had been worrying and disconcerting, although,
not totally surprising. Howard had strode into the Union
Council chambers to find the place commandeered not by
callow freshmen, but the leading hard line demonstrators
and dissidents of the day; those who had cut their teeth on
the Vietnam War and gone to gaol for it. Howard would
never take on a Harry van Moorst or an Albert Langer
by design. He'd always keep his distance from any serious
debate, he would skirmish and no more on the issues that
drove these types of men. After all, he was only a man of
the theatre, a faker and these people were for real, and any
humour in Howard was lost on them. But there he stood
face to face with the leaders of the protest movement, the
bellowing bursts of nonsensical babble that had propelled
him up the stairs, petering out in the heat of their glare.
They set upon him not just with words. They knocked
the wizard hat from his head and stripped him of his black
cloak, hanging both out of the Union Council windows
on broomsticks like heads on pikes. The students on the
barricades below roared an approval more befitting a war
criminal. Howard barked back tamer than a poodle. The
gig was well and truly up, he had been exposed: an agent
of the vice-chancellor, a henchman for the establishment;
Howard Starr stood accused of selling out for a bag of silver
dollars. 'Judas,' they all but cried.

Howard asked me if I'd like another cup of tea.

I shook my head as he poured himself a fresh cup.

'What about your father?' he asked.

I told him Len thought the Performing Arts Centre-thing was a good idea.

Howard reflected on that. 'So he knows about me.'

'Well…not as such. Not yet anyway.'

Howard sat quite upright. 'I'd like to meet him.'

The prospect of Len meeting with Howard was somewhat daunting. I told him that *was* a great idea, but that Len travelled a lot, so getting hold of him was difficult.

Howard's face darkened with suspicion. 'Wouldn't your Dad prefer to sell it?' he asked.

I was almost indignant. 'It's not his it's mine,' I protested, 'at least as long as this Shady Green character can't be found.' My voice was animated and loud in the small room.

'You could be a very wealthy boy,' Howard said.

The notion of wealth carried with it an image of a target on my back. I wriggled in my seat.

A hint of a smile played at the moist edges of Howard's mouth. 'Money attracts the worst types.'

My jockettes were riding uncomfortably up my arse.

'You need help managing that,' he said.

For one disturbing moment I thought he could read my discomfort.

'I really should meet your father,' said Howard.

I looked at Howard with a 'lost for words' expression on my face.

'Not a good idea?' he added with what was more apparently a smile.

It was a shit idea. 'Maybe,' I said. 'But Len likes to do everything himself.'

'Len's your father?'

'I call him, Len, sometimes. He doesn't mind.'

'What does Len do?'

'He runs a truck business.'

Howard cogitated upon this. 'What sort of trucks?'

'Big ones. Semis.'

'Big ones,' he mused.

'He builds them,' I said.

'He's an engineer?' Howard asked.

'A boilermaker.'

'Could he make a set?'

'A set?'

'A theatrical set. For a stage.'

'Oh, Len can do anything.'

'I really should talk to him.'

I wanted to say that I didn't think Len would be interested. 'He pretty much just does trucks.'

Howard wrote on a pad in front of him. 'But he's good at that sort of thing?'

I nodded.

'We have to keep moving on this,' said Howard, as he tapped pensively on the pad in front of him. 'I'll tell you what I could do. What if I knocked up a set for you inside the Ballet Shoe Factory—.'

'I'm not sure if we're really that ready to go ahead—'

'—nothing too elaborate. Wouldn't cost you anything. A mini-set. Just something you could show Len that you've got in mind.' Howard ruffled his ball of curly hair. 'Come on!' he said. 'What have you got to lose?'

What did I have to lose? 'He likes musicals,' I said.

For a moment I thought a pained expression might emerge upon Howard's face.

'Musicals?' Howard asked.

'*Hello Dolly, Mame, Showboat.* Mother and Len go to all of them.'

'*Hello Dolly, Mame…*' Howard repeated slowly like the

words of a curse.

'Cabaret?' I added.

'Oh, Cabaret,' said Howard brightening up, 'that's quite a good one.'

If there was one thing I couldn't stand it was a musical. All I knew were the names and the bits of the song Len would murder in the shower, and ululate when he'd dash naked from the bathroom to the main bedroom.

'Could you do one of them?' I asked.

'Maybe *Cabaret*,' he said.

'That'd be a good one.'

'They'd definitely like that?' Howard asked.

'How big would it be?'

'The actual set?' he asked.

I nodded.

'Not too big…more of a mock-up.'

'Could you see it from the street?'

'No, only if you looked through a window.'

Howard stood up in the manner of someone who was about to close a deal.

The room felt somehow smaller as though it had shrunk. Howard's large head loomed above me. I had an overpowering desire to leave. I stood up and took a step towards the door. 'I've really got to go. They'll be expecting me back.'

'So?' he asked. 'Should we?'

I was almost at the door.

'Well?' he asked.

He held his hand out.

I looked at the empty palm of his very white hand.

Howard laughed quite warmly. 'Well I'll need some keys,' he said. 'I'll have to be able to get into the Ballet Shoe Factory. I won't want to get done for breaking and entering, would I?'

Without a second's hesitation I reached into my pocket and deposited the keys to the Ballet Shoe Factory into his outstretched hand.

'I'll send you the set design. See what you think. *Cabaret?* Right?' Howard said following me at a distance down the hallway.

Not for a second did I take my eyes from him as I backed down the hallway.

The prospect of redemption was never far from Howard's mind, and with it the overpowering need to retaliate and stick it up the vice-chancellor and the student political heavies, and anybody else who thought Howard Starr was just some lightweight, neo-fascist narcissist with an eye for the main chance. But Howard's mind kept coming back to the war and the recent runaway success of *Hair* the musical. What about *Hair, The Ballet?* An anti-war blockbuster that raked hearts and softened hardened souls, and stirred the energies of the editorialists and the opinion-makers. A production that got people off their backsides and out in support of the activists, and draft-card burning draftees, in mass condemnation of the government's witless subservience to US military paranoia, and the never-ending need for the US imperial war machine to find a war somewhere. Now that would be something.

PART TWO

A STRAPPER'S TALE

TWENTY-ONE
A STRAPPER'S TALE

From the moment Tick Tock placed the key to the Ballet Shoe Factory in my hand at the hospital, and said, '*Remember*,' the warning lights should have been flashing. I should have known that he wanted to remind me of something more than just feeding the chooks. That concentrated look as he stared into my eyes for some recognition of what he asked. But at the time, the giving of the key had seemed the most important thing—and I had nodded my acknowledgement of *its* secrecy only.

I chose the chook pens for my place to read A Strapper's Tale, as private and quiet a place as I could find. And before long I realized that it was the story that he wanted me to remember. The story he'd told me in the chook pens when I was not quite nine. A tale of secrets not to be told until the time was right. Secrets, so important, that he'd written them down, lest they be forgotten and lost for all time. Yet too confidential to share with anyone, other than a little boy, his grandson, whom he thought of as his friend. The memories came flooding back, images then the actual words that Tick Tock spoke until the words on the page and that time in the chook pen with Tick Tock were one and the same.

*****

Tick Tock told me to sit on the little wooden bench beside him. The little wooden bench from where the absent rooster would customarily command and crow the break of day. I remember swinging my short legs in and out through the dry straw of the chicken coop, scuffing a pair of tracks. I had been reluctant to sit on the bench. The rooster would make a big fuss if any of the hens sat on the bench, and I believed the rooster would think as little of me as he did of the hens, if he should return and find me there. I did not wish to be chased around the coop like the hens, running for their lives, the ugly coxcomb of the rooster bristling, as he pecked and strutted and scared them aflutter, their wings flapping and their wattled throats gulping and squawking. Tick Tock assured me that the rooster was back in his pen and he would not disturb us.

This was a special day, I was told, for the hens had had their chicks and did I want to see them? I said I certainly did. Tick Tock reached into a wooden box at the back of the coop. He lifted out a handful of fluffy, scrawny, yellow and white chicks that cheeped and cheeped. Their little heads danced around so violently that I thought they could hurt themselves with such sharp movements. Tick Tock asked if I would like to hold one, and I told him yes, and he gave me a chick that I held as gently as I could for fear of hurting something so soft, brittle and full of life. He said I should stroke the chick, which I did, and I saw that he was doing the same, all the way from the crown of its little egg-shaped head to its scrawny rump. 'They are very beautiful when they are young,' Tick Tock had said, and I had nodded. 'They are very beautiful, Tick Tock,' I replied. He gave a bare dip of his head and smiled back at me which I have never forgotten because he did not smile often, and I knew he was very happy in that chook pen with the chicks and the hens and me.

Tick Tock stroked the chicks over and over, and in this time his eyes seemed to go very far away. Whenever this far away look came over him I would think that he was thinking about the War and Uncle Pat, and that was what I was thinking in the chook pens. Then all of a sudden his eyes regained more than their normal intensity and he said very quietly, 'I'll tell you a special story. One you can never tell.' His voice was low and seemed to speak of secrets. 'Do you understand?'

'Can I tell Dad?'

'No,' said Tick Tock, 'no one at all.'

No grown-up had ever spoken like this to me before. I swung my short legs even faster in and out and through the straw, a deepening pair of tracks now plainly visible.

'Mother?'

'Not even your mother,' he said, and I thought he might smile again but he did not.

'Not forever?'

'There will be a time, but it is a time well into the future. Not one you need to worry about right now.'

Tick Tock moved up on the bench right alongside me and placed his chick at his feet. I, too, took the chick from my lap and placed it on the scuffed straw at my feet. I had wondered what type of story it would be.

'Anyhow you probably won't remember much of my story, but that is as may be,' he said. 'It is the story of someone you do not know and may not ever know, but in any event it is the tale of a strapper.'

*****

A Strapper's Tale

In 1918 it seemed like the whole world was at war because in a way it was. Only later did people come to call it the Great War said Tick Tock, but nothing great about it at all. Just another war but a bigger war than the rest of them.

The story, he said began one wet morning, in the suburbs of Melbourne not far from where we sat. It had rained heavily overnight and down it still fell in a light patter. A young slightly-built man—a boy, really—a horse strapper for a living, waited out the front of a large Edwardian residence on the high side of Ballarat Road, just beyond the spur where the Geelong Road came to a sharp end.

All the houses in this stretch of road were of some size and substance, many belonging to those connected with the so-called Sport of Kings, horse racing, for down the road on the flat plains adjoining the Maribyrnong River, was the home of racing, Flemington Racecourse.

The owner of the house, a well-known horse-trainer, eventually came out with his coat wrapped tightly about him. The young man jumped in the front seat and the trainer, after some trouble, starting the big black Buick, pulled out the choke, and the V8 roared down the hill, the windscreen wiper swishing the rain away.

The day was different from almost the start. Soon after they arrived at the track, the young man saw a shifty-looking fellow in a coat with his collar pulled up, handing a sheaf of banknotes to a jockey behind the stables. A little later, when the strapper was in a stall, low and out of sight, brushing down a horse, the two men had a conversation right outside the stall. While the strapper, in his crouching position, could see neither of the men, he recognised one voice as that of the jockey, who'd been talking to the man in the coat and had taken the bundle of notes.

'The boys understand,' said the jockey in that unmistakeable, squeaky, child-like voice typical of jockeys.

'They've got their money?' asked the man.

'They know what to do,' confirmed the jockey.

'If anything other than this nag here gets up,' and the man rapped the stable door so sharply and loudly that it made the strapper jump, 'there will be hell to pay.'

'It'll be My Time Flies by a length and a half. The boys have got it worked out,' said the jockey.

'I hope so,' replied the man, 'I hope so for all your sakes.'

The strapper stayed hidden behind the belly of the horse while it nuzzled at a bucket of oats in a corner of the stall. The footsteps of the jockey and the man grew faint as they clicked over the cobblestones and away from the stables. Cautiously, the strapper got to his feet, took a look outside and then resumed brushing the horse slowly and mechanically. The horse he was brushing was My Time Flies, a big bay gelding, not a metropolitan win to its name and at least fifteen-to-one with the bookies in Race 5 at Flemington, on the next Saturday of racing. What he had overheard was clear and unmistakeable: Race 5 was to be fixed and My Time Flies would be the winner. The jockeys, and who knows whomever else, had been paid handsomely to make sure that happened.

I interrupted Tick Tock and asked him if race-fixing was wrong and he told me it certainly was. So did that make the jockeys and maybe the strapper criminals? Tick Tock told me that I was jumping the gun and that it'd be better if I waited for the rest of the story. I told him that I liked the strapper and I hoped nothing bad happened to him. He just nodded and said I'd have to wait and see.

My Time Flies shifted and snorted in the almost empty stables. Most of the trainer's other horses were swimming at the river or being ridden trackwork. The strapper was waiting for the veterinarian—My Time Flies had shown signs of shin soreness. As he wondered how long the vet would be, he couldn't help calculating his winnings if he put £10 on My Time Flies at 15-1. That would be enough for a large deposit on a modest house in Williamstown. If he should wager the entire amount of his savings— £35—that would be more than enough for a very large house, and something more besides. Soon the numbers and their combinations whirred in the strapper's head, until he could almost feel the wads of waxy £10 notes in his tight-fisted grasp.

Now the strapper did not get paid much for his job because his job was a job of love for horses and not a job of work, and often, when people did jobs for love, people would not get paid much. To afford a house in William-stown of the type his fiancée wanted, the strapper had taken a second job. And today the strapper could not wait to get to that other job, as a lookout at the Starting Price book-makers, or the 'SPs' as people knew them.

I asked Tick Tock if the SPs were criminals. I asked him because sometimes in our house Len and Mother talked about the old days and the SPs as if they were outlaws and they might, at any time, have been run out of town. He told me that those were different times, very poor times when people struggled for jobs and food—nothing like now. A bit like Ned Kelly? No not the same as Ned Kelly although others might care to differ he replied.

Cavanagh's Tote took bets on horse races all the way up and down the east coast and the southern states. As a lookout, the strapper was the one who stood out back of the tote where the passage from Nelson Place met the lane—Little Nelson Place. As a rule, he'd sit on the cross-joists of the timber fence that ran down the lane. From here he could see right the way to both ends of the lane. The strapper's job was pretty simple, his instructions were clear. If he saw anything suspicious, and especially, if he saw the cops, he had to blow as hard as he could the silver whistle that Mr Cavanagh had given him.

On this day the strapper had waited quietly at the door of the Tote that was just ajar. Beyond where he stood was out of bounds for a mere lookout. Inside the Tote it was busy: people were yelling, phones were ringing, betting chits were being passed around. Sheets of butcher's paper with the fields for Saturday's races, Flemington, Randwick, Doomben and Morphettville, hung off the walls. The strapper could just make out the races for Flemington. His eyes ran down the races. When he got to the race he was interested in—Flemington Race 5, he stopped and stared: No.1 Man Ray 5-1, No.2 The Tide Is Running Evens, …No.12 My Time Flies 20-1. 20-1? The odds were even more than he had expected. For every pound he bet he could win twenty times that much! If he put the £35 on, he would get back—he could barely think of a number this big— £700.

For a minute or so the strapper waited to be noticed. In due course Mrs Cavenagh bustled by and through the small gap in the doorway he inquired of her, in a low and respectful voice, if he could put a bet on for his father who was not well enough to make it down to the tote. Mrs Cavenagh relayed the request to Mr Cavenagh. He got up from a small desk and came to the door. After looking the strapper up and down Mr Cavenagh said, in a thick Irish brogue, that his father's money was as good as anybody else's. He asked the strapper what horse did he have in mind, and the strapper said, My Time Flies and it was running in the fifth on Saturday at Flemington. Mr Cavenagh did not know that the young man worked as a strapper by day. And although there was nothing wrong with working as a strapper *and* a lookout at the Tote, it was, nevertheless, a fact of which he was unaware.

Mr Cavenagh grimaced when the strapper said the name of the horse, as if it didn't have much of a chance of winning. He suggested Man Ray was a more proven animal, a last-start winner and handily-weighted. The strapper replied that he thought his father had pretty much made up his mind. With a sigh Mr Cavenagh said a man's money was surely his own, he could spend it anyway he pleased. Nevertheless, he asked the young strapper, as a favour for himself, to tell his father what he had said about Man Ray.

Without telling a soul, not even his fiancée, the strapper went to the bank the very next day and withdrew the entire £35. He went straight to the Cavanagh's Tote after his work at the track. Luckily, Mr Cavanagh wasn't in, and one of his men, a sidekick took the bet with a smart aleck remark about where would the strapper be getting a sum like that. When the strapper said he got it from his dad, the sidekick all but slapped his sides laughing. Yet despite any suspicions the sidekick might have had of where the £35 had come from, he took the bet and gave the strapper a betting slip as a receipt.

Never before had the strapper held anything as valuable, so he thought, as this little piece of paper, as good as a cash cheque for £700: Flemington Race 5 Horse 12, *£700/35* scribbled and hardly legible but if My Time Flies won, worth every penny it stood for. Of that the strapper didn't harbour a doubt.

Tick Tock was a pound the same as a dollar? For a moment the old man was quiet and thoughtful and then he told me that a pound had been worth about twice as much as a dollar. Do we still have pounds? I persisted. No, we only have dollars now. We got rid of all the pounds. And I know that for many years after that I wondered about this fact. About why we would get rid of all the pounds if they were worth twice as much as the dollars.

Up until Race 5 the strapper had brushed and saddled and led all his other horses in relaxed circling around the mounting yard just as he usually did. Then the trumpets announcing Race 5 had blared. It was as if My Time Flies knew something was wrong. He reared and bucked and snorted. The strapper struggled to hold him. The jockey asked what was wrong. No amount of rubbing and patting could settle him down. It took an age to get him in the starting gates. For a while the strapper even worried that the stewards might scratch him.

When the barrier gates opened My Time Flies was left standing. By the time the field had gone 100 yards My Time Flies was tailed off last, on the fence, behind a wall of horses. The strapper screamed for the jockey to do something, certainly to get off the fence. It couldn't win from there. And never had an idea that he could make £700 seemed so fantastic, so stupid and so greedy, than it did, as he watched My Time Flies running last and struggling for a run.

But as if by some plan or design, suddenly, the leading horses collided, cannoning into one another and buckling back into the rest of the field. With the field spreadeagled, the jockey of My Time Flies saw his chance. Crying, 'Use the whip, use the whip,' strange words for any strapper, he roared My Time Flies on. In the shadows of the finishing post My Time Flies put his nose in front. The strapper thought his heart had stopped beating. My Time Flies had won, and so too had the strapper—£700, a fortune.

A chilly wind was blowing down the lane behind Cavanagh's Tote when the strapper got there just after 6. Although Jim Cavenagh was a rich man and the strapper knew he'd made many big payouts before he had an uneasy feeling in the pit of his stomach. The strapper opened the back door to the tote and stood at the edge of the room, waiting to be noticed. Mr Cavenagh and Mrs Cavenagh were there, and so, too, a bookie's clerk, whose face hovered just above the page of a large book inked full with entries like the new one he was making. Mrs Cavenagh saw the strapper standing there, but did not greet him. She left the room to make a cup of tea so she said.

Mr Cavenagh turned to face the strapper. 'I suppose you've come to collect?' he asked.

The strapper removed the betting slip from his pocket. Mr Cavenagh's eyes briefly dropped to recognise one of his own betting slips and stretched out a hand. He took the betting slip and handed it across to the bookie's clerk, who quickly read the betting slip, and then with a set of keys opened a cupboard down by his legs. After hearing what he thought might be the tumblers of a safe, a thick wad of banknotes was passed to Mr Cavenagh, who didn't give it a glance.

'I honour my bets even to cheats,' said Mr Cavenagh.

But Tick Tock the strapper wasn't a cheat I cried. He just found out by accident. I'd got off the little bench and was remonstrating with Tick Tock. That's not fair. He won the race fair and square. Tick Tock told me to quieten down. But the man, Mr Cavenagh, is wrong and that's not fair. It took a little while for Tick Tock to get me to resume my seat. He said he wouldn't keep going unless I sat down beside him and listened.

Afraid, that whatever he said, might prevent him getting the money, the strapper stayed quiet.

'The boys tell me you're the strapper for My Time Flies. You didn't tell me you were a strapper, did you, son?' Mr Cavenagh waited for some sort of answer. 'You see, I'm not a man who believes much in coincidences. And when a lookout puts this much money on a rank outsider and I find out he's the strapper, and the horse gets up, I call that a run of coincidences.'

'I haven't done anything wrong,' pleaded the strapper.

Mr. Cavenagh held the money out to the strapper. He reached for the money slowly and cautiously, anxious, that it might be reefed away at the last moment.

'Son, you don't have to take it, you know.'

The strapper looked at Mr Cavenagh, doubt etched on his face.

'I will honour my bets even to a little thief like yourself. But if you think I'll let you get away with it you've got another thing coming. The cops won't lift a finger to help a snivelling little thief like you.'

The strapper thought of his fiancée and the house and all the other things the money could buy, and snatched the money from the SP bookmaker's grasp.

'Don't take it, son,' warned Mr Cavenagh.

But the strapper took the money all right. He raced down the backdoor stoop stairs and out through the long, thin backyard. As he pushed open the gate to the lane, a lookout jumped down from the fence and yelled to someone closer to the Tote. The strapper sprinted along the lane aware that there were two men following him. Trembling, he scrambled over the high, timbered back fence of the place that he knew as the Ballet Shoe Factory. It was dark and quiet. He thought he'd be safe there, huddled behind a big tree.

Moments later the strapper heard Cavenagh's men, talking hard up against the backfence. He knew it wasn't safe to stay put. If they jumped the back fence they would find him in no time. Over in a corner of the backyard the strapper spied the opening to a large drain. Drains like this one, near to the bay, were common in Williamstown. And then rain began to fall.

The strapper dashed the short distance to the drain and in a trice had ducked his head and was inside. From the darkness of the drain the strapper watched a pair of arms and then a head and then a set of shoulders of one of the lookouts come over the fence. Reluctantly he backed further up the drain. Within a few seconds, first one lookout and then the other leapt into the backyard and began to search.

While the strapper had expected the drain to smell like rotting garbage or standing water, something awful, it did not. The drain was musty, as if it had been recently dusted with a fine powder of cement. It had a peculiar distinctive smell, a rinsed or washed smell that now smelt like something else he couldn't quite put his finger on. The strapper figured it was only stormwater and what harm could there be in that? Hesitantly, he backed even further into the drain, and was glad he had, when the legs of the lookouts crossed in front of the drain's opening. Cornered, he couldn't stay where he was. He either had to make a break for it or go further up the drain. Then he remembered the drains that ran beneath Smithfield Road and under the track at Flemington. The ones that he and his mates used to avoid paying admission on race days. The strapper hoped that this drain, like the ones at Flemington would connect to a larger one, and eventually come out some distance off, somewhere safe. The strapper set off blindly down the drain and, once again, it was lucky he did, because not long after a lookout had appeared, looking into what would only be darkness. But if the lookouts couldn't see him he could certainly see them, even if it was through a grey spidery veil of rain.

The strapper walked slowly and steadily. It was not easy walking in the drains on their slippery surfaces and in the dark. How much time had passed he did not know. He'd been walking non-stop in a near pitch darkness broken only by the nightlight let in by the occasional metal grates overhead. But he was too scared to stop, consumed with fear that rats might get him, sinking their razor-sharp teeth into the soft pink of his flesh.

At the thought of the rats I'd pulled my legs up on to the bench and nestled closer to Tick Tock. He took one of my hands and held it firmly within his. His hand was very brown, much browner than mine which was really quite white and smooth: wrinkleless. Not like Tick Tock's.

The strapper supposed the drain was following the street-lights of a major street, as the light that shone through the grates, was enough to show the water in the drain as an inky-blue in colour, and the bars of the grates in clear reflected criss-crosses. When he came to the next grate he noticed a small stoop of narrow steps directly beneath it. He climbed up. Pressing his face to the cold metal of the grate he tried to see what was above. Wet weeds tickled his nose. But all he could see was a full moon and clouds sliding by as clear as bones in a doctor's x-ray. He tried to push open the grate. The grate wouldn't prise loose no matter how hard he pushed.

The strapper worried that he'd been walking in an enormous circle and had at some point crossed under the lane back near Cavenagh's Tote. He did not want to pop up jack-in-the-box-like anywhere near the Tote. And for the first time it occurred to the strapper that being in a drain on a wet night might not be the safest of places.

Progress he measured in steps—he guessed about two feet to a step. Although the height of the drain let him walk mainly upright, the base was curved and the walls slippery with a mossy lichen-like growth such that every slip and stumble was almost a fall and progress overall was slow.

Having counted five hundred steps since he peered through the grate, the strapper calculated he had gone about a thousand feet, in a direction that he thought was north, directly away from the bay. The rain now weighed upon him. A dread took hold, as he imagined the trickle of water that lapped around his ankles, rising and filling the drain. Reaching down in the darkness the strapper felt for the level of the water with the tips of his fingers. No longer was it a thin tendril of water licking the soles of his boots. It was now, distinctly higher, covering the toes of his boots. An awful shiver shook the strapper. He was tempted to retrace his steps. To go back to the little stoop of steps, where, he could, at least, push his mouth and his nostrils through the bars of the grate, and savour every molecule of fresh air that flowed through from the outside world. But would he be safe, even there, if the waters filled the drain to overflowing? Could they rise that high?

But the strapper did not turn back. He quickened his step. Soon after a shower of light appeared up ahead. It was geometric in shape, and seemed to hang from the ceiling, the dust motes within it, shimmering like sequins. When he stepped into the light the dust motes parted and he saw above him a metal grille, much larger than the grates he had seen before, open to the night sky. Arching his back he called out, 'HELP HELP.' His voice sounded foreign and high-pitched, and echoed long and deep into the drain. He listened for a response, but the only sound was of his voice's echo growing soft and finally disappearing altogether. It was as if it had travelled somewhere else too far away to hear.

Just beyond the shower of geometric light was a kind of junction: a pair of drains emerging like an oversized pair of sunglasses. Each of these drains was made of small, undressed, red bricks, the pointing of the mortar clear in every row all the way to the ceiling of the main tunnel, which was slabbed in sandstone, richly yellowed and honeyed in colour, as if it had been dunked for a century in syrup. Above one of the drains was an inscription—*Shady Green's Pipedream*. Whether the writing was the work of a child or a lunatic he had no idea. All the same, the strapper thought that the mention of someone's name had about it a hint of civilisation, and so it was, when he peered intently down the drain signposted *Shady Green's Pipedream*, that he thought he could see light at the other end. With the vision of emerging safely more in prospect, the strapper set off with purpose down the right fork of the tunnel.

It sounds like a trap to me Tick Tock. That's what it sounds like to me. I'll bet it's a trap! The bad guys are down that tunnel. It's like their secret hiding-place or something. You never know was Tock Tock's reply.

The strapper's pockets were bursting with money. Great, tight packed wads stuffed in every pocket, and a few more besides down his underpants causing no little irritation. The money in the strapper's mind was as good as spent. He would buy just the sort of house that Maisy wanted. That is what he wanted too: nothing else. How excited she'd be when he told her he had all the money they needed. She would not have to go to work, and it made him proud to think of this. His wife would be like one of the wives in places like Toorak and Malvern, who had all day to get the house just right, all neat and tidy with a beautiful hot meal on the table when he got home from work. He could almost smell the roast lamb and the mint jelly and the scent of onions that would come steaming off the plate set before him, like he was some kind of medieval king. Yes the strapper looked forward to the day he could tell his mother and father that Maisy would stay home to look after him, and the children, they could now easily afford to have.

But, all this, he knew, was fanciful, not much better than a dream and it was only the surreal netherworld of the drains that could allow such imaginings to happen. Mr Cavenagh was a righteous man who felt wronged. Only time could heal his wrath. Nowhere in Melbourne would be safe for the strapper. Where could he go? He reached inside a trouser pocket and clasped a wad of money just to make sure it was really still there. Water trickled through his hair and down his back and he shook with the cold. All this money he thought and what was it really worth? Would anyone believe him, when he said, he had had nothing to do with the race-fix?

The darkness seemed to come even closer as if it was touching and reaching into him. He got to thinking that he might head north to Brisbane. The strapper had never been there, but he knew he would like it. A warmer climate to live in was what he had always yearned for. Maisy would love it, too; he knew she would; at least for a while until the race-fix blew over. They would have to elope. It would be a great shame that they couldn't have a proper expensive wedding at the Yacht Club for all their friends and family with no stinting on the numbers. Yes that is what he would do, as

soon as he got out of the drain, he would head to Spencer
Street Station and catch the Southern Aurora up north. He
would send Maisy a telegram telling her where he was. It
would say:

```
'DEAREST MAISY A MOST UNLIKELY AND UN-
EXPECTED TURN OF EVENTS HAS HAPPENED
FULL STOP DON'T BELIEVE WHAT ANYBODY
SAYS FULL STOP PLEASE MARRY ME PLEASE
SAY YOU WILL FULL STOP I WILL WAIT FOR
YOU HERE FULL STOP DON'T SAY WHERE I AM
OR THAT I HAVE SENT THIS FULL STOP LOVE
VAL.'
```

He would stay at the best hotel in Brisbane and Maisy
would know this from the details upon the telegram. She
would love to stay at a beautiful hotel. He would send the
telegram to where she worked, so that it could not be intercepted by her family. He would write a letter to his parents
and tell them he had done nothing wrong, and not to worry,
and he would come and see them as soon as this was possible.
This letter he would send to Maisy, too, and she could post it
locally from Melbourne before she left to join him, to make
sure that the postmark didn't betray his whereabouts.

Now the strapper was apparently so lost in his thoughts
that he hadn't noticed his boots were splashing in the water.
Up ahead, a point of light, no more than a pinprick of
brightness, pierced the dark and signalled him to move on.
The weight of the water was heavy on his boots as he lifted
them above the rising surface of the water. Despite the water
having risen to just below his knees, he told himself there was
no need to panic, he was almost there; no more than twenty
yards from the apparent end and light was flooding in. The
drain opened out to twice its width and twice its height. It

was then that he saw he was trapped. Covering the opening, imprisoning him like an ancient portcullis, was a massive grille of rusted iron bars, as wide across as a lion's circus cage, firmly fixed into the brickwork of the drain.

I told you! I told you Tick Tock that it was a trap. I was so excited that I'd guessed it right. I might have been shouting, I can't remember. But I was certainly standing and waving my hands about. Tick Tock patted me on the knee and nodded his head in agreement. I was way too smart for him.

The strapper stumbled in slow motion, despairing of his misfortune, reaching out and grasping the bars of the grille: indeed trapped. Beyond the grille lay the river itself, with nothing else in between, an expanse of slow-moving muddy gray water. The strapper's head sank against the bars. He watched the drain's leaves and twigs eddy and gather in the joins of the iron bars, before freeing themselves and sailing out to the river in jerky little movements. His heart filled with despair and hopelessness as he contemplated a pitiful end, washed up against the grille of the drain, entangled in all its rubbish.

Then he heard a scraping noise. In a darkened alcove behind him was a series of iron rungs going vertically up the wall of the drain. Hand over hand, the strapper climbed up, until perched on the second highest rung, he reached up and touched a metal manhole cover that was quivering and scraping, seemingly of its own will. Overcoming his immediate fear and hesitation at what might be causing the movement, he pressed against the manhole cover. In the instant that he did, the manhole cover rose and revealed a dark young man with a great frown upon his face.

'What ya think ya doin' down there?' said the dark

young man.

'Thank God,' said the strapper and he did not care that he had mildly blasphemed, so pleased was he that salvation was at hand.

The young man was quite dark-skinned and thin, and dressed poorly in clothes that hung lank and loose, as if they had somehow lost their grip of whatever bone and muscle lay beneath. He regarded the strapper as if he had uncovered something undesirable.

'Told you boys about comin' here. Told ya what I'd do. Warned ya, I did.'

The strapper had no desire to quarrel with the young man on a matter of which he had no knowledge nor did he have any intention of staying a moment longer within the drain. But as he began to climb the final couple of rungs, the young man placed a hard, weathered boot upon one of his hands, and pressed so it could not be removed.

In alarm, the strapper looked up. 'The water's rising in here,' he pleaded.

The man scratched his forehead in mock disbelief. 'That be right? Who would have thought with all this rain?'

'I can't stay down here.'

'What are you doin' in there in the first place, then?'

'It's a long story,' and with that remark the strapper cast a look down at the rising water.

The young man produced a spear from behind his back and waved it at the strapper. 'Back in there with ya. Go on now.' The strapper retreated down the rungs of the drain's ladder. In a flash, the young man, with the spear in his hand, was in the drain, the manhole cover back in its place, pushing the strapper further back into the drain. In the eerie moonlight, in the echoing chamber of the drain, in what must have been almost three feet of water, the young man and the strapper stood face to face.

'You're not coming out here, at any rate,' said the young man. 'And you might not be coming out at all, unless you tell me why you're really down here. Sick of you lot muckin' with my things.'

The strapper, sensing he had no choice, and all too aware of the rising level of the water, told the young man what had happened. He told him the whole story of the race-fix and the Cavenagh's Tote, leaving out only the amount of money he had won.

'So you're lookin' for some place to hide?'

'I had to get away.'

'I can understand that,' said the young man and a knowing smile creased his dark skin.

'The water's getting deep,' said the strapper.

'Pair almost drowned here last month.' The young man chuckled. 'Thought they were goners, they did, before I came along and saw their sorry faces...right about where yours is now.'

The temptation to roar obscenities tore at the strapper. Water streamed through their legs and for the first time the strapper felt his weight shift under its power. Was this dark-skinned young man with strange fiery eyes some sort of madman?

'Could just leave ya there, ya know? Could do that. Mmm?' The young man waited a few moments. In the next instant the young man pushed past the strapper and disappeared into the blackness of the drain. The strapper followed. What other choice did he have? They walked for a time in a silence broken only by the splash of their boots, one behind the other, the young man always a few yards ahead, the strapper's right arm extended, afraid he'd run up the young man's back. The strapper was content to be led. His confidence was borne of the notion that any man who could walk with assuredness in darkness was a man who could find a way out. From time to time the young man had stabbed the water with his spear and, on one occasion, snared what was apparently an eel, that twisted and writhed, forcing the strapper to recoil from he knew not what at the time. Good eatin', is what the young man had said, 'specially with the mussels you get from the rocks.

After a while the young man and the strapper entered a very different system of drains where water did not flow. Suddenly the young man halted, and spread his arms wide. Both men blinked. Up ahead a single kerosene lamp did its best to light the lofty proportions of an enormous tunnel that appeared still under construction, neat piles of gravel and powdery cement mix—a shovel and a pick sticking out of one—lay upon an unfinished slab of concrete that stretched two hundred yards into the distance. Projecting from the wall, every twenty yards, were giant ventilation fans the size of jet engines. It gave the impression of an industrial project—a bomb shelter or train subway, perhaps—not quite finished.

'Prince of drains,' the man said. 'No one much comes here. Except those, of course, who can't get out.'

Fear came upon the strapper afresh, his sense of isolation was acute—no cry for help would be heard down here.

Part of one side of the tunnel had been turned into a kind of bedroom—big bright rectangular carpets, a mattress with some blankets piled untidily on top, and beside it a small mahogany bedside table. But what struck the strapper the most was the painting. The walls and even some of the ceiling were painted in a dense, elaborate surreal and un-settling style: hands reaching from the wall, open mouths in silent shouts and hot suns and sparkling stars dotted, apparently with purpose, throughout the concrete canvas.

'Home,' said the young man.

Was the young man serious?

'You don't live down here?' said the strapper.

The young man stared unashamedly straight back at him. 'Better than you think Mr High and Mighty. Nobody will find you down here.' He raised his spear a foot off the ground and shook it violently. 'And don't worry 'bout those damned louts. If they come back, they'll feel the point of me spear.' He shook the spear again for good measure.

The strapper wiped his lips with the back of his hand. 'What do you eat…and drink down here?'

'Plenty of water. You seen that. Most of it good.' He pointed at a large, filmy glass flagon that the strapper guessed might have originally contained sherry, the liquid within it tainted orange. The strapper imagined a mouthful of sweet, distasteful, sherry-flavoured water and reflexively swallowed a gulp of saliva.

'Food?' The strapper croaked.

The young man held up his spear like a trident.

'Beach. River. Close.' He could sound like a caveman.

'Right.' The word had been uttered with no conviction.

The young man regarded the strapper closely. 'You plannin' on leaving?'

Should the strapper reply honestly? Was that the wise thing to do?

'You wanna go. You can go,' said the young man interrupting the strapper's deliberations. 'I won't stop ya. What do I need with ya? Eh?' There was no menace or threat in the young man, seemingly as agreeable to whether the strapper stayed or left.

'You won't stop me?' The strapper's eyes might have betrayed a lack of confidence in what the young man had said.

'I've pretty much taken you out right now, fella.'

The young man picked up the lamp and walked over to the bedside table. 'Got another one of these,' he meant the lamp. 'Very good for readin'. Ya like to read?'

The strapper replied that he didn't read much and the young man shook his head in disappointment. 'A man's gotta read,' he said, 'and this is a good place to read,' and pointed at the stack of books, two feet high on the bedside table.

The young man might also have remarked that the tunnel was a very safe place. He could see anything coming from one hundred yards off in either direction. On cue a rat hustled towards them from the far depths of the tunnel, its nostrils quivering. 'Don't mind the rats,' he said, 'they've got other more juicy things on their mind.' The rat scurried past not paying them the least of notice, its sleek dark form disappearing beyond the light.

From afar, at first, came soft muted reverberations, and then as they came closer, a louder pounding upon the earth: the unmistakable sound of galloping horses. The strapper looked at the young man in dismay. 'You knew. I told you!'

'Now…'

'I told you everything and you've taken me to the most dangerous place of all.'

The strapper thought he was back at Flemington race-course. Mr Cavenagh's men might be standing right above, searching for him, intensifying the hunt. 'It's not what ya think,' smiled the young man.

As the hooves pounded overhead the strapper could not imagine anything but the worst.

The young man maintained a puzzled ease in the face of the strapper's discomfort. 'Williamstown. It's the ole track at Willi'.

'Williamstown?'

'Williamstown racetrack. Right above us.'

The sound of horses pounded overhead.

'What d'ya wanna do? Go back? Wanna go back where ya came from?'

Although the strapper desperately wanted to get out of this subterranean network of drains and tunnels, there was something strangely safe and reassuring about where he found himself, and the company that he had found.

The young man's twinkling muddy-brown eyes gazed searchingly upon the strapper. 'Are you stayin' or goin'?'

PART THREE

THE BALLET SHOE FACTORY

TWENTY-TWO
MY TIME FLIES

Len had just returned from Brisbane and doing the rounds of Tick Tock's old haunts. Mother had been firmly of the view that the search up north would not come to anything. Her conviction was anchored in the belief that she knew everything about Tick Tock that was worth knowing. If Shady Green was such an important friend of Tick Tock's, then there was no doubt in her mind that she would already be well and truly aware of his existence.

Surrounded by lots of little piles of paper on the floor that I guessed were notes from the trip north, Len lay reclined in the Jason, watching TV distractedly, with a glossy hardback edition of Norman Vincent Peale's '*The Power of Positive Thinking*' in his lap. Every now and again, he'd look up and talk to the TV over the top of the rims of the spectacles, he wore halfway down his nose.

Len shuffled in the Jason, searching for some extra comfort in the hip region. 'An old mate of Tick Tock's in Brisbane mentioned a horse race. A long time ago. A big scandal.' He continued to shift in the Jason, probing for that elusive, additional relief or greater well-being, that the Jason wasn't quite delivering.

For a few seconds, Mother and I didn't realise Len was talking to either of us.

'Am I working on this by myself?' Len grumbled.

Mother and I both took our eyes off the TV and focused on Len. 'Brisbane? What was that about Brisbane?' Mother asked.

'A horse race. A big scandal,' Len mumbled into his book.

Mother cocked her head on the side. 'What sort of scandal?'

'A race-fix.'

Mother's head was pretty much still cocked on the side, if marginally more in the vertical. 'Tick Tock and this Shady Green involved in race-fixing? Who said this?'

'Think that's possible?' Len, with no small amount of discomfort, leant over the arm of the Jason and scrounged on the floor amongst the bits of paper. He picked up a ragged newspaper clipping from The Argus dated 27th March 1918, and held it up. 'Seen anything like this?'

My Time Flies Connections Under Investigation

The connections of both My Time Flies and The Tide Is Running were questioned at length yesterday by stewards in relation to the running of Race 5, The Havelock Handicap which witnessed the rank outsider My Time Flies score an improbable victory over overwhelming favourite The Tide is Running. It is understood there was a late plunge on My Time Flies whose recent indifferent form and maiden status aroused the suspicions of stewards and whether or not the race was run on its merits.

My mother read the clipping with seeming interest. 'Is this the whole story?'

Len's small eyes narrowed. 'I'm not a detective agency.'

'Quite.' My mother hated being left in the dark.

As if to bolster the argument, Len added, 'Tick Tock was an SP bookmaker.'

'Hardly. He was just a lookout.'

'Tick Tock could have known what was going on. I mean he would have been sitting on the backfence of Cava-nagh's Tote in 1918, *and* don't forget, he was a stable boy at Flemington at the same time. That's two different ways he could have been involved.'

Mother didn't like where this was going. 'Tick Tock's been dead for a matter of weeks and you're accusing him…'

'Hang on hang on I'm not accusing Tick Tock of anything. Just of knowing and if he knew…'

'And if he knew…what?'

Len took his glasses off and laid them across *The Power Of Positive Thinking*. 'Now don't get angry,' he said as he saw that Mother was becoming exceedingly angry, 'but how do you think he ever got the money for a place like the Ballet Shoe Factory?'

My mother stood up with her arms crossed. 'I know where you're going on this Len and I don't like it.'

'He said he won it on the races. Didn't he?'

'That's no secret, Len. He told everybody that.'

'Not when he first won it he didn't. He didn't then. He did much later when everyone had forgotten about the race-fix. But at first, he said he got the money from selling his Sicilian uncle's fishing boat. Didn't he?'

Mother's face clouded in thought. 'But nobody believed all of that anyway.'

'That's what he told Maisy.'

'Mum was seventeen when she got married. She would have believed almost anything to get out of the house.'

'And the race-fix is why he went to Brisbane.'

Mother thrust the clipping back at Len. 'He went there for the weather.' She stood up and fastened an apron about her waist with a furious knot. She'd cook rather than listen to this.

Len wriggled in the Jason from impatience and discomfort. 'Has someone been sitting in the Jason–' he began to say, 'look I know all this stuff about his thin Sicilian blood, but that's not the reason he left Melbourne. He went to Brisbane straight after he had a falling out at Cavenagh's Tote. That's when he left, he used to say it himself. But falling out over what?'

'He had an argument with the Cavenaghs.'

'About what? Did he ever say about what?'

My mother sighed. 'I can't remember, Len. The Cavenaghs blamed Tick Tock for a big payout. Tick Tock never said what it was, as far as I can recall. He did say it wasn't his fault and we all believed him.'

Len picked up the newspaper clipping, 'Nothing about this horse…My Time Flies?'

'Never heard of it.' Mother gave the impression of trying to think. She closed her eyes. The cat miaowed for food in the kitchen. Over in the corner of the lounge in a flickering of light the TV went to an ad break.

'Tick Tock didn't go to Brisbane because of the weather and all this bullshit…'

'Well that's what he told us. That's what he told anyone who bothered to ask,' interrupted Mother almost indignantly.

'But that's not why he went in the first place,' insisted Len.

'Why then?'

'He had to go.'

'Len can you just come out with it. Why did he have to go?'

'I think Tick Tock knew the race was rigged. I'd like to bet he borrowed every penny he could get and put it on My Time Flies with the SPs. Not to make too fine a point of it, the Cavenagh's Tote. If you've ever really wondered where he got the money for the Ballet Shoe Factory from, that would be where.'

'And you know all this from a newspaper clipping?'

I held my breath. There was an empty ringing sound in my ears.

'I think this Shady Green is still around.'

I swallowed hard.

'For heaven's sake Len how do you know all this?'

'I met someone in Brisbane who knows him.'

A nervous tingling rode down my spine like it was filleting flesh from bone.

'You've found this Shady Green?'

'No.'

'No?'

'An old guy in a geriatric ward knows him.'

'An old guy in a geriatric ward?'

'On a heart-lung machine. He says he knows him.'

'Might be mistaken.'

'Don't think so. Insists he knows him.'

'He's not senile or something.'

'Don't think so.'

'How old is he?'

'Old. Eighty plus.'

'And you believe him?'

'I do.'

'So where's Shady Green now, then? Did he know that?'

'No he didn't. He hadn't seen Tick Tock or Shady Green for years. For most of that time this guy's been in hospital.'

'So this Shady Green is still very much a mystery man.'

'Shady Green is certainly elusive.'

'Maybe you don't know your father as well as you think.'

Len may as well have thrown a jerry can of flaming fuel over Mother's head. 'Don't tell me I don't know my father. I know him better than you, better than anyone, so don't tell me that.'

Should I tell them Tick Tock's story about the strapper? But how could I? I'd been sworn to secrecy—it didn't matter how long ago. I had promised Tick Tock not to tell.

TWENTY-THREE
SHADY'S MATE UP NORTH

When Len came in the front door, he walked straight down the hall to the living room, the only sound he made, was from the jangle of keys hitting the crystal bowl in the middle of the dining table.

Mother popped her head around the kitchen door and asked, 'Is that you, Len?' and he didn't reply because he couldn't hear over the TV, he'd just switched on. She went to where he sat and asked if he was hungry. Len said he wasn't very hungry, he might have something later. Mother asked if anything was wrong, and he said, there might be. She asked what was it? Not the gout again? Len said it wasn't the gout. Was it this damned Shady Green business? No it wasn't that. What then? He said he didn't know for sure but he'd seen a doctor today. You've seen a doctor? What had the doctor said? asked Mother. The doctor said it was his kidneys. His kidneys? What's wrong with your kidneys? And she'd sat on the footstool of the Jason at Len's feet.

'Is it...something serious?' she asked.

Len said, it wasn't cancer, but they wouldn't know everything until they got the results of the tests back, and if she didn't mind would she move because she was sitting in front of the TV and the Channel Nine News was on, and Len never missed the News. Mother went the colour of clean, white cotton sheets and headed back into the kitchen where she began stirring with a large, wooden handle a pot of I-do-not-know-what. She stirred and stirred whatever was in that pot and Len watched the Channel Nine News with none of his usual running commentary.

Two days later the doctor gave Len the bad news that one of his kidneys had stopped working altogether, and the other one, the so-called good one, wasn't really a good one, as it was just hanging on. Len would need to go on a dialysis machine. He asked for how long? The doctor said, off and on, maybe forever. Len said he'd prefer to die rather than stay hooked up to a machine. Len asked, if he could get a transplant or something. Well, said the doctor, we can hope and pray that someone comes along and donates a kidney. Hope and pray? asked Len, as if Len might hope and pray that the welds and rivets in a semi-trailer's pressurised hydraulic container might go the journey without blowing sky-high. 'Mr. White,' the doctor had explained with a wide and expansive gesture of arms, 'there is still much to be learned about the business of transplants and although there is a terrific amount of research going on both here and around the world, in the meantime, the good lord is sometimes as good a place as any in which to reside one's trust.' Len muttered something to the effect that the good lord may have had something to do with him getting the disease in the first place, so he sure as hell had no intention of speaking to him in any terms, other than angry ones.

The doctor, who was someone Len and Mother knew quite well, advised Len against this in no uncertain terms. He told Len, that there was no point getting the good lord offside with blaspheming; that wouldn't be in anyone's interests.

Besides said the good doctor, he, himself, had witnessed any number of little miracles when it came to the restoration of a patient's good health. Len asked if he was saying that he needed a miracle. No the doctor said, what he really needed was a new kidney. In any event the good doctor assured Len that he would be the first to know of any prospective donor.

Len, although somewhat disturbed by the knowledge he had only a solitary dodgy kidney, had left the doctor's surgery with a firm resolve to get a new doctor. When he had finished telling Mother the results of the tests, she began to cry. Len said, don't worry, please get him a beer, and in the same breath he indicated he'd get another medical opinion as the one he'd got, seemed to rely more on the bible, than anything the good doctor would have learned in medical school. He told Mother he didn't want anybody else to know what he had. He didn't think it was any of their business. He'd put up with the dialysis and get the first kidney available. To him it was as simple as bleeding brakes.

Len had delayed going back to Brisbane for another meeting with the old invalid friend of Tick Tock's, Tom Forbes, who professed to know Shady Green. This week, he said, he felt better, and he'd made arrangements to return to Brisbane to visit Tom Forbes, at the same place, in the ward of the public hospital at Mount Druitt, in outer Brisbane. Len asked if I wanted to come. 'I'll miss school,' I said. He said school could wait. 'Sometimes there are more important things than school.' Mother was not happy about the travel plans, but given the circumstances and Len's health, she would hardly object.

In the cab from Brisbane Airport Len warned me not to show any signs of shock or horror at what I might see in the iron lung ward of the hospital. Tom Forbes was in poor health and mightn't have long to live. I only needed to introduce myself as Tick Tock's grandson to explain my presence. Len advised me to listen closely to Tom Forbes, as the mechanical whooshing of the iron lung machine, would make him hard to hear.

Tom Forbes was in the third machine from the end in a ward of a dozen patients, only their heads showed from the great metal cans that kept them alive. The hydraulic push and whoosh of air for each machine rose and fell, as if it was the synchronised breath of a single living organism. Each artificial breath came and went like it might be the last.

Paul Moore, our solicitor, Len and I formed a semicircle where Tom Forbes's head protruded from the machine. He had seen us coming through a mirror attached to the back of the iron lung machine.

Tom gave a knowing, wan attempt at a smile, twisting his head very slightly as he spoke. 'Back so soon.' Due to a shortage of breath, he spoke monosyllabically and deliberately like, 'back-so-soon.' His head looked tiny and as if it was bolted on to the iron lung machine which, itself, resembled a 1950s robot lying on its back. When he moved his head, I kind of expected the whole tank-thing to make a corresponding adjustment.

Len adjusted his position forward a half step so that Tom could look more directly at him. "Brought the heav-y ar-till-er-y.' He tapped a knobby finger on my arm and I introduced myself.

'Tick Tock's grand-son, eh?' Tom Forbes said.

Maybe the freckles made the resemblance hard to see.

'We wanted to talk to you a little more about Shady Green,' Len said.

We looked at Tom Forbes in the rear-view mirror in the same way we would if we were in the back of a taxi, and he was in a sense a long way away, miniaturized by the dimensions of the little rigged-up mirror.

'Do you know where he is?'

'He comes and goes,' he answered.

'But he's up here? In Brisbane?'

'Likes it warm, you know?'

The overhead fans whirred slowly and noiselessly through the thick Queensland air. A nurse in flat, white shoes padded softly down the aisle between the two banks of machines. Len took a further step forward so that he was in front of Tom Forbes's slightly inclined face. The repetitive soft compressor-like pulse of the machines beat the still air in a steady, muffling hush, a permanent reminder for everyone to be quiet.

Len moved his good ear closer. 'You know Tick Tock died?'

Tom's head shifted and his eyes met Len's. 'Word gets round.'

'Left this Shady Green with most of what he had,' Len said, in a voice that had ratcheted up in volume just a little.

'Is that right? Well now. Great shame tho' his dy-in' when he did.'

'Why's that?' asked Len.

'The ros-a-ry beads. Af-ter all these years lost he would have got Pat-rick's ros-a-ry beads back.'

Len and I knew nothing about rosary beads.

Tom Forbes worked his mouth. 'Shady could-n't wait to give 'em to Tick Tock.'

'What do you mean, rosary beads?' Len persisted.

'Tick Tock's eld-est boy, Pat-rick. Shot by a Jap snip-er. In the jun-gles of New Guin-ea.'

'But these rosary beads I've never heard about them,' said Len.

'Had 'em when he died. Dig-ger mate took 'em off him for safe-keep-ing. The Nips got him lat-er too. Then no one

knew who they be-longed to un-til an old dig-ger mentioned them to Shad-y up here in Bris-bane and he tracked
'em down and i-den-ti-fied 'em.'

Tom Forbes stopped to take a big gulp of air. 'He'd be on
the way down to Melb-ourne, for sure,' he said.

Len nodded in agreement and produced the newspaper
clipping from his pocket, unfolding it in front of him. 'Ever
heard of My Time Flies?'

A complex grid of creases mapped the concentration of
Tom Forbes's old face. 'Oh sure.'

'The racehorse.'

'Sure, the race-horse in the…,' Tom wheezed, and tried
to adjust his position in the chamber, 'race-fix.'

'He told you about that?'

'Tick Tock told me.'

'About the race-fix?'

'Tick Tock had nought to do with it. He just got luck-y.'

'Tick Tock didn't tell you about Shady Green?'

'What 'bout him?'

The effort to speak might have been tiring Tom, who
closed his eyes. Never before had death and life seemed
so close together. I counted ten discrete whooshes of the
machine before Tom finally opened his eyes and turned to
me.

'Got an itch. Driv-ing me cra-zy. Care to help an old
man…a good friend of Tick Tock's?' he asked.

Len told me to put my hand through the lowest porthole
in the chamber, the one nearest the bottom of his leg. I
reached tentatively through, and scratched the blue cotton
of a hospital gown.

'Low-er,' he said. 'It won't kill you.'

I scratched lower and harder and Tom closed his eyes
seemingly in some zone of pleasure.

'Does-n't take much to make an old man hap-py, does it, son?'

My hand worked away at his leg.

'You can stop now,' he said. Tom Forbes looked up in the mirror at the faces that stared back at him. 'If Shad-y Green is like most old things, they pick a peace-ful and fav-our-ite place to go when it's their time.'

'Is he dying?' Len asked.

Tom Forbes signalled with his head, that he would like someone to rub his face with a flannel that lay alongside where his head rested. Len took the flannel and gently wiped his brow, and when Tom Forbes wiggled his lips, duly moistened his lips as well.

'Shad-y's got the em-phe-se-ma so it'll be get-tin' him some time. But with the beads on him he'd be headin' Tick Tock's way for sure.'

'To Tick Tock's?' asked Len.

'Of course. What did they call it? That place he spoke of all the time…as if it was the best place on earth…a fun-ny sort of place…a type of fact-or-y…I think…thought it was a spec-ial kind of place.' Tom clearly struggled to remember what this place was called. 'He's a bit of a strange one is Shad-y. A bit sort of mys-tic-al.'

'Was it the Ballet Shoe Factory?' I asked.

Tom gave a stifled laugh that strained the muscles of his face. 'That be it young fell-a.'

'The Ballet Shoe Factory?' queried Len.'

Tom Forbes nodded his head quite vigorously. 'Yeah. Bit of the black-mag-ic in him. Know what I mean?'

Tom Forbes shut his eyes. The effort to talk had exhausted him. The nurse came alongside the bed, took one look at Tom Forbes and said that would have to be enough for the day.

*****

On the flight back Len's head lolled about in a fitful sleep, jerking him awake with abrupt, loud snores. I sat beside him saying prayers that would ensure our safe arrival back home. In sleep he looked older and mortal, and when he started awake it was as if he'd seen a genuinely frightening thing. The whites of his eyes were shot through with red, and he'd begun to yell before he realised that whatever it was, had not got him yet. I wished whatever he was thinking would go away, and wondered for just a moment, what life would be like if he was dead.

TWENTY-FOUR
A STRAPPER'S TALE (UNDER THE GRAND-STAND)

To read the Strapper's Tale was like reading the story of a movie I'd seen long ago. Where the words conjured up distant almost forgotten images and made them clear and bright. Side by side I'd sat with Tick Tock in the chook pen, hanging on every word of the most wonderful story I'd ever heard. A story that came back to life with every page I turned:

It was not long before the strapper came to the conclusion that it might not be such a bad idea to spend a little time out of sight and out of danger. The plan he'd hatched to go to Brisbane could wait. And so it was settled between the two young men that the strapper would stay for a few days, at least until the ruckus at the tote and the track had died down, and he'd a chance to think things over.

A few days stretched to a week and from a week to a month. In that time the two young men lived as closely together as two people could. It was only as night fell that the strapper typically became restless, and the knowledge of the darkening shadows in the outside world cloaked him with the courage to leave the safety and secrecy of the tunnel alone. The young man, too, would also routinely leave the tunnel about this time, returning with neither food nor any indication of where he had been. One time the strapper had asked where he had gone and he'd been told in an angry voice to mind his own business. But on this night, when the strapper knew it was almost the time for him to leave the tunnel, he decided to follow the young man on one of his evenings out.

The strapper tracked his companion's twilight shadow from a distance, aware of the young man's uncanny ability to see and navigate in near darkness. From time to time the young man disappeared from view and he would hustle along in his anxiety not to lose him altogether. The moon was full and in the open wasteland along the river, the strapper hugged the low coastal vegetation. All the while a southerly breeze beat steadily into his face.

For a time the lighthouse beacon at Gellibrand Point seemed to point the way. But then the young man veered away from town and across the windswept Williamstown racetrack in the direction of the old grandstand. The strapper hitched his old jacket high about his neck as the wind whistled through him. In the dark shadows of the grandstand, the young man disappeared from view. The strapper quickened his step. A minute or so later the strapper stood, guardedly, where he thought he had last seen him. He climbed about the stonework until he came upon a set of stone stairs that led underground. Down he went, one slow step at a time, securing his purchase on the sandy surface that covered each step, before safely moving to the next. Soon there was no light above and only a square of darkness before him, having reached some kind of landing or entrance. The darkness beckoned him onwards.

The room was simple, square and genuinely tomb-like and the young man was on his hands and knees in the middle of the room with a candle on one side of him and the shining light of a lamp on the other. He was rummaging through a small bag, distinctly blue in colour, a sort of navy blue. The young man must have sensed the presence of the strapper and turned around. Even though some distance away, the strapper could see the concentrated expression upon the young man's face. The young man momentarily registered the strapper's presence and then turned his attention back to the bag.

At some stage in the telling of the story I remember that Tick Tock had stopped. He had told me in a serious tone that this was a very grown-up story. My eyes must have looked at him in wonder and anticipation. Tick Tock said he wanted to tell me because I would find out later, this sort of thing always got out and he wanted to tell his side of it. The trouble with people, he said, was that their minds were all made up and that was most of the reason that the world got into the trouble it did. He said I was young and my mind was not made up, and that in some ways, I was very like him. I remember telling him that I didn't think I was anything like him, as he was old and whiskery and grey and I went to school. He may have smiled I don't quite recall.

Then the rooster had come out and began to run amok. After Tick Tock had shooed the rooster away the chicks were still in a very excited state, squawking and dancing across the straw and going in and out our feet. Tick Tock bent down and picked up one of the fluffiest chicks. He informed me that although the chick was only a humble little creature, it learnt all the same. It had eyes and ears and something would come of all the things

it saw and heard, and some of these things it saw and heard,
would stay with it forever. Tick Tock said if he could not tell
this story to me, he would tell it to nobody. The story, he said,
would come to me from far away and it may not reach me for
a very long time. 'By the time it reaches you, I think you will
understand,' he said. 'Will it be travelling as fast as the speed of
light?' I asked. No, he said it wouldn't be travelling anywhere
near as fast as that, but like all the rays of light you don't see
coming or going it would one day just be there, and you would
know when it was.

The strapper heard the faint whir of a zip unzipping.
Reaching into the little blue bag, the young man took out
a number of objects. What they were he could not see. So
by the shadowy and flickering light of the candle he crept
a little closer.

With his head bowed the young man told the strapper
that the little blue bag was a Navy issue bag that he'd got
when he signed up for fighting in the War. It seemed to the
strapper that his companion didn't look like any returned
soldier, certainly not a sailor. The young man had read his
thoughts and said he had fought in no war. 'But the bag?'
inquired the strapper. The young man explained that every
sailor gets a bag even those that in the end don't choose to
go and fight. 'But how'd you get to sign up?' inquired the
strapper, the question betraying no small measure of mysti-
fication. 'They can't make you, can they?' 'No,' replied the
young man, 'they can't make you and they can't stop two fool
boys volunteering if they're of a mind to either.'

He explained that it all happened on the spur of the
moment, after he'd drunk half a flagon of sherry with a mate,
who he said everybody knew was nuts. Down to the enlistment office they'd gone as full as ticks. If only the old navy

enlistment officer hadn't been so old and his eyesight not so poor they would never have made it through. He said the true gravity of the trouble he'd likely brought upon himself only dawned on him when he was handed the little blue navy bag with the words, 'Guard this with your life.'

Honestly, the young man said, until that day he'd never given the War a lot of thought. It was always in the papers and on the radio, of course. But his Pa had died before it started and he'd no uncles who could have gone. All he had was a bugger of a step-pa, forever drowned in grog, who showed no propensity for 'venturin' beyond, what his Ma called, the Devil's Triangle of local hotels.

It was two months later the young man said that his ma got an official letter hand-delivered to home. Just from the official crest on the outside of the envelope his ma guessed what it might be about without opening it, just like he did. She handed it to him without a word. He had to report for training at the Naval Dockyard at 0800 hours on the 15th March 1918. The young man said he threw the letter to the ground and said he wasn't going. 'But the letter,' she'd said. 'They'll make you go.' 'I'll hide,' he'd replied. 'Where?' Her speechless face had drawn a blank. 'I've found a place,' he told her. But he couldn't tell her where the place was. All he said was that he'd be safe. She should tell the authorities that he'd gone bush looking for work.

'Doesn't everyone want to fight for their country?' I'd asked. Tick Tock said the fighting was very far away. On the other side of the world. They're always fighting over there my nine-year-old self informed Tick Tock. To me Europe was a warring place. That's what they did. Napoleon and Bismarck and Hitler the whole lot of them were Europeans and fighting was what they seemed to do most.

The young man stopped speaking and in his eyes was a look of innocence and wrongdoing and a shy searching for forgiveness. The strapper understood that the young man had deserted, he had refused to go and fight. 'Why didn't you go?' the strapper asked, 'Did you lack the guts?' The young man replied that he didn't know whether he had the guts or not. All he knew was that he wasn't ready to kill anyone. The strapper knew that his companion was not the sort of man he would ever call a coward. He had saved his life and cared for him in the tunnel. He couldn't help but feel pity for someone that he now considered a friend.

'What was in the bag?' The strapper had asked. 'That my friend,' replied the young man, 'is the greatest secret of all.'

TWENTY-FIVE
HOWARD VEERS FROM THE SCRIPT

Howard had delivered a large envelope containing sketches of a set design he was working on. It was for a production of *Hair, The Ballet*, in what would be a spin-off of the spectacularly successful, *Hair* the musical. But what about *Cabaret*? Hadn't we agreed on a production similar to that? And a ballet? This was no *Cabaret*.

I was aware that parts of *Hair* were performed in the nude, so it was with both misgivings and some excitement that I removed the drawings from the envelope. There was one large drawing and two smaller ones, all drawn to scale with multiple architectural perspectives. The overt psychedelia of the original *Hair* production had taken on a more militaristic and apocalyptic aspect, and if the profusion of tropical foliage and the bamboo hut set was any guide, the urban revolution had shifted to the jungle of, presumably, Vietnam.

Howard had sent a note accompanying the sketches,

Dear Michel
Enclosed are preliminary sketches for the sequel to the blockbuster production of *Hair*, to be titled, *Hair, The*

Ballet. Can't you just see the headline on the opening night: *Ballet Shoe Factory Lives Up To Its Name?*

I know we spoke about *Cabaret,* but on reflection, I think this will work much better. I am, like your father, quite an enthusiast of the right type of musical, and I want to follow up quickly on the huge success we had with *Hair* (I was an associate producer on that). At the same time I want to *work* the anti-war theme as hard as we can (I'm sure you'll agree with me on that one!). You'll be wondering, I'm sure, that 'This is a ballet not a musical.' Yes, a ballet has to have dancing, but it's also got to have music. I propose a score comprised of the biggest hits of *Hair,* the Musical and a smattering—perhaps your father has some ideas on this—of popular songs from other musicals like *Cabaret.* Also bear in mind, what better opening night for The Ballet Shoe Factory than the performance of a ballet.

My initial idea is to allow the public access to as many parts of the pre-production phase as possible. The general thinking here is audience involvement. Along the lines of, where we get the audience to join in with the cast in the last Act of *Hair* (the Be-in), and taking it that little bit further. The advertising pay-off from this early public engagement should not be discounted. Flesh sells tickets. Believe you me!

I've had another wander around the Ballet Shoe Factory and I think it is even more suitable for the theatre than the first time I had a look. It's a perfectly wonderful place to mock-up the set design. I'm already moving on that.

Let me know your thoughts,

Howard S.

P.S

To give you some idea of dimensions, if you look at the big sketch of Saigon, that will stretch well over half the length of the very large part of the premises that faces the backyard and those beautiful trees.

Was Howard proposing that the public be invited to what would, in effect, be naked rehearsals of the play? Was that what he meant? A chorus line of dancers with luxuriant tufts of pubic hair danced before my eyes. In the wings of the stage stood the police and the vice squad shaking their heads at the rampant, moral squalor that cavorted brazenly and without any inhibition. The fellows swirled their private bits like propellers and the women almost uniformly looked dreamily into the middle distance, stripping petals from the stems of flowers until, the deflowering accomplished, they stroked the clean, long stems in a none too subtle sexual reference, which even the Old Plod would decipher as acts that had all the criminal elements they needed for grossly obscene behaviour. One by one as the chorus line shimmied within reach of the wings, the vice squad would hook them off the stage, a constable's hat covering the offending parts.

Howard Starr had recovered from the shock of his impending eviction from the storeroom at the back of the University Theatre. This kid, Michel White, had arrived like manna from heaven. Howard kicked himself for not thinking of moving off-campus sooner. Suburban theatres in Carlton and Fitzroy were flourishing, Why not leafy bayside Williamstown, the historical heart of Melbourne?

As far as Howard could work out, the Ballet Shoe Factory was in great shape, even if it was abandoned. He'd been around to visit three times to make certain of its suitability, and not once had anyone been there.

Howard thought he had a better chance of convincing Michel White of the merits of *Hair, The Ballet*, if he could erect all the major sets upon the Ballet Shoe Factory site itself. He wasn't sure the kid would really understand how good it could be, without him seeing the real thing. He did not want to take the chance of putting together a few flimsy sketches and a toy-sized mock-up, and then the kid showed them to his old man, who simply dismissed them over a TV dinner. No, he would go all out to impress him, knock his socks off.

After dabbling with the idea of *Cabaret*, Howard decided that a sequel to *Hair*, in the form of a ballet, had the makings of another blockbuster for him. He would leave the prospect of nudity open to speculation for as long as possible to pique public interest, keeping the outrage of newspapers and TV proprietors at least warm. The set design would be psyche-delic and alarming. The war would be ever-present and he had an idea for a small dirigible—something the size of a Japanese mini-submarine—that would float above the stage, and in a climactic ending explode in a massive gelatinous burst, the smell of burning petrol—artificially contrived—overpowering and frightening and he hoped, unforgettable for the audience.

The walls would be veritable frescoes of hippie power and Haight-Ashbury, the symbol of peace and love everywhere. The scale of the production meant that the sets would need to be assembled inside the Ballet Shoe Factory. The exquisite little carpenter's model he turned in his hands did little justice to his grand vision. Howard gazed upon the model, turning it this way and that, as he weighed up the risks of surprising Michel and building the full set design. Whether or not the Ballet Shoe Factory was actually Michel's, he refused to dwell upon. What harm would be done? He was hardly damaging the place. If they didn't like it, well, he'd dismantle it all and take it away. The bigger risk was that the kid or his father didn't buy the idea, and peering at the model, he was not convinced that it was enough. He would take the chance. The set designs were in full-miniaturised mock-up as it was, they wouldn't take long to complete.

'Big envelope.' Mother said walking past. 'I told you about those swimming pool brochures.'

I pushed the drawings back inside the envelope. 'These are the last. Promise.'

Mother grimaced and shook her head.

The image I had of naked dancers sashayed across her chest. My heart spluttered at how shocked she would be, if she knew, that I was capable of conjuring a pornographic movie in which she sort of starred. Tits and bums revolved around Mother so that she was no less than a projector screen for my involuntary, carnal imagination.

I blinked forcibly three times in an effort to switch the images off.

'Are you all right?' she asked. 'Have you been taking your drops?'

She was referring to both my susceptibility to conjunctivitis and the blinking she associated with its onset.

'Yes,' I said.

'You'll be as blind as those poor aborigines if you don't,' she warned, the equation between blinding glaucoma and a garden-variety non-existent conjunctivitis was virtually complete.

If not for the irrelevant warnings about the swimming pool brochures and Len's illness, I might have summoned the courage to show Howard's sketches to him. Len had not gone into work for the third time this week. Invariably, he was to be found propped up in bed, in front of an 11 inch portable TV, that sent him dozing off, with his mouth wide-open, and *The Power of Positive Thinking* splayed on his chest. In his intermittent, but prolonged rests at home, Len had become an expert on soap operas, and acquired a couple of favourite shows that he couldn't bear to miss. Mother said it was unbearable having him around all the time; he'd even offered to cook, which was something she would never allow. She didn't want Len in the kitchen, he might reorganize everything.

The dialysis treatment was for Len little better than being on artificial life support. Apparently, the waiting list for a kidney donor was about two years. Len couldn't believe—when young healthy people were dying in droves on the roads—that there could be such a long wait. While he knew that hospitals couldn't just tear a kidney out of every corpse that came their way, he wanted something done. That very week he'd prevailed upon Mother to go into the Royal Melbourne Hospital and sign the whole family up for organ donorship. A kind of public commitment, that he hoped, in its own small way, would strike a chord with those at the front line of organ administration and assist, more specifically, in getting Len further up the donor queue. Esther and I had taken great umbrage that as guardians of our welfare, he and Mother had signed away bits of us to God-knows-who. 'Why do you care?' he'd asked. Esther had inquired with caution—not at all sure of the answer that would be forthcoming—if he'd personally take the still warm kidneys from his children's barely stopped breathing bodies, if we were amongst those, run over by the proverbial bus. There might have been a twinkle in Len's eyes when he replied that he couldn't see any reason why not. Esther stormed off. Although it didn't help that the lead item on the News that was running in the background, featured an horrific multi-fatality pile-up on the Hume Highway.

Apart from the developing saga of Len, the biggest news was confirmation from our solicitors, that in the absence of Shady Green being found within the next four weeks, Tick Tock's will would be probated in my favour. This news prompted me to buy a pocket diary into which I posted two entries, one for today and one in four weeks time,

Diary Entry
Tuesday 23 November 1969

Found out today when Mother was talking to Myra on the phone and she did not think I was around (let alone listening), that the will would be probated before Christmas, if this Shady Green can't be found.

P.S I looked up probate in the dictionary and it is apparently when the executors of the will can tell whoever needs to know, that the new owner is a certain someone else, which in this case is me.

In a sign of optimism, in much the same way, as I would have counted down to Christmas when I was younger, in carefully placed crosses on a calendar, I made an entry in the diary four weeks ahead.

Diary Entry
Tuesday 23 December 1969

I am reliably informed that by this date the keys to the Ballet Shoe Factory will be mine for good. Len is in and out of hospital so that has slowed him down in his search. But there is always Aunt Myra and Uncle Alf to worry about, as they go on and on about getting their fair share. Mother worries that they might take it to court. Len tells Mother they know they'd lose and besides, they might enjoy having something to complain about for the rest of their lives. Anyway, they've really stirred up the other relatives into getting 'their share' and they're coming around tonight, and I've suddenly realised that I should be writing this under today's date 23 November 1968, and so am in two minds, whether I should cross this out and rewrite it in there.

As my diary noted, Aunt Myra and Uncle Alf were coming around tonight. I would make myself scarce, but did not intend to miss a thing. The living room had good acoustics; what they said would carry to my little nook in the hallway.

Aunt Myra began by saying that it wasn't fair that a young boy (she didn't even use my name) could acquire something of so much value. Mother interrupted and reminded her that they'd been through all this before. Len then said it was no 'cast iron certainty' that I would get anything. Aunt Myra made a sort of snorting sound of disbelief that this unknown fellow—Shady Whateverhisname—was anything other than the product of imagination. Aunt Myra asked Uncle Alf to speak and there was a bit of a gap in the discussion, until Uncle Alf could be heard to say, that they might have to sell the house to pay for a course of treatment for his condition. Mother asked, 'Which condition would this be?' Aunt Myra erupted and accused Mother of never having liked her. I heard a few sniffles, which I figured was Aunt Myra, and that meant a real bout of the waterworks wasn't far away. Len, in a quiet and tired voice said, that if they needed a little financial help from him, they should ask for it. I crawled to where the hall met the living room and stuck my head around.

Aunt Myra was not appeased. 'It's not the point. It's not the point at all.'

To which my mother responded in a spray of exasperation, 'What is the point, Myra? Tell us, what is the point?'

Knowing Mother as I do, she would have been suppressing news of Len's dire kidney condition with some effort. She would have loved to sock that news to Myra like a killer uppercut, but she knew Len would not approve. Len didn't win by having people feel sorry for him.

Was there the potential for the opening up of negotiations? Myra seemed to think so, replying in a confidential tone, 'Surely there is enough for all of us. After all, we're not greedy. Can't we just have a bit of an understanding, nothing in writing mind, that after the will is probated, that the Ballet Shoe Factory will get sold and we all get an equal share of whatever it's worth.' Aunt Myra had never sounded so reasonable.

There must have been a full ten seconds silence before Len spoke. 'But Myra, that's not what Tick Tock asked to happen. And in any event we may get nothing.'

Her chest heaved with frustration. 'You're not on about this Shady Green Whatshisname nonsense again are you? I wouldn't have thought you of all people would be sucked in by that.'

Some diplomacy was clearly in order. 'Look, Shady Green is quite real. We just haven't found him yet,' Len replied with an even-handedness that probably surprised himself.

Aunt Myra said she didn't believe any of it; he was just making it up. Len assured her that nothing was being made up. Why, he asked, would they make it up? Myra responded that she didn't have the answer to everything. 'This is all smoke and mirrors, so Michel gets the lot, isn't it? That's what it's all about, isn't it? We all stay blindsided by this non-existent person until it's all too late and hey presto you get the lot.'

Len told Myra and Alf about Tom Forbes in the iron lung machine.

'Now you're listening to some character in an iron lung machine rather than your own flesh and blood.'

Len said that Tom Forbes thought Shady Green might be headed this way. He didn't mention the rosary beads. That sort of thing would upset Mother.

Aunt Myra clapped her hands together. 'Holy smokes Len and why wouldn't he? You think that's some kind of coincidence? A final journey? He's coming to collect, Len, that's what he's coming to do. Coming to collect at,' she was on her feet now pointing at everyone in the room, including a finger pointed disconcertingly at the stairs to signify all the children upstairs, ' all our expense.'

Len's face seemed confused as to what he might say next.

It might have seemed to Myra that standing up was unduly confronting and so she resumed a seat. 'OK,' she said, 'Just to make sure everything is on the up and up…what I mean to say is… to make sure we're looking at this the right way, why don't we all go and meet this Tom Forbes character?'

There was no hesitation in Len's reply. 'I don't think that's a good idea.'

'Why ever not?' she asked.

'The man is dying, he doesn't need a posse at his bedside.'

Mother had maintained an admirable reserve until this point, but no longer. 'Myra, it's got nothing to do with you or Alf or me for that matter. Haven't you asked yourself, why Dad left the Ballet Shoe Factory to this Shady Green in the first place? Have you asked yourselves that?'

'Don't need to. Tick Tock was not himself when he died. That's the only explanation any of us need. Besides you're just saying this because of Michel.' Myra folded her arms to mark the significance of what she had said.

Len answered the claims. 'Tick Tock was as sane as you or I. The fact that he kept to himself is no sign of madness, nor is tending to the chooks as much as he did, for that matter. It's a puzzle why he left it to this Shady Green and I don't have an answer for that, yet. But I will find it.'

'Spying now are we?' Esther's voice floated over my shoulder.

I rose slowly from the soft cushion of the carpet.

'You're the one with all the answers, aren't you, sport? I mean you know why, don't you? Poor old Len, sick as he is, traipsing around the country, when you know already.'

'I told them about Shady Green,' I answered less than honestly.

'You told them bugger all, sport, and you know it.'

She, of course, was right.

'I'm right aren't I? You've hardly told them anything, have you, sport?'

I wished she'd stop calling me, sport.

'You're actually quite a devious little bugger, aren't you? I've caught you out before in your disgusting little habits,' the pissing on the lawn in druid-like circular formations, clearly at the forefront of her mind, 'and this spying and skulking here is just another side to your deceptive and warped personality.'

I was very tempted to hold up the mutilated finger, but without a wider audience it wouldn't have had the same effect. 'I don't have time for this.'

'We all saw you in the chook pens with Tick Tock. We saw him talking to you all those times. Yabbering on at ten to the dozen when we couldn't get a word out of him. He told you everything about this Shady Green. He did, didn't he? That's what he would have been talking about all those times and that's where he would have told you. Isn't it?'

'Is that you, Esther?' It was Len.

'Yes, dad,' she said, sweetly and distinctly. In a much lower voice she added, 'I'm up here with the craven, little creature who would otherwise be known as your eldest son.' She poked her tongue out.

'Why don't you come out and say hello to your Aunty Myra and Uncle Alf,' Len called out.

'OK, just a minute,' Esther shouted, her voice loud in the hallway and at odds with my undisclosed presence. And under her breath, 'And why not your perverted eldest son as well, who listens in on conversations, and might care to confess some of his nasty little habits…which includes being less than truthful and…'

I retreated down the hallway.

'Coward,' she called out.

'Bitch.'

'Ooo, now I know I'm right.'

It was disturbing that my sister was so close to the truth. She had always had a sixth sense about such things. What as good as broke her heart was she'd never been able to prove my guilt on anything that really mattered.

TWENTY-SIX
VIVIAN UP CLOSE AND PERSONAL

Stunned by an afternoon which had ended in a double-period of religious instruction, I staggered from bus to train to yet another train like a punch-drunk featherweight. Kenny reefed the carriage door open and I followed in his slipstream. We had not exchanged a word on either the bus or the train. Spending time with Kenny could involve long periods of silence. It was as if Kenny knew what I would say, before I had even thought of it. He'd say, 'Don't even think it, friend.'

I was so disconcerted by Kenny that I didn't notice Vivian sitting directly opposite us with her legs crossed. She was reading *Jane Eyre*, the waterfall of hair covering her eyes. Her fringe so straight it drew a line like an eyebrow sectioning her head into a top and a bottom part. Yet she was still so painfully pretty.

My eyes dipped to the schoolbag in my lap.

There was no indication she even knew I was there.

'Weakness of the flesh?' uttered Kenny in a low, instructive, vibrating voice that approached in pitch the hollowness of an echo. Kenny visually examined me. Was my most heartfelt desire so obvious?

Brenda stormed into the carriage and dropped down next to Kenny. 'How's it going, handsome?' she ventured. For the Kenny of old there would have been no finer opening line than that.

Kenny forced a smile and a slight tilt of his braced neck in recognition.

'Still a bit sore?' she inquired, her teeth bared in a wince of shared pain.

I heard their conversation as if they were on the other side of the world.

What if Vivian had some massive disfiguring scar right across her forehead? A big Z for Zorro thing?

'You've got to get out more, Kenny,' worried Brenda, her fair, dark moley arm draped solicitously over one of his knees.

In that kindly, almost morally patronising way that was becoming Kenny's standard form of delivery, he replied, 'Brenda, those friends of yours are doing me no favours at all.' Kenny referred to the girls at the party who had taken a singular interest in turning him away from God, as if God was the enemy of sex, and to have sex with Kenny would show Kenny how wrong God could be.

Brenda was somewhat nonplussed. In a voice only Kenny and I could hear, she whispered, 'You still like girls, don't you?' Her voice quavered in desperation.

Kenny looked her straight in the eye. 'Not in the way you mean.'

'Oh Kenny, please don't say that.' Brenda shrank back against the seat.

There was no hate or ill will evident on Kenny's face, no sign of seeking revenge. Kenny was knuckling down to a lifetime of celibacy. 'I couldn't be happier,' he said with real authority.

'But how…' Brenda began to say. 'But how can you just turn your back on…it?'

Kenny stood and patted Brenda on the shoulder. 'Don't worry so much. It's the best thing that could have ever happened.' He cast his coat over his shoulder and wandered into the next carriage to join the other boys, whose level of care for Kenny's new social orientation did not match Brenda's.

Brenda watched him leave with a determined and sad expression upon her face. She growled in exasperation and slid forward on the seat, proclaiming, 'I'm not giving up on that boy, yet.'

In his own way Kenny was exhausting. It was impossible to relax or think of anything other than Kenny's transformation while he was in the vicinity. To change the topic I said, 'Gerry said to say hello.' This was a total fabrication.

Brenda eyed me with a guilty expression. 'I was too afraid to ask.'

'He's much better.'

'Is he? I really thought he might…you know.' She wrote Gerry's obituary with a shrug of shoulders.

I thought Vivian might have looked up from *Jane Eyre*. Something had moved, maybe she'd turned a page.

'Oh no. He's fine.'

Brenda's face brightened.

I felt compelled to say, 'Well he's not that fine he's still in hospital.'

Her face tightened as if she'd recalled the knife going in.

'Hell of a scar,' I said. 'Cuts right across his shoulder.' I made a diagonal cutting motion across my shoulder blade.

'Don't…' she said, 'I can't bear to think about it. Kenny and Gerry in the same week. I feel so responsible.'

In an effort at maturity, as much for Vivian as for Brenda's benefit, I said, 'The idiot who stabbed Gerry is the only one responsible. That's who they've got to find.'

Vivian's presence made conversation difficult. Whenever I snatched a glimpse she was engrossed in the book. I didn't see her turn a page. I teetered on the edge of doing just about anything that would get her to look at me. Mentally, I tried to sweep aside the dire social consequences of failure, as I prepared to do the bravest thing I had done since the apocalyptic occasion of Linda X.

'Why don't you ask her?' Brenda said.

What? I didn't know what she meant.

'Vivian. It was her boyfriend.'

The bikie who stabbed Gerry was Vivian's boyfriend? The guy who almost pissed on me down the side of the garage?

Vivian placed *Jane Eyre* face down on her lap. 'He is most certainly not my boyfriend.'

Brenda stood up. For once it appeared she didn't want to fight. 'Well he used to be. Anyway,' she addressed the question to me, 'do you think Gerry would like me to pay him a visit in hospital?'

One look at Brenda and Gerry's dad would draw only one dark and, as yet, incorrect conclusion. 'He's only able to…ah…see family and …ah…close friends,' I stuttered.

That was Vivian's boyfriend? Don't panic I told myself! He was an attempted murderer, the authorities would have to lock him up.

'Well you make sure you tell Gerry that that was a very chivalrous thing for him to do…to stand up for a girl like that.' She took a couple of steps, her hands gripping the overhead straps, monkey-like, for balance. 'Now,' she said, with a wistful backwards glance, 'for something I can do something about, Kenny Roberts.'

For apparent emphasis Vivian removed the book from her lap and placed it on the seat next to her. 'He is not my boyfriend.'

I looked at Vivian uncertainly.

'The guy who hurt Gerry.' She made sure I knew whom she meant.

'The guy who almost stabbed Gerry to death?' I corrected.

Vivian crinkled her face, mildly annoyed. 'I *used* to go out with him.'

She seemed uncomfortable. Her eyes blinked bewitchingly beneath the fringe. I couldn't think of a thing to say.

'I didn't know he was going to be there.'

'That's OK.' What would Gerry think if he heard me say, that's OK?

'I heard you mention he's going to be all right.'

'Right as rain,' I said. 'Take an awful lot to kill Gerry.' A nine-inch knife had almost done the job.

'She's rather keen on him.'

'Gerry?'

She smiled. 'Kenny'

The smile was a showstopper. A girl had never smiled at me like that: not a trace of derision in it.

'Kenny?' I wanted verification.

Vivian smiled. 'She seems to like him.' She made no attempt to avoid the 's's' as they each slid into a 'th', a little hiss like the tyre puncture of a child's bicycle, a not unattractive sound.

'Oh…yes…she does in a way.' I could hardly tell her that Brenda had helped push Kenny out onto a sexual wasteland.

A few seconds of silence hung in the rattling carriage, the leather strips that dangled from the overhead bars swayed just a little, as the train swept into a corner. A Linda X would—apart from the fact she wouldn't have spoken to me civilly in the first place—have stuck her head back in *Jane Eyre,* and for good measure, raised it above her eye-line to block all view of me and effectively terminate the conversation.

'I hear your grandfather owned the Ballet Shoe Factory.'

I thought her voice sounded rather beautiful. And seeing how she spoke with her eyes, it came across the small distance between us intimately, as if we were at a candlelit dinner alone.

'He died.'

Jesus was that all I could think of! Well of course he'd died. That's why she would have brought it up.

'I'm sorry,' she said. For a moment she gave the impression she might abandon any further attempt at conversation.

'No, of course not. The hospital did it to him.'

'The hospital?' she inquired.

Everybody blamed the golden staph, nevertheless, the laws of slander were quite severe. 'Well he was old, too. That certainly didn't help things.'

She straightened her head. The fringe briefly uncovered her eyebrows: she had a regular pair. And as far as I could see, there was no deforming scar beneath the fringe.

'Brenda told me that you'd inherited the Ballet Shoe Factory. It's the most wonderful house I've ever seen. Like something out of a fairy tale. Have you...inherited it?'

I shrugged. 'Sort of...it depends.'

'What does it depend on?'

If I was not an heir of some kind, would that pretty, auburn head dive straight back into *Jane Eyre*?

'The lawyers are sorting it out.'

'Oh.' She did not understand.

Maybe I should lie outright and condemn the chances of any Shady Green to oblivion. 'I think it's just technical.'

'What will you do with it, then?' She uncrossed her legs. My eyes followed her perfectly bronzed legs. She smoothed her short plaid uniform into the crease of her thighs.

I tried to purge any filthy thoughts, to, as the Brothers would say, 'Get my mind out of the gutter.' Killer would have been in a state of ecstasy in such proximity to what no doubt he could almost smell. If my face matched the contortions of my mind, Vivian probably thought I was in considerable physical pain.

'We're going to put on plays.'

Without a second's hesitation she asked, 'What sort of plays?'

'Like *Cabaret*.'

'Oh. Singing and dancing.' Her snub nose did its best to wrinkle.

'Musicals.'

'You like musicals?'

'My mother and father do.'

'Oh.' She must have thought I'd be a lot of fun.

'We're still working on the script,' I lied.

'Do you write too?'

What did she mean, *too*? What else did she think I did? I thought that the world thought I did nothing.

'I sort of collaborate.'

'Collaborate?'

'We're a sort of team. Howard Starr and me.'

'Howard Starr…that's a name I know.'

I could tell she was mulling the name around in her head.

'He specialises in musicals,' I said.

'When's the first show?'

Was she asking for an invitation? Could this be some kind of date?

'Pretty soon,' I said. Her expression conveyed the need for greater certainty. 'A couple of weeks,' I added.

'How do you get a ticket?'

I looked at her with some vacancy. 'I'll get you one.'

Vivian smiled appreciatively.

The first real date of my life *only* hinged upon premiering a musical.

Brenda sauntered back into the carriage. 'Make love not war,' she said and gave Vivian and me the peace sign.

I gave Brenda a look that said, Sorry?

Brenda snuggled up next to me like I was her kid brother and whispered in my ear, 'Offered to... you know...give of myself...with Kenny...point-blank refused.' She cast a look of helplessness at Vivian. 'Boys, eh?' Vivian gave her that fabulous cave-woman stare from under her fringe.

Brenda sighed. She seemed to be transitioning to another realm of preoccupation. 'Now tell me, Michel White, if the rumours are true.'

I was not the sort of person for whom rumour generally found any interest.

'Come on,' she said, urging me to confess.

Vivian watched with interest.

'What?' I asked.

'Don't you hold out on me Richie Rich. I hear they've offered you a fortune to knock that old Ballet Shoe Factory down.'

Vivian stared at me her eyes blinking.

'I don't know anything about that,' I answered honestly.

Vivian picked up *Jane Eyre* and held it in front of her face. I doubted if she was reading it.

TWENTY-SEVEN
HOWARD STARR ENTERTAINMENT PRESENTS,'*HAIR*, THE BALLET'

Tick Tock might have been horrified to see what psychedelic and fantastic changes had been wrought within his beautiful Ballet Shoe Factory. The effect was surreal and spectacular. The transformation from classic, bespoke, ballet shoe manufacturer so complete, that if it were not for Howard's consistently sympathetic and emblematic use of all things ballet: from ballet shoes to barres to full-length mirrors to the costumes themselves, instantly recognisable in the set design as those from *Firebird, Swan Lake* and *The Nutcracker Suite*, variously arrayed on ceiling-high panels, that revolved as easily as a newsagency's postcard holder, to reveal a different, but just as eye-catching scene, on the reverse sides, you would never have known this had ever been the salon for the making of ballet shoes.

Not *Hair* the musical, this would be *Hair, The Ballet*, a different form of the production, which didn't involve any sell-out of the original or pulling of punches. Indeed the impresario could sense his real potential emergence into the commercial mainstream *and* that of the critically acclaimed.

Something he had not always thought possible, but when he stood back and appraised the near-complete set design from various compass points of the old salon, he now saw as within his grasp.

The windowsill seemed a good place for Howard to liberally fluff his flouncy, black tresses—giving them air he called it—so that in the reflection of the mirror, on the other side of the salon, even he thought he resembled a very credible white version of a hip, afro'd, black American. The thought that he, himself, could be an important and galvanising promotional tool for the production, had more than once crossed his mind. And sitting there, in the reflection of the mirror, it was clear to him that there was no safer or for that matter better pair of hands for the task than Howard Starr.

An appropriate change of business name that might project a more ambitious tone and corporate amplitude was something that Howard had been toying with; a recognition that Howard Starr Theatrical Productions in its plain, dead ordinariness of describing exactly what he did, somehow just didn't seem to cut it. Howard Starr Entertainment had sprung to mind, and despite the populist ring that didn't sit altogether too comfortably with Howard's generally elevated sense of self and taste, he was satisfied, all things considered, that it best described his theatrically corporate future. The flyers and the tickets would be headlined:

Howard Starr Entertainment
Presents
'Hair, The Ballet'

It would not be plain sailing. There was the trademark nudity, one of the hallmarks of *Hair* the musical, and how that could be incorporated within *Hair, The Ballet*. All the nudity business in *Hair* the musical had been massively overblown by the media, confined as it largely was to the entire ensemble gathering just for the finale of the show. But the promoters had always been shy of telling the musical-theatre-going-public exactly how much gratuitous nakedness there actually was, when it was clear that without it, the audience numbers would not be remotely as great.

Howard considered the concept of *Hair, The Ballet* a triumph of inspiration that came upon him like the shattering filament of an incandescent, electric light globe, when the Michel White kid had uttered the words: Ballet Shoe Factory. An integral part of the vision was the male tendency to reduce the whole balletic artistic creation to a ridiculous prancing about in well-stuffed codpieces. Howard would turn this almost pathological male preoccupation on its head, and resolve the need for nudity with the mere hint of nudity, by having the cast perform throughout in flesh-coloured bodystockings. The men would be appropriately upholstered in codpieces of varying shapes and sizes, so that for those for whom the codpiece was a source of some titillation their enthusiasm would be undinted, and for those for whom the codpiece was simply a standard piece of ballet equipment, it would be a case of 'nothing to see.'

Annoyingly he would have to, at least in part, accommodate the White parents' taste in musicals. The kid had mentioned *Cabaret*, which as musicals went was something he could live with. Howard was tossing around the idea of cameoing a role for himself, as Emcee, conducting a cabaret chorus line. There were other sequences of *Cabaret* he was sure he could fit in, without destroying the integrity of his vision for *Hair, The Ballet*.

Above all else, Howard would ride the anti-war sentiment and the rich commercial seam he knew he was tapping into, and which on his rough calculations could be a heart-stopping dollar gross to put him at the top of any pantheon of impresarios.

TWENTY-EIGHT
A STRAPPER'S TALE (THE TIME CAPSULE)

For days I had wondered what could be in that little blue bag. Title deeds? Painting brushes? That book he had in the Cave: *The Arabian Nights?* And then I remembered:

'It's my time capsule,' the young man said referring to the little blue Navy bag and brightening a little. The strapper had no idea what a time capsule was. The young man explained that he knew that his time was just about up, living like he was in a subterranean world. He said he had always wanted to go and live somewhere warm, and the months in the drain hadn't changed his mind. But the time capsule asked the strapper? Mementos of my life nothing more than that he told his companion.

The strapper leant over the bag and peered inside. On top was an old, pink, satin ballet shoe and beneath it packet upon packet of photos bound by string. To satisfy the strapper's obvious interest the young man took out a packet of photos.

The first was a picture of an old lady with a kind plump face, who the strapper wrongly assumed, was the young man's grandmother. The old lady was sitting down. In her lap she had a ballet shoe.

That's Mrs Gorham! That's Mrs Gorham I had cried. I would have recognised her anywhere. Tick Tock said yes, yes I was right and patted me on the knee to be quiet.

The young man said: 'That's Mrs Gorham.' 'Whatever happened to her?' asked the strapper. The young man replied that Mrs Gorham had had a stroke.

I remembered I started to cry. I didn't know what a stroke was but it sounded like another name for dying. Tears ran down my face and under my chin and I did nothing to stop them. My throat tightened and I struggled to breathe. I asked Tick Tock if there'd been a mistake. He told me to listen, listen, but he didn't say she wasn't dead. Although it was just a story it felt like murder to me.

Well, said the young man, early one evening the boys found her lying on the floor of the salon with a sewing needle and a leather insole just beyond her outstretched hand. At first they thought she was dead. Then she opened her eyes.

I was hanging on every word. Mrs Gorham was alive. She was still alive.

She tried to talk. But her words were nothing more than mumbles. With a couple of boys at either end they had loaded her as seemly as they could on the horse and buggy and driven her to the big hospital in Footscray where all the eminent doctors worked. The doctors said it did indeed look like she'd had a stroke and everyone feared the worst. And while Mrs Gorhan didn't die she never returned to the

Ballet Shoe Factory, not for a farewell not for one minute and the boys left one by one. By the time a man looking after Mrs Gorham's business interests showed up to tell the boys that the Ballet Shoe Factory was to be shut down, there was only a handful left: the young man one of them.

I remember thinking this was the saddest day of my life since the time my dog, Scottie, got run over by the nightman.

'And the ballet shoe you see at the top of the bag that's one of Mrs Gorham's,' the young man said in answer to the strapper's prying eyes. Next, he removed from the pile a night-time photo of the Ballet Shoe Factory—an extraordinary shot that bathed the Ballet Shoe Factory in a white halo as if it was an electric light globe and a radiant heat reached from it high up into the atmosphere. The young man declared it as beautiful as any temple: 'It's my *Taj Mahal.*' Then he fanned the photos like they were a deck of cards. Every other photo was of the Ballet Shoe Factory. Not done with, he delved deeper into the bag, extracting an even thicker pack of photos. He fanned these like the first in a wider arc across the floor. Once again every photo was of the Ballet Shoe Factory. There couldn't have been an angle or perspective that he'd missed. It was as if he had been some kind of official photographer of a landmark public building or a shrine.

The strapper's eyes must have betrayed his thoughts. Was his companion of the last couple months not just a bit eccentric but maybe quite odd? Mad, even? The young man asked him if he thought he was crazy? Not crazy exactly, was the strapper's response. His companion nodded sagely. 'Yeah, you think I'm crazy,' he replied. He managed a wry grin. 'I can't explain it. I only wish I could,' he'd said. 'But when I sit outside that beautiful, white house under that big elm tree there's nowhere else I'd rather be.' The strapper listened intently and tried to understand this love for a place, but this admiration, devotion, almost idolatry of the Ballet Shoe Factory was more than curious.

'You are surprised…my friend,' said his companion with a smile because he knew those words of friendship would seem unfamiliar coming from him. Still smiling, the young man reached back into the bag and withdrew a primitive camera. The strapper momentarily recoiled, as he believed he might take a picture of him. Laughing, the young man said he was a bigger chicken than him, a comment that would ordinarily have offended the strapper, but in the circumstances, he felt that he could let pass. His companion told him, that it was to the Ballet Shoe Factory that he stole out every night, armed with the camera. Why not just keep the little blue bag with him in the drain? asked the strapper. The young man replied that he didn't want to get caught with the evidence. He gave the strapper a knowing look that the strapper understood to be a reference to the money in *his* pockets. The strapper asked him about the Navy and what was he going to do about the little blue bag? It being well known that the Navy would search high and low and never rest until they got its property back. The young man said he'd been thinking about that and he was not convinced that taking the little blue bag back would be the end of the matter. The authorities, he said, would pursue him forever, whether he took back the little blue bag or not. 'But what about when the War was over?' inquired the strapper. 'The Navy was a vengeful thing,' the young man replied. Even with the War finished, they'd come and get him and lock him away. The strapper said that he didn't think the authorities would be as bloody-minded as that, but who was he to know, he was only a humble strapper and lookout. 'Why keep the bag at all?' asked the strapper. The young man conceded that this was a good question to which he didn't know the right answer. He said, he could not destroy or abandon what belonged to his country even though it was only a little blue bag.

The strapper told the young man, he wanted to leave soon too. He was thinking of Brisbane, far away from the Cavenagh's Tote. And so it happened that on the following day, the two of them, left the tunnel together like the old friends they now were and caught the train to Brisbane. For a year, the two young men lived together in a boarding house. The strapper pined for his fiancée and the young man pined for his beloved Taj Mahal. The young man had kept some of his photos with him and he carried them everywhere. And ritually, every afternoon, under a big Moreton Bay fig, in a square near Brisbane Central railway station, he'd get the photos out and pore over them. The strapper would watch and wonder if staring alone could wear out the image. And in part he was right—the sun did what staring couldn't; day by day the images faded just a bit, not that the young man seemed to notice or care.

In the meantime, after a year of letters back and forth between the strapper and his fiancée and waiting for a sort of 'all-clear' the strapper's return to Melbourne was arranged and a date set. Maisy had agreed to marry him and big Jim Cavenagh had passed away, removing any lingering doubt that he might still exact revenge. The strapper promised to visit the young man in Brisbane every year, sure as taxes. The young man had said he didn't have to. The strapper insisted that that was what he was going to do. As he said it it all sounded a bit hollow and weak. Was this how he would show his gratitude to a man who had not only saved him from almost certain death but who had befriended him when he was most in need? A man who had asked for nothing in return. A man who had bared his soul to him.

So the strapper got to thinking. And the more he thought the more he came to the realization that there was only one way to express his gratitude because there was only one thing in the world that the young man might possibly want: the Ballet Shoe Factory.

Did he get the Ballet Shoe Factory for him, Tick Tock? Is that what he did? I know I was excited because in the back of my mind I wasn't sure if Mrs Gorham was properly dead. And if the young man had the Ballet Shoe Factory he could give it back to Mrs Gorham or let her come around to visit or something like that. Do you think he should? asked Tick Tock. Yes, yes I cried. He loves it more than anyone. Tick Tock cast a strange look at me, as if he'd seen something new and undiscovered. He hugged me tight, and for a moment, I couldn't breathe. 'Tick Tock,' I cried, 'I can't breathe.'

TWENTY-NINE
'THIS IS NO CABARET'

'Len are you doing anything down at the Ballet Shoe Factory?' Mother inquired with some curiosity, as if she had suspicions that he was.

Len looked up from *The Power of Positive Thinking*. 'Last chapter,' he noted, 'still hasn't told me a thing I don't know.'

I happened to be passing through on the way to the fridge. 'The Ballet Shoe Factory,' I said, half-volleying the question into a proximity with Len, where I knew he could hear.

'What about it?' asked Len.

Mother with a mild frustration, borne of the knowledge, that nothing she said was apparently heard at first instance asked, 'Are you doing anything down at the Ballet Shoe Factory?' The words were uttered slightly slower in the repetition.

Len laid his glasses on top of the book. 'Like what?'

'Marge Froggett just rang and she mentioned all this activity down there as if I knew about…'

I was on the Malvern Star and pedalling flat-out to the Ballet Shoe Factory before Mother had finished the sentence. Half a block from my destination, I could hear the choral strains of *Hair's* anthem, '…Gimme head with hair/ Long beautiful hair/ Shining gleaming/ Streaming flaxen, waxen…' floating across the roofs of houses. By the time I threw the bike up against the fence at the back of the Ballet Shoe Factory, it was clear that a full-scale dress rehearsal was in progress.

Shady scrambled around in the ruins of the grandstand, convinced that the little blue bag would still be buried where he left it over forty years ago. Eventually he found it, covered with weeds and damp sandy soil. With the first wipe of his hand he uncovered the Navy insignia.

Never had the walk back from the old racecourse to the Ballet Shoe Factory seemed so long. To Shady the little blue navy bag was as conspicuous as walking a monkey. For every person he saw coming he turned a corner. For every sound he heard his heart skipped a beat. Scuttling along as fast as he could he finally reached Little Nelson Place. But something was wrong. Up ahead there was an almighty commotion coming from the Ballet Shoe Factory. He approached the high back fence with a measured step and cautiously peeked over.

On the other side, in the backyard, was an extraordinary-looking fellow, pacing up and down outside the window of the salon—golliwoggy in appearance, like one of those Fuzzy Wuzzy Angels in New Guinea that helped the ANZACs during the War. This fellow appeared quite mad, walking about the backyard and peering through windows, inclining his head this way and that, talking to himself about who knows what. Shady, for a time, thought the fellow was talking about fish for he called out 'cod' a couple of times.

Shady smiled at the antics of the man, finding them

increasingly hilarious the more he watched. The man could have been mistaken for giving a paid performance. If Shady had the breath to spare he'd have laughed. A burst of rock music started up from within the Ballet Shoe Factory. It was only then that Shady noticed all the figures moving about in the salon—the crazy fellow had been a formidable distraction. Shady considered going over the fence. He also considered the possibility that the mad, prattling fellow might be odder and more demented than he even looked. The reality that the fellow was a genuinely certifiable, criminal nutcase who had just wandered onto *his* property, couldn't be dismissed lightly.

Mother wasn't wrong! Things were certainly happening at the Ballet Shoe Factory.

An old man dressed in wintry clothes with a bag at his feet —another smaller bag blue in colour squeezed in on top— was peering over the back fence. I kept a cautious distance. A cast of characters cavorted from one end of the salon to the other. At first I thought they were all completely nude. 'Jesus,' I said out loud. Len and Mother and Aunt Myra flashed photographically before me in a foretaste of 'Please Explain'.

'They're good, aren't they?' It was the voice of the old man who had quietly sidled up beside me.

I jumped.

The old man entertained a rueful smile. 'Didn't mean to frighten.'

My first impression was that I had been accosted by a derelict who'd been attracted by cheap, lascivious entertainment. For all I knew, there was a whole sanatorium of his type, up the road somewhere, making their way down. I took a cautionary step back.

The old man seemed to be struggling for breath. 'You ought to see the ringleader. Now he's a marvel. Wait for him.'

I was disinclined to say anything to this rheumy-eyed, dishevelled, oddly sooty-skinned man with a duffel bag by his side.

'Here he comes,' he said, and pointed out Howard Starr pirouetting with a member of the cast.

On the verge of averting my eyes from what I feared was pornographic revelling, I realized that the cast were not nude after all—covered as they were from neck to toe in flesh-coloured body stockings, all too realistically skintight.

My sense of relief must have shown such that the old fellow thought I had acknowledged him in some subtly pleasant and engaging way. His ancient grin broadened.

Back over the fence, Howard had returned inside. I tried to interpret what the set design actually depicted, although the colours struck a visual blow even from a distance. Had Howard listened to a word I'd said? *Cabaret*?

'Is it some sort of theatre?' asked the old man.

I was tempted to say this was a very recent development of which I was only partially aware. 'It's been a bit derelict.'

The old man looked at me a little surprised. 'Doesn't look too derelict.'

No, it appeared more invaded than derelict.

'Don't see much of this where I come from,' commented the old man as he removed his hat and wiped the sweat from his brow.

For a moment I thought he was referring to the brazen acts of apparent debauchery, but when he tried to hum along with the music, I decided he meant the theatrical and musical aspects of the production. 'Where's that?' I asked.

'Brisbane. Not much theatre up there.'

The not so random thought that this old man might

be responsible for the destruction upstairs and the signs of recent habitation began to settle like a fine spray of vermouth over a very dry martini.

'She's a beautiful building, isn't she?' the old man said, his head arched slightly back to frame the Ballet Shoe Factory and the single-engine Cessna that had so far spelt the letters 3 X Y R O C in the sky, and which in another thirty seconds or so, would complete with a K and an S, its message in the sky.

This old man couldn't be, could he, the mysterious, much-sought-after Shady Green? He did seem strangely familiar.

'George,' he introduced himself, and held out a hand.

My insides quivered. He was just as I'd imagined from Tick Tock's story: the colour of his skin, the baggy clothes, his eyes of melted chocolate.

'And who would I be talking to?' the old man inquired.

'Oh,' I said quite forgetting my manners, 'I'm Michel White.'

The old man regarded me closely, adopting a manner that seemed to doubt my identity. 'Are you now?'

Did this old man know me?

'Give us a bunk up?' he asked. The old man apparently wanted to go over the fence.

Instinctively, I cupped my hands like a stirrup. After two failed attempts, he finally managed to wedge an unsteady boot upon my laced fingers, and with a hand balancing upon my shoulder, launched himself over the fence. There was a dull thump from the other side. I scrambled to look over the fence. The old man lay on the ground with his arms outstretched. He looked stunned, but not unhappy, in a state of some genuine repose. 'Are you all right?' I asked.

A curious boyishness played in his eyes. 'Right as rain.'

'You haven't broken anything?'

The old man surveyed the sky and the disintegrating radio station signage upon it. I imagined he was trying to make sense of what 3XY ROCKS were. He clambered to his feet. 'Can you throw my bag over?'

It was not my custom to leap the back fence when I usually had a key to the front door.

'Well, aren't you coming?' the old man asked.

The old man made for the chook pen and I followed at a slight distance. Inside the empty chook pen there was still plenty of evidence of chickens: bits of feather, stale feed and the sharp smell of recent droppings. He circled the chook pen like a rooster looking for hens. At one point he grasped the chicken-wire, his fingers curled around its rough hexagonal pattern, and scanned the backyard, its big tree and the salon. Finally, he sat on the little wooden bench and slapped his knees in a sign of contentment.

When he sat down on the little wooden bench I decided I had no other option but to follow him in. The old man sat nearest to where the rooster would have roosted, in the place where Tick Tock would normally have sat. I took up a position near the gate. The chook pen—for all the care Tick Tock had taken of it—already showed signs of dilapidation: gaps in the grey wood planking and the wire in places rent free of the chook pen's frame. A fix was in order, if it was to be a proper working chook pen, again. Still, I thought, it wouldn't take much. A hammer and a few nails would do it. Len could manage it in no time.

'My grandfather loved his chooks,' I said.

There was the sound of distant laughter from the salon. The old man's breathing laboured audibly in the relative quiet of the chook pen.

'Do you know who I am?' asked the old man.

I forced myself to say the name. 'Shady Green?'

The old man took a deep breath. 'George is my rightful name, but no one calls me that. Val, your grandfather, I believe you all call him Tick Tock, was my best friend.'

'You saved his life,' I said.

'He told you that?'

'Right here, he told me,' and I pointed at the bench.

Shady contemplated the empty space beside him on the little bench, in the manner of someone who could see back in time, and then, suddenly, and seemingly having recollected a matter of importance, he reached down to the duffel bag at his feet and began to riffle through its contents. 'I've got something here you may be interested in,' he said in a sharp intake of breath, cut in half by the effort to bend over. When he raised his head, he had a scroll of papers in his hands: the title deeds to the Ballet Shoe Factory. 'You'll be needing these,' he said.

I reached for the title deeds with an uncertain hand. Could this be true? Or was this a trick of some kind?

Shady pushed the title deeds closer to me. 'Told Tick Tock I never wanted anything like this.'

'But didn't you save his life?' I asked.

'Tick Tock exaggerated.'

'Tick Tock told me the whole story.'

Shady nodded, seemingly impressed. 'Not many people know the full story,' he said.

He waved the title deeds in front of my face. 'Don't you want them?' he asked.

'You're just going to give them to me?'

He pressed the title deeds at me.

'You don't want them?' I asked, amazed.

'No,' he replied firmly, placing the title deeds beside us on the bench. He leant down, rummaged further in his bag and took out some old faded photos of the Ballet Shoe Factory. 'These are more than enough for me.'

'But don't you want the real thing?'

He showed me one of the photos. 'It's all in the head, anyway.'

'But what if I just knock the whole thing over. Destroy it. That's what a developer would do.'

Shady shrugged his shoulders.

'Don't you want to know what I would do with it?'

Shady's eyes blinked wearily. 'What?'

'I've told everyone that I'll turn it into a Performing Arts Centre.'

He gestured to what was going on inside the Ballet Shoe Factory. 'So are you?'

'But it might be worth a lot more if I just knocked it down.'

'That's up to you.'

I looked closely at him. 'But what if you came back next week and it was just a pile of rubble?'

'Look, son, nothing lasts forever, not even me.' He gave a wan smile. 'This place was here for me when I needed it. When I was young and I had nothing. No money. No prospects. I needed inspiration. Something even more than the stars and the planets. Mrs Gorham and the Ballet Shoe Factory gave me that. They were my Taj Mahal.'

'That's why Tick Tock bought it for you.'

'No need. I had it anyway.' And he tapped his knuckles against his forehead. 'I had it all here.'

I was almost angry on Tick Tock's behalf. 'So my grandfather was too generous? It was a mistake leaving it to you? And now you don't care what happens to it? And what about them?' I pointed to the salon where the music blared and the figures twirled. 'All that craziness doesn't worry you?'

Shady narrowed his eyes. 'Should it?'

His nonchalance was infuriating. 'It'd bother me if I owned it.'

'I don't think of myself as the owner,' he went on. 'That's why I want you to have these.' He thrust the title deeds at me again.

'Are you mad?' I blurted. 'It's worth a fortune. My relatives would tear it down without a blink and put up a block of flats on it.'

'What's wrong with flats?'

The old man raised the brim of his hat, so that he had a better view of the tall, grey, ugly complex of Housing Commission flats, rising high above the grand Victorian terraces. 'Places like that give less fortunate people the chance of a decent place to live.'

'*Decent?*' My eyes raked the sixteen-storey pebble-creted monstrosities.

'They'd get good views of the bay from up there,' said Shady squinting into the sun.

I tried again. 'A place like the Ballet Shoe Factory can disappear just like that.' I snapped my fingers as the image of a wrecking ball swung before my eyes. 'You're happy with a bunch of greedy property developers making off with whatever they can out of it?'

Shady now tapped his head twice empahtically with the knuckles of his right hand. 'It's all been up here, all these years. This is where you need to have it—the grey matter. Every time I shut my eyes I can see the Ballet Shoe Factory. Clear as crystal.'

Shady stood up, eyes shut, and stepped through the narrow exit of the chook pen for the broader realms of the backyard. As he walked he described the minor landmarks— the massive elm and the signature at the base, the drain's height against a man that he measured with several chops of his hand against his forehead. When he reached the salon, he spread his arms wide and opened his eyes. '*Voila.*'

In a brutal interruption to Shady's brief demonstration, I asked, 'Why are you here then if not to collect?'

He smiled gently. 'As we get old we get a bit soft and sentimental too. Logic doesn't always win out. But It's lucky that I've come here today because I've bumped into you.'

'Why's that?'

'Well, as I say, I told Tick Tock I never wanted it.' He meant the Ballet Shoe Factory. 'But Tick Tock just went ahead and bought it and put me in the will and all that.' Shady took off his hat and fanned his perspiring face. 'I expect you know about all that now.'

I told him both our names were in the will. Mine after his.

Shady nodded thoughtfully. 'It was the only thing in the end that I wanted. That my Taj Mahal was looked after when I was gone. That it went to a person Tick Tock trusted. That was the important thing.' he said. 'Anyway let's see what all the fun and games inside are. It looks like they're having a party.'

Shady held the title deeds out to me, as if they were the final part of the argument.

Soon we stood at the bottom of the main stairs, bathed in the rosy blush of the atrium's stain glassed windows. Music played loudly. Shrill voices rang out in rehearsed unison, reverberating along the passageway to the salon. When I opened the thick heavy door to the salon I held my breath.

A jungle of tropical fernery and tree-sized pot plants blocked our way. The foliage was thick and heavy, and we needed to push our way through. The density of the vegetation made the salon hot and steamy like a greenhouse.

A conga line of singing cast members, bound together by intertwining coils of green, camouflaging vine threaded its way through the undergrowth. We followed its snaking progress to a clearing on the far side of the salon, which had been transformed into a kind of Vietnamese town square replicating colonial Saigon. In this part of the set the theatrical, militaristic presence was heavy. Soldiers marched backwards and forwards with automatic rifles over their shoulders—marine-like hup two three four hup two three four, a gun carriage with three soldiers dragging it, and upon an overhanging Juliet balcony, jutting out over the salon, several girls wearing traditional white Vietnamese leaf hats, waved and shouted with great enthusiasm at all the soldiers that passed within range. They, too, were in flesh-coloured tights, their apparent nakedness mitigated only by the odd piece of floral decoration.

Howard stood in the middle of what was meant to be a very small paddy field: an improvised irrigation moat full of running water, separated by two thin stripes of a type of faded, yellow material that swayed like wheat in wind. He was giving directions to two actors, one of who was painted jet-black and the other albino-white, the latter's dyed snowy hair falling in a wave over his shoulders.

Howard saw me and waved. 'What do you think?' he yelled. 'I'll be over in a minute.'

What did I think? The scale of the works and the number of people rendered panic futile. I could hardly call something this far advanced off. My brain worked on excuses to Len and Mother that would sheet the blame home to an overly enthusiastic impresario. A weak green light for a mock-up of a set design did not mean wholesale renovations to the Ballet Shoe Factory and an invitation to a cast and crew for a full-scale dress rehearsal.

I mouthed dismay.

Howard strode to our side. 'Fantastic, isn't it? Coming along rather well, don't you think?' He didn't pay Shady any attention.

Shady stared about him bug-eyed. For a moment I thought he might have taken it upon himself to expel the infidels from his holy place, but all he said was, 'Young people certainly know how to enjoy 'emselves.'

I looked into Shady's face for a sense of outrage or genuine shock, something more than—astonishment.

A stagehand called out to Howard, and despite him saying, 'Look I'm right in the middle of something,' he promptly made off in the stagehand's direction.

I guess it was the neighbours or perhaps a passer-by, who must have alerted the police. A Victoria Police riot van pulled up in the lane. Policemen spilled over the fence in a strategic advance that seemed to presuppose resistance and mayhem.

The effect upon Shady was both immediate and awful. His struggle to breathe intensified, clutching at his throat, as if he might dig his way to an air passage with his fingernails. 'The police,' he croaked, distraught, that after all these years they still were after him. Grabbing his bag he lurched through the set and the chaos of a cast that had realised there'd been a raid. While Shady was under no illusions the police had come for him, the cast had little doubt this was the heavy-handed work of the State's Chief Censor, and he was after them. Nor was Howard Starr in any doubt. In defiance, he turned the music up, climbed the little balcony and exhorted the cast to go about their business as if nothing was amiss.

Shady staggered into the backyard.

Through the salon window I watched him struggle to stay on his feet. Should I follow and try and help him?

The police raced throughout the set. The realization

that the cast were not nude apparently deemed insufficient to prevent a general round up. A cop called out, 'Hey there's some kid pervert in here.' I dived into the nearest copse of thick foliage and waited for several pairs of large, black, police-issue shoes to hurry past. 'He went this way,' said one of them. I squinted through palm fronds for a way out through the confusion.

When I reached the backyard I saw Shady and his duffel bag disappear into the drain. I darted after him. Seconds later a voice bellowed, 'I know you're up there.' The police stood at the entrance to the drain, undecided if they'd follow. 'Don't make us come into that bloody cesspool to get you,' one of them warned.

THIRTY
SHADY STRIKES A MATCH

Shady had strained to duck his head beneath the lip of the drain. He knew he'd been crazy to bring that little, blue Navy bag back. Perhaps the authorities would reduce the sentence for good behaviour. After all it was the only wrong thing he'd ever done. No, he thought, it doesn't matter if it's three months or thirty years he wouldn't go to gaol.

The disorientating echo of the drain made it impossible for him to tell the distance of the pursuing voices. An absence of torchlights gave him hope that the police had given up any chase. Some minutes had passed with no sound beyond his own clattering boots and the wheeze of his chest. Shady slowed his pace and soon his breathing resumed a more steady rhythm.

There was an unusual smell in the drain. Shady thought it must have come from a tannery discharge. It was in fact the smell of gas. The emphysema made one smell like any other smell. Shady passed the distinctive odour off as unpleasant and nothing more. Instinctively he knew which way to go. After a time he arrived at the place he had once called home: the Cave. From the duffel bag Shady took out a torch and switched it on. It took a couple of minutes for his eyes to adjust to the thin cylinder of light. But time hadn't dimmed the brilliant colours of the frescos that adorned the wall nor the night sky that twinkled from the otherwise pitch-dark roof. Shady lay down and briefly reacquainted himself with his work. A draught of air from the river channelled down the middle of the Cave, drying the sweat from his face. Although he wasn't hungry, he thought something to eat might make him feel better. He decided he would have a little rest, catch his breath and cool down. Then, refreshed, he'd catch a fish and cook it on the little fold-up gas stove he had brought in his bag. It never occurred to him to wonder if the fish would bite.

Shady's weakened physical state was the only reason I'd managed to stay in touch with the shadowy outline ahead that occasionally came into view, whenever he passed beneath a grille, and was momentarily lit by outside light.

The smell of gas in the drains grew stronger the further I went. It was too late to turn back. Shady was my only way out. I had refrained from yelling or trying to overtake him in the dark, for fear of giving him a fright. But presently, Shady emerged into a wide spectrum of light, and shortly after, so too did I.

Shady knelt in the middle of the concrete floor fiddling with equipment he'd dragged from his bag.

'George,' I said as quietly as a whisper at Sunday Mass.

He raised his head, possibly unsure he'd heard a sound at all, his pupils tiny in the shocking large whites of his eyes.

'What are you doin' in here?' he asked, more in surprise than anger. 'Down here is no place for you.'

'Are you all right? I saw you run off…'

'I'm fine. I'm fine.'

'Just the way you ran off worried me that something

might be wrong.'

Shady beamed. 'You're just like your grandfather, aren't you? Everything is fine. This place is, as you know, like a second home to me. A bit of a rest down here in the quiet and then I'll be on my way.' Shady coughed and wheezed.

My eyes itched. 'Is that gas?'

Shady peered down the tunnel in the direction of the offensive smell. 'The damned tanneries. There should be a law against them. Right,' he said, 'let's get you out of this dusty, smelly old place.'

He led me a short distance to a ladder with metal rungs that ran up the wall of the drain to a manhole cover above. When I reached the top rung he told me to push hard and the manhole cover would prise loose. After several hard shoves the manhole cover lifted and a bright blue sky filled the circular opening. By the time I turned to say goodbye, Shady had gone. I turned and stared into the blackness of the drain, the harsh naked sunlight spotting my vision. For a time I was convinced that he lurked in the shadows. But he had not even waited for me to replace the manhole cover.

Shady extracted the portable gas-fire stove from the duffel bag. He sat the little stove on its folding stand and attached a gas bottle. For the first time, what he smelt, he recognised as gas and, wondering if some of the gas had escaped from the bottle, he sniffed the valve. Shady confirmed to himself a leak he thought to be of no particular consequence, stood up and brushed dust from his hands down the sides of his trousers. 'Right,' he said, 'now for the fish.'

It took longer than he expected to catch the fish. The Kororoit Creek waterline was low. The petro-chemical factories and oil refineries that spread along the creek's banks might have had something to do with it. From a cupped handful of water he determined that the water was brackish but not unpleasant. The fish, he eventually caught, a flounder, was small, no more than nine inches in length. In the old days he would have contemplated throwing it back. Shady decided that the size of the fish matched his modest hunger, and besides it had taken over an hour to catch. He scooped the fish into his jacket pocket, careful not to put it in the pocket with the matches.

A siren sounded from the oil refinery. Shady reasoned it was a change of shift. Distant figures appeared at the different levels of the plant's superstructure, working their way down the flights of metal stairs. A thick plume of smoke rose from the top of the refinery cracker. Fire licked from the cracker like flame from a medieval dragon.

Into the drain Shady climbed with the fish carefully laid from hand to wrist and held before him like an offering. He gutted the fish upon a cleared section of the concrete floor and then, placed the fish laterally across the stove. An eye stared back from the fish but not at him. Shady reached into his pocket for the matches and was thankful he'd remembered to keep them away from the wet dead fish. Taking a match from the box he turned the gas knob of the little stove to full on. The gas escaped with a distinct hiss. A large rat scuttled past on the other side of the drain. Shady raised his eyes from the stove and the imminent lighting of the match to watch the rat go by.

Somewhat numbed, and blinking, just to see, he held the match poised in the air alongside the matchbox. All of a sudden he began to cough, bone-shaking shuddering coughs that made his back arch and jolted the rosary beads free of his shirt, dangling from his chest. His face contorted with pain, Shady rolled on his side and sucked the noxious air in short, shallow breaths, holding the match in one hand

and the matchbox in the other. For a few sweet moments, he felt the muscles of his back and legs and arms involuntarily relax. Conjuring a picture of the Ballet Shoe Factory in all its luminous glory, he felt strangely content.

A vision of a watchful Tick Tock surrounded by chickens rose before him. The hand holding the match reached out to touch this image of Tick Tock. The apparition, at first, did nothing so comforting as beckon for him to come or extend its arms in an embrace, only bestowing liberal quantities of shell-grit on the ground for the chickens. But then the apparition came towards him and reached for the rosary beads. It took hold of the beads and ran its fingers around the beads one by one. The apparition smiled and nodded its appreciation. It was a rare Tick Tock smile and, although, Shady supposed he was dying, he was happy.

In a life that now could be measured in blinks and with the gas swirling in his nostrils, and his head spinning, Shady slowly drew the match along the rough striking surface. As Shady blinked a final time he glimpsed a flash of light.

THIRTY-ONE
GREAT BALLS OF FIRE

The ground of the old Williamstown racecourse pulsed and rolled and trembled as if it was the epicentre of an earthquake. A thunderous, rumbling murmur emanated from deep underground. Throughout the old racecourse and down by the creek, all the way to Hobsons Bay, great balls of fire emerged from the network of drains that had exploded when Shady struck the match.

Explosion followed explosion. The ruins of the old grandstand submerged into the shattered terrain. The drains collapsed like melted honeycomb. For those, by chance, standing on the hills of the rifle range, they would have seen, just south of Kororoit Creek, not far from the old racecourse, a flash of light and then a fiery, red line trace along the creek, disappearing for a few seconds, as it passed under the creek's waters, and reappeared on the far side, tracking for the oil refinery. Smoke ringed the dusky sky from Williamstown to the fireball in North Beau Vista, where the mighty oil refinery stood wreathed in flames.

Dust and smoke billowed from the drain, covering the backyard of the Ballet Shoe Factory in a fine grainy haze.

There were no signs of the police or the cast. On the verge of leaving, I noticed some figures weaving within the jungle of the theatre set. I stood right up to the window of the salon and looked inside. My face, appearing suddenly in the window, forced my mother, who happened to be standing directly on the other side, to reel back. She shook her head in accusation. I'm no Philip Wilkinson, but I could read her lips, and she'd said, 'Here he is,' to Len, who was emerging from stage right amidst the field of what was meant to be wheat, flexing in a breeze manufactured by a large Electrolux fan. Len eyed me, as seriously as he could, for a man attired in a light blue safari suit.

Had they seen the police raid? And the cast? Howard Starr? Jesus, what would they have made of him?

Mother hugged me. She had tears in her eyes. 'You're filthy.'

I hadn't noticed.

'Look at the state he's in, Len.'

Len didn't judge a man by how dirty he was. 'At least he's safe that's the main thing.'

Mother almost smiled in relief. 'We thought with the refinery explosion you might have got caught up in it... and then we decided to come over here, and my god, what carryings-on...never seen anything like it.'

Len and Mother had arrived while the police raid was in full swing. Len didn't care what the Chief Censor thought, he just wanted to see the cops' search warrant which the local constabulary in their zealousness had overlooked. Len told them to get off the property before he called the Melbourne Criminal Investigation Bureau and reported the lot of them for trespass and assault. The police had dispersed reluctantly, with the parting shot, that they'd be back soon with all the necessary papers in order. For cast and crew and Howard Starr, Len was something of a hero. Howard shook Len's hand and the cast congratulated him with liberal slaps on the back. He was unused to such displays of emotion and tried to tell them to stop, but they wouldn't. One tall, handsome, young fellow had hugged him clear off the ground. To break it up, Len insisted they had to leave before the cops returned. They had obeyed and dispersed like it was a command.

Fine particles of dust filtered through the air of the salon.

Len acknowledged the brilliantly realised cameo of Saigon around us. 'Hell of a job.'

'Len!' exclaimed Mother.

'You did this?' he asked me, undeterred.

Mother seemed put out. 'This is the first we've known about it.'

'I was going to…'

'You were going to? Look at it! All this hasn't arrived in the last shower. Has it?'

'I didn't know…'

She folded her arms anaconda-like as if she was strangling herself. 'Howard Starr, ring any bells?'

'Howard Starr…' I said the words only to give myself time to think.

'Don't push your luck,' warned Len.

Luck was not something I thought I had tapped into a large vein of.

I explained the limit of any understanding that I had with Howard Starr—a mock-up of the set design at no cost to me. Len thought this had been a reasonable arrangement.

'So this is all Howard Starr's idea?' asked Mother doubtfully.

'You mean the set?'

'Yes.'

Len interrupted, 'You do know there's been a huge explosion at the oil refinery in North Beau Vista.'

'Well, yes, I could hardly miss the explos…'

And as if Mother had had more time to appreciate how bad I really looked she asked 'Why are you so filthy?'

I would not tell her I'd been in the drains.

'The beach.'

'To get like that?'

'Stinking seaweed's everywhere.'

One did not roll around in seaweed, but it might have explained the unnatural odour of the drains.

'Mmm…' said Mother suspiciously.

'Done a good job with all this–' Len took a few steps to his right, and whacked his arm in a mild test of strength against the woodwork frame of the French colonial balcony that overlooked the replica Saigon town square.

'Howard's meant to be pretty good.' I briefly pondered the impresario's immediate whereabouts.

'Len! Just look at the place,' exclaimed Mother.

As though under instruction, Len took another look around him. 'Yeah you should have said something.'

Mother berated Len with her eyes.

It made no difference to Len: when it came to the war, he was resolute in his hatred. 'If this helps stop those stupid bastards in Canberra I'm all for it.'

It was time to own up. 'I met Shady Green,' I confessed. It hurt to say.

One of Mother's hands flew to her face.

'Where?' asked Len.

I pointed at the back fence. 'All the way from Brisbane. Right there. He just came up to me.'

Len's face hardened. 'What did he want? I presume he knew, he'd inherited the Ballet Shoe Factory.'

'He showed me the title deeds.'

'Cheeky monkey,' said Mother.

'Well, that's it then, son. The man's got title that means all this,' he looked around the salon, 'is his.'

I feigned disappointment.

'All this work on the set design might be for nothing,' Len guessed.

'He'd want it to go on.'

Len's chubby cheeks flapped in surprise. 'He told you that?'

'Good as. In the chook pen.'

'You had a chat in the chook pen?'

'Like with Tick Tock?' asked Mother.

'Exactly like that,' I said.

'Had he come to claim it?' asked Len.

'He'd more like come to see it,' I replied.

Len's and Mother's faces displayed confusion.

'Only to see it?' asked Len.

I explained that Shady Green had an obsession with the Ballet Shoe Factory since he was a boy and lived in Williamstown. I couldn't tell them the story of the Cavenaghs and the drain and the little, blue Navy bag, but I was sure Tick Tock wouldn't mind if I told them about Shady's Taj Mahal.

'*Taj Mahal?*' queried Mother. 'For him it was the Taj Mahal?'

Len smiled in a sort of shared understanding of what a thing could mean to a man, even a simple boilermaker like himself. 'The Taj Mahal, eh?'

'That's what he called it.'

Len scratched his chin. 'Was he all right in the head?'

'Dad! Oh yeah. He has all his marbles.'

This seemed to please Len. 'Did he say where he was going?'

What should I say? 'He was going home.'

'To Brisbane?' asked Mother.

'Going home is what he said.'

'But do you think he meant Brisbane? He's come an awful long way for just a look at his beloved Taj Mahal,' said Len.

I couldn't tell a lie about a thing such as this. 'I don't think he meant Brisbane.'

Len stared straight into my eyes. 'Where then?'

'I can't say.'

Len's belly poked a little further over the belt of his trousers, as he made the effort to stand straighter. 'Can't say or won't say?'

I shrugged my shoulders.

Len sucked in some air that in turn sucked in his gut. 'You've seen what greed has down to that filthy fat swine of a boy, Nigel? Haven't you?'

Reluctantly, 'I've heard.'

'Well if you know where this Shady Green character has gone, for your sake tell us. We don't want that hanging over our heads.'

I had to fight back the temptation to tell them that Shady Green had almost certainly been obliterated by the fireball that had rocked most of the western suburbs. But I didn't tell them. Shady was a sort of secret: a strange man from a distant time and place. A figure from a dream who was larger in life than he had ever been in a dream. I, alone of our family, would know what he was like. Just like I, alone, knew *all* the story. I would not kill him off. Shady would, for a little while longer, remain an eternal figure, shrouded in mystery.

This was the way I wanted it. This was the way Tick Tock would have liked it.

Len hitched his safari trousers higher. 'Son, you leave us with no choice. You say this Shady Green exists, that you've even met him. We have to look for him until we find him. The Ballet Shoe Factory will remain his, until then, whenever that might be.'

'What about the ballet?'

Len looked uncertain. 'It does seem a pity to let all this go to waste—'

Mother gave Len the sternest of looks. 'Len, the vice squad raided it—'

'Those stupid bastards don't know what they're doing either,' said Len.

'Shady liked it,' I said.

Len raised his eyebrows. 'You're not just making that up?'

I nodded. 'He liked it a lot.'

'Well…,' he mused, 'seeing the property's his and he liked it, I don't see why we can't keep it going—'

'But Len, the police—'

'Marg, would you stop going on about the damned hypocrites that are running this country, and just for a minute humour me and let me run my bit of it the way I want.'

Hair, The Ballet would go on and be the finest piece of anti-war propaganda the state had ever seen. The reviews were rapturous. *The Melbourne Times* proclaimed it, 'The defining spectacle of our time,' and *Farrago* 'As funny as it is obscene.' Howard couldn't have scripted it better himself.

Howard's star was in the ascendant. Success followed success. Broadway beckoned. His beginnings in a storeroom off a goods ramp became the stuff of legend. His alter ego as El Maestro passed off as just one of those mad things young people do to get ahead, and the arrangement with the vice-chancellor nothing more than a witty little dinner table anecdote to amuse devotees.

THIRTY-TWO
LAST TRAIN TO ESSENDON

It was the final day of the school year. The last time in 1969 I would make the journey from Beau Vista to Essendon. The last chance I had to speak to Vivian, before we all went our separate ways for summer.

The Beau Vista to Newport leg of the journey was too short to be sure of making successful contact with Vivian. Besides, there was always an element of settling in, and sometimes disarray at Beau Vista, as late arrivals stormed through the carriage doors to beat an impending departure.

No, I would make my move on the second leg. This section was long enough to make my move, but not so long that I had to sustain a conversation beyond any safe limit of inventiveness. None of the stations in this section of industrial hamlets— apart from Footscray, by which time I'd already have been committed by action—was busy enough with passengers to interfere with my calculated encounter with Vivian.

I planned my encounter with Vivian for mid-way between Newport and Seddon. If there were an empty position beside her, I would sit there. If not, then I would stand and hold a leather strap, and from that vantage point direct a scintillating and hopefully engaging piece of conversation in her direction.

Len, at my insistence—his face an oval of bemusement at the request—had driven me to the station ten minutes earlier than usual. I boarded the 7.10 a.m. train as its first passenger and took a seat strategically close to where Vivian would invariably sit. The distance between us would be discreet. My position mustn't appear unusual. I didn't want any of my fellow travellers passing comment. This could puncture my temporary courage. On my calculations I should be facing Vivian and her two MLC girlfriends. The distance I needed to cover was no more than eight feet. I certainly didn't want any long walk down an aisle. The streetsmart like Brenda might guess what I was up to and follow my progress like some kind of unfolding romantic train-wreck. Two or three paces should be OK. I'd rise from my seat without being noticed, cover the distance between us in a trice and, before she knew it, I'd have started a conversation. I'd know within seconds if she were interested. Should I fail, only those very close or very watchful would have witnessed the rejection. I'd be back in my seat almost as if I hadn't moved. Any collateral damage would have been minimised. By the time the rumour-mill had established as a fact my failure to romantically pull it off with Vivian, we'd all be on holidays. Seven weeks from now when the new school year started, they wouldn't care less what had happened on the last day of the previous year.

The day before as I ran Gerry through my plan, he just shook his head in disbelief. He was at home, in his pyjamas, on the couch, a light blanket covering him to the waist: a genuine convalescent. 'You have no idea, do you?'

'What do you mean? Have I missed something?'

'You can't plan these things. Something always goes wrong.'

'Like what?'

Gerry rubbed his stubble in the annoying mannered way of a man who'd had it most of his life. 'How the hell should I know? Or you know? Anybody know? I mean anything could happen.'

'But,' I began to protest, 'if I'm sitting where–'

'You might be sitting just where you planned and then the unexpected, the complete left-of-field, right-out-of-the-blue thing, that not even Einstein could have predicted will happen. And then you won't have a plan.'

I was getting a little angry. 'Well what do you suggest that I do then, huh?'

Gerry let go of what passed for a beard. 'Why don't you just talk to her and forget *how* you plan to do it. Just do it.'

'No plan?'

'No plan.'

I couldn't think about doing it without a plan. But from the moment passengers got in the carriage it was as if they were part of a conspiracy to make it all go wrong.

To sit as I was—the only person so far on the 7.10 a.m. train—was mildly unsettling, a bit like sitting in an empty bath. I figured there was a good chance Kenny would sit next to me by the window. Since his conversion, he had taken to looking out the window for most of the journey. He would be the perfect, silent witness for what I had in mind.

Brenda, who was normally one of the last to arrive, and would habitually sit two rows further away at the back of the carriage, had arrived first and sat down next to me. She gave me a concerned look. 'What's wrong?'

I shrugged. 'Nothing.'

To sit next to Brenda was to sit under a social micro-scope. If Kenny decided to sit somewhere else there was a reasonable chance that Brenda would follow him.

Vivian's two MLC girlfriends did the right thing and sat in precisely the seats I had mentally allocated to them. They had allowed enough space for one more passenger to sit beside them: Vivian, who would get on at the next stop, Seaholme.

Within a few minutes most of the school contingent had arrived—except for Kenny. Finally, he stooped through the open door. He noticed Brenda, and for a few heart-stopping moments I thought he would do as I expected and continue down the aisle. Instead, he unshouldered his bag into the overhead luggage rack and sat down beside me.

Brenda beamed. 'How are you, handsome?'

Kenny smiled in a detached way that he wouldn't have prior to his 'conversion'.

'He's looking good. Don't you think, Michel?' Brenda was deadly serious. She hadn't given up on re-converting Kenny.

I was more concerned about what was happening to the plan. 'Yeah...he is.'

Brenda shot me an angry look for the disinterested response. 'Well *I* do Kenny...and I'm a girl so it matters more.'

Kenny lifted a cheek muscle in partial recognition of Brenda's insight.

The railway crossing lights dinged, the driver blew the whistle to depart and the Red Rattler chugged free of the platform.

I had no doubt that as soon as I raised my backside from the seat to talk to Vivian, Brenda would wonder what I was up to. Before she saw where I was going she might even guess. Through a blur of oncoming panic I imagined the worst that could happen. Mentally, I shook my head and looked past Brenda out the window at the passing backyards and clotheslines, some already laden with washing, the sheets starkly white in the hot early morning sun.

Vivian would sit at Seaholme Station, on the green bench, where she always sat, at the far end of the platform. Her bag would be on her knees and her arms folded upon the bag. The door of the part of the carriage in which the two MLC girls sat would line up with the green bench. Vivian would walk in a straight line to her intended seat in the carriage. A blind woman could do it.

The train rattled into Seaholme. The platform and the waiting passengers came into view. The green bench was empty. There was no Vivian anywhere on the platform.

Brenda flirted with Kenny.

He regarded her with the faraway eyes of a desexed tomcat. 'I wish you'd stop doing that,' he said.

'This?' Brenda asked, as her fingers played with the muscles of his forearms.

Kenny gave a forlorn smile. I think Brenda had managed to tickle him.

The pit of my stomach was a knot of nausea. I despaired. I'd done it again. A whole year had gone by and I was no closer to getting a girl. Gerry was right: all that planning and nothing to show for it.

I stared past Brenda and Kenny out the window.

The Red Rattler swayed as it cut across the marshy, river flatland of the old Williamstown Racecourse. The forward carriage bent into view as the track curved. The red of the carriage's paintwork showed as a tawny brown faded by the sun. A smoky haze hovered above the debris of the destroyed oil refinery. Passengers crowded against the windows of one side of the train to see how much damage had been caused by the blaze. Amazingly nobody died because all the men had just come down off shift. But all the hospitals in Melbourne were full of injured, mainly burns victims, dozens of them. Mother kept telling me to count myself lucky. The cost of it all was something else again. I couldn't look.

As the train passed over Kororoit Creek, in the distance along the bank, the dark shadow of a drain's opening showed. For a moment I thought it might have been where I'd farewelled Shady Green. No, on reflection, that drain was a little further up the creek.

A sprinkling of people walked through the ruins of the grandstand. They had come to see the effect of the explosions. A man picked up a small block of rubble and cast it in the direction of the creek. It failed to carry to the creek, landing in the thick sedges of the creek's bank.

'You're ticklish,' Brenda announced as Kenny squirmed under her grip up against the window. 'Michel!' She wanted recognition for her efforts.

The look on Kenny's face might have been revulsion. Brenda was pretty frightening to look at first thing in the morning.

The whole year was going down the romantic drain. First, Lisa, now Vivian: an endless cycle of failure. Next time I would listen to Gerry and throw all caution to the elements. I had to take more risks.

I slumped against the back of the seat and looked around the carriage. From behind framed cracked glass an anti-vivisection advertisement glared. Couldn't Victorian Railways have gotten something less confronting to divert its passengers in their travels?

Newport station signal box appeared. We crossed the

railway crossing on Melbourne Road. The train slowed into Newport station. Self-pity and hopelessness devoured me.

Fellow students reached for bags. Brenda briefly refrained from annoying Kenny. The leather straps overhead hung slightly off the perpendicular. A window slammed shut. The Newport station waiting room shot past and within its shadows stood, Vivian.

I have never seen her get on at Newport: she must have been running late for Seaholme station and raced the train by car. A nervous sensation wound its way down my spinal cord, as if some nerve endings had been severed. Yet another chance beckoned. I would make my move as originally conceived: on the second leg. There wouldn't be more than fifteen minutes to get the job done.

Student travellers were creatures of habit. They would continue the trip to North Melbourne in the groups in which they had travelled from Beau Vista to Newport. It was as if they'd been programmed for the day. Vivian was screened from view by the walls of the waiting room. I stood half a dozen paces away with Brenda and Kenny, and resisted the temptation to walk a little closer to the waiting room, and re-establish, sort of forensically, that Vivian was still in there. I didn't have to wait long. The connecting train was barely a minute behind us. The new, shiny, blue and steel Harris train flowed into the station on a gust of wind. Vivian emerged from the waiting room with the MLC girls, and we all stood waiting for the train to stop. Brenda, Kenny and I reformed in the earlier seating arrangement, and Vivian took up a seat between the MLC girls on the other side of the carriage, just one configuration of seats further down the aisle.

The last passenger to get in the carriage pulled the silver, knobbed handle of the carriage door shut and the train pulled swiftly out of the station. Vivian took a book out of her bag and laid it in her lap. I knew from the illustration on the front cover that it was *Wuthering Heights*. I'd hoped she'd have a book *and* I'd read *Wuthering Heights*. My hopes lifted. A sense of rare optimism welled within me. The nervous tingling had stopped. I wiped the sweat off my hands onto my grey school trousers: no sweat stain showed. I wouldn't know until I stood, but my legs seemed to have stabilised. I was confident I could stand and make the walk of my life. 'One bold step for man, one giant leap…' etc. The syntax of this had always worried me and as the train decelerated into Spotswood, I realised that what I thought had been a few seconds of final musings, had lasted a full minute. I had miscalculated and now waited for the next stop, Yarraville. Neither Brenda nor Kenny had noticed my backside briefly leave the green vinyl seat-cover.

The train stopped at Spotswood station. My heart pounded. The wait for passengers to board was painful and prolonged. What was the hold-up? There were never many passengers at Spotswood. Brenda tickled Kenny who laughed uncharacteristically loudly, almost a cackle. They paid no attention to me and my particularly alert state.

I tried to resolve on the opening line, something about *Wuthering Heights*. I searched for inspiration on the floor of the carriage that was remarkably clean compared to the Red Rattler's. The carriage doors had opened and shut, but I hadn't looked up. I thought I had the line and was sounding it in my head, when a pair of scuffed, black, boys' school shoes walked into my line of sight.

'Look what we've got here, Killer. Le Frog mumbling some mystical froggie chant.' John Carson and Killer dropped their school bags at my feet. 'We haven't disturbed you have we, Froggie?'

John Carson and Killer had Brenda's attention. Kenny took advantage of their appearance and faced out the window.

'You've gone all white, Charles? Have we interrupted something? Are you communing with some dead European?' John Carson's trademark smirk distorted his face in apparent mirth.

'What are you doing here?' I blustered.

The train roared on its journey. We would reach Yarraville in less than a minute.

'It's a free country, Charles. But, if you must know, Killer's looking for a new car. The Datsun expired on the weekend. We've just looked over another one Killer saw for sale in *The Trading Post*.'

I could feel rising panic as the train slowed into Yarraville. Two more stations left on this leg. The presence of John Carson and Killer made any advance towards Vivian the most public of spectacles. My confidence and enthusiasm were wilting.

Brenda finally acknowledged John Carson with a frown. John Carson reciprocated with an arrogant tilting back of his head and a jutting chin.

'Good party,' said John Carson sarcastically, in reference to Gerry's near-death experience.

Killer pulled a book out of his bag and began to read standing up. 'Yeah, great party. I'll bring a gun for protection next time.' He slowly turned a page of Henry Miller's, *Sexus*.

Brenda adjusted the position of her head to identify what Killer was reading. 'Are you reading that for the sex?'

Killer seemed lost for an answer.

She answered for him. 'It might be the closest to sex *you* ever get.'

Kenny shook his head at the passing houses.

The train had stopped at Yarraville and was now on its way to Footscray. In a few minutes we would be at the North Melbourne interchange disembarking for the final leg.

John Carson and Brenda traded gentle verbal fisticuffs all the way to North Melbourne. Killer blocked any view of Vivian I might have had. When the train stopped, John Carson assumed I'd walk with him to the new platform. We crossed the station flyover together, Killer a step or two behind attempting to read as he walked. I hoped he'd fall onto the tracks. That was the sort of diversion I needed.

I feared my forecast of seating arrangements would be obliterated by the presence of John Carson and Killer; wherever I sat they would sit. If I moved they would follow. There would be no getting away from them.

As we descended onto platform 3 the connecting train to Broadmeadows (via Essendon) screamed into the station. We hurried down the ramp worried that it might leave without us. I hadn't seen Vivian since leaving Newport station. Disconsolately, I stepped through the doorway of the carriage with John Carson and Killer in tow.

The carriage was crowded and some passengers had chosen to stand. First, I saw the empty seat, and then I saw Vivian sitting directly beside it. I would have to walk straight past both. As I drew level with her, all sense of risk and loss and embarrassment disappeared. I dropped down beside her like I'd got the last seat in a game of Musical Chairs. Vivian shifted her bag with her foot without looking my way, and for a moment I thought I'd sat on her dress. One of her girlfriends giggled. I looked up at John Carson, who briefly hesitated, as if he might stop and stand above where we sat. I was beyond caring. John Carson and Killer stepped past, but not before they had so clearly registered the beauty of the girl whose lap I'd almost sat in. I saw Brenda out of the corner of my eye watching us. She tapped Kenny on the knee and he turned to observe us out of politeness to Brenda. A sarcastic comment from her and my fragile resolve would shatter like cheap china. She regarded me with a kindly and merciful expression that nearly nodded in approval. Kenny's big, dumb, bovine eyes conveyed a rare under-standing. Hanging from a chrome rail on the other side of the aisle John Carson leered in an effort to put me off. He had guessed.

Vivian turned a page of the book and smoothed it to the edge with the tips of her slender, tanned fingers. As I tried to summon the nerve to speak she turned the book over and laid it cover up on her lap of blue and white cotton. The drawing on the cover depicted Heathcliff and Catherine at the base of a large tree beneath a glowering sky. They both looked expectantly into the distance: he portrayed a deep melancholia, she appeared radiant and happy. Vivian raised the cover of the book for me to see more easily. '*Wuthering Heights*,' she said. 'Oh,' I replied. I asked, disingenuously, what was it about. She paused, quite deliberately, before she answered. Then in that beautiful, sibilant lisp of hers she told me it was a sort of love story, not something I'd be interested in. I assured her that I would. I would be very in-terested. 'I don't want to ruin it for you,' she said. I assured her she wouldn't be doing anything of the kind. 'Well', she said, with a knowing look, 'I don't know how it turns out. When I've finished, I'll give it to you, so you can find out for yourself.'

Despite my best efforts, we did go to Narooma for holidays that year. I fretted that Joanie would show up at the Motel Montague as a temp. She was neither seen nor was she mentioned in my presence. I think Mother had got wind of Vivian from Mrs Roberts, and kept dropping hints that suggested I might be going out with a girl. I heard Len say to her, 'You'll know soon enough.'

Vivian had dropped *Wuthering Heights* around to my place before we left. She'd written an inscription on the inside cover in indelible black ink:

I hope you love this book as much as I have. Tell me what you think of it when you get back.

Happy Holidays

Vivian

THE END